A MOTHER'S CRY

by Jane Kirkpatrick

Dedication

To midwives everywhere.

Prologue

1843—Milwaukee, Wisconsin Territory

Adele Marley laid the infant on her mother's breast. The umbilical cord looked barely long enough, but something more was wrong, very wrong. Adele's mouth felt dry, and she reached with one hand still centering the child on its mother while pressing a clean cloth against the woman's birth chamber. Blood soaked the rag in seconds, staining the bedsheets, Adele's hand. Everything looked red.

"It's all right." Adele spoke to the mother, hoping as she did that she'd be forgiven for the lie. "Feel your daughter. Pretty dark hair. Fine as goose down. You've delivered a treasure to the world." The woman groaned, and Adele helped her place a weak hand on her daughter's head. "You did it."

"I did it," Serena Schultz gasped. "I did all things through..."

"Him who strengthens me." It was the verse Adele had given the woman for comfort all through the pregnancy. It was a prayer as well as a promise. Serena gasped in pain. In Adele's few short years as a midwife, she had never seen so much blood.

"Serena? Stay with me. I'll send Arthur for the doctor. Arthur!"

The man appeared, hair up in sticks from rubbing his hands through it in worry, eyes rheumy with waiting, hoping. Adele heard Serena's breathing change. "God be with this woman, this child, this man," she prayed under her breath, so as not to alarm Serena.

"What's wrong? Serena?"

Adele touched Arthur's shoulder. "You have a healthy baby girl, Arthur. Polly, isn't that what you said you'd name a daughter?" Arthur nodded. He reached for his wife's hand. "Polly's healthy." Serena gasped, her breath shallow and short. "Go get the doctor, Arthur. I'll do what I can." She knew it was too late. Arthur hesitated.

Adele stared at the woman's face, pale as piano keys. The placenta moved from her as her breath exhaled. Adele cut the umbilical cord. Then she watched as a presence moved up through Serena's body like a breath, floating across the woman and disappearing at her eyes, passing without a sound from her body. Serena, no longer full of life and struggle, lay still, her face peaceful.

"Serena!" Arthur pushed the infant aside then, and Adele stood in time to catch the slippery babe and hold it to her breast.

"I'm so sorry, Arthur. So sorry. But you have a daughter to care for now. A beautiful child. Serena would have—"

"I did not want a child!" His eyes rained tears. "Serena—" He held his wife to him, her limp arms unable to wrap comfort around her husband or her child.

"I'll hold the baby until you're ready." Adele held back sobs.

"I have no care what you do with that child. None at all. I never want to see her again—or you. If you hadn't told Serena she wasn't too old to have a child, if you hadn't—"

"She's only thirty-two, Arthur. It was a quirk—" Adele stopped. She knew that anger was the brother of grief. Her words would only fuel the fire of loss that burned within him.

Adele swaddled the child. "I'll find a wet nurse." It was her nature to set necessary things in motion. Her own grief would have to wait. She held the baby to her and stood to heat watered milk she knew the child would need. False sustenance it was when what she truly needed was her mother's love, her father's care. Neither was to be.

March 2, 1843. A midwife means "with woman," and tonight that was so in such a mournful way. At times I feel helpless in being "with woman" during times of uncertainty and fear. The beginning of the first stirrings of life is so wonderful, and I am "with woman" until the moment when the child cries into living, eyes staring at the candlelight, wanting to connect with someone even before they want to suck. I knew Polly, who sleeps beside me, before she was born. I was there when her mother felt the quickening. There, when she startled Serena with her kicks. She was "Paul or Polly" then; it did not matter. She was life, and I was there with her.

But I must not let my heart fall too deeply in love with little Polly. It is the gift of midwifery to be present at the hour of birth, to speak courage and potency to the mother, to tell her that she is capable of delivering this new life into the world. "I can do all things through Him who strengthens me." That's the verse I gave Polly's mother. And she did do it, deliver this child. But midwifery is also a curse when things go wrong. Even with the child thriving, a good midwife knows never to fall too deeply in love with another's child, because that love cannot be returned in an unconditional way. Such surviving children belong always to another. No, a faithful midwife learns to love, to cry, to pray, and to say good-bye.

Chapter 1

SOMETHING UNUSUAL THIS WAY COMES

Sixteen years later
1859—Western Wisconsin

Adele Marley stood at the postal window, staring at the letter.

"It's from that new banker," Cora Olson, the postmistress, told her. "There." She pointed. "The return address. Jerome Schmidt, Esquire."

"Probably a printed flyer announcing something at the bank." Adele pushed the envelope into her grip along with the German Almanac from Milwaukee and a letter from her friend in the new state of Oregon. She was careful not to disturb the thread and needles she'd purchased earlier from the other end of Cora's store.

"I haven't seen any other letters like that one," Cora said. "I'd say it was a personal message of some kind. See the handwriting? Lots of flourish. Don't you want to open it? In case you have to stop at the bank and take care of something before you head home, you know."

"I thank you for your insights." Adele looked the woman in the eye even though she wanted to stare at her broken eyetooth. Adele didn't let on that a trickle of sweat had already begun seeping beneath her corset.

"Might be a legal concern." Cora's raised voice floated as Adele reached the door. "That 'Esquire' after the name means lawyer, doesn't it?"

"You have a nice day now."

Adele hurried out to her buckboard, the boxes of supplies already loaded by Cora's husband, who lifted his hat to her. Adele nodded back, her eyes dropped in modesty beneath her bonnet. She grasped the wood smoothed by years of hands and stepped up into the seat of the wagon then lifted the reins, snapping them to let the mule know she was ready.

What would the banker want with her? The note against her farm was paid annually, with interest. She owned the land but, like most farmers, borrowed operating expenses each year, expenses paid off with the sale of her milk and butter and the occasional heifer. She had a bull that brought in breeding fees, and with selling excess wheat she grew and her midwifery, she and Polly did quite well. She'd even been able to supply a widow with five children all the milk they needed until they could afford a cow of their own. She hadn't asked for a loan extension of any kind. No, the letter couldn't be about the farm.

The new banker was a lawyer, but—*Arthur*. After all this time. Adele pulled up the reins just before crossing the bridge of the Buffalo River outside of Mondovi, the small town she and her husband had moved to in western Wisconsin five years before.

She dug in her satchel for the letter, breaking the wax seal with her gloved finger. Arthur had moved away from Milwaukee, long before Adele and John and Polly headed west. They had no idea where he'd gone. They'd left notice with a lawyer where they could be found, though Arthur had not. But this was what Adele feared, that Arthur would come looking for them or send someone else. With John gone—God rest his soul—the possibility of the loss of Polly sent a searing pain into her side. Her hands trembled as she opened the letter.

May 2, 1859

Mrs. Adele Marley from Jerome Schmidt, Esquire.

I have a question of some urgency that I would like to discuss with you. I will arrive at your home on Tuesday, May 10, at 3:00 p.m. Tea is not expected.

Cordially, Jerome Schmidt, Esquire

He was coming to her home? Tuesday—this very afternoon!

Adele stuffed the letter back in her bag and flicked the reins, her lips moving to unspoken prayers. She'd send Polly away for the afternoon. One look at the slender girl with walnut-colored hair compared to Adele's stocky frame and aging yellow strands would only remind the lawyer that Adele was not Polly's mother. Polly, such a jewel in Adele's life, full of sparkle and yes, lately, a bit of spit. Polly, reminding her of life and living and that there is a time for everything; even sadness must not last forever. Maybe being a mother didn't last forever, either.

I'm not Polly's mother. I have to remember that.

She'd send Polly to the widow Wilson, give her eggs to take—yes, that would work. She'd deprived the girl of the trip to Mondovi for weekly supplies, telling her it was because the garden needed planting. Adele often found excuses not to let Polly be out and about. She was being protective. And there was no sense in Polly being frightened by changes blowing in the breeze. Adele would keep her composure, but she'd fight for this girl as much as she'd fought to keep Polly's mother alive all those years before. Then, forgetting her earlier promise to remember Polly's birth mother, Adele spoke out loud to the mule: "Polly belongs to me, and I'll make sure that lawyer-banker knows it."

Chapter 2

THE SLANTED SEAT

Jerome Schmidt preferred action. The bank ran itself, what with Miss Piggins, old as dirt, looking after reports and such. So this task came at a good time. He didn't intend to remain long in this small village, but it had given him respite. He had eyes on Oregon, but then, what adventurous man didn't? Maple leaves glistened in the light breeze, and the white bark of the birch trees gave his old blue eyes comfort. At forty-two he wasn't that old, though of late, he'd felt that way. He inhaled the scent of spring in this western Wisconsin hamlet, taking in the variety of greens popping out in the woods, lilacs primping for their May performance. He preferred this to the bustling city of Milwaukee, where a man could barely get a good night's rest with the drayage firms delivering supplies at all hours, steamships and trains blowing their whistles. Sounds of progress, yes, but constricting, too. Refuge, that's what he'd found here on the Buffalo River, and a chance to start over and keep his commitments to his family, such as it was.

He rode his big gelding into the widow's neatly tended yard, spied the stock tank at the end of the hitching rail, and dismounted, letting his horse drink as he surveyed the two-story house framed by lilac bushes. A good tight barn stood to the side with the edge of a new planting of what looked like oats in the distance. Six cows chewed their cuds lazily near the barn, surrounded by new grass. The fences could use repair. Hollyhocks would add to the bare outhouse. He tied the horse to the rail in the shade of a giant maple then approached the house. Chickens scattered. He noticed the porch post wobbled when he touched it. Yes, a little fixing might help. Before he could knock, the door opened. The woman's glare surprised him.

"Mr. Schmidt, I presume?" Adele took the lead. She was glad she'd decided to do so, as his presence was imposing, with his well-trimmed beard sporting a hint of silver within the auburn and eyes as blue as her Willow plates. One eyebrow arched higher than the other, making him look. . .intimidating. He was taller than most of the farmers she knew, and he'd have to duck through the door. The seven-foot ceilings might make him feel enclosed, which was good. He had no right coming here without invitation, setting the date and time, giving her no chance to protest or even prepare. What if she'd waited until tomorrow to go to town and get the mail? He'd have shown up and she wouldn't have had time to send Polly away. It was not coincidental that Jerome Schmidt's letter offered a measure of preparation. She thanked God for that.

"I am," he said and removed his hat. He ran his hand through his maple-syrup-colored hair that didn't match his beard at all.

"I only this morning received your letter. A busy woman doesn't have the luxury of picking up her mail daily."

He stepped back. "My apologies. Perhaps the letter wasn't posted when intended."

His admission surprised her, and she gentled her voice. "Yes, well, that does sometimes happen in a busy bank." She thought back to the date on the letter, a week previous. But still. Let Mr. Schmidt, Esquire, be a little uncomfortable. In fact, when they entered the parlor, Adele directed him to "the chair." It had belonged to her grandmother, who had cut the front legs down two inches so the occupant tipped slightly forward, a little off balance. Maybe Mr. Schmidt wouldn't be as likely to stay as long as he would if he could settle himself and lean back in a nice soft leather seat and take over the room let alone the conversation.

Jerome Schmidt took the seat, his knees awkward as he slanted forward. He frowned slightly but didn't complain.

"I have tea," she said. "Would you like cream? It's very fresh."

"No, nothing. I know I'm imposing."

"Nonsense," she said. "I'll have tea. You may as well, too."

"If you insist," he said. His voice was deeper than her John's had been, but not unpleasant.

At least he had manners enough to admit his imposition. She took a closer look at him as she handed him the small cup. Slender as a poplar shoot. He probably couldn't push a wagon stuck in the mud like her John could. A narrow face with a full lower lip, which she noticed he chewed, as though nervous. She decided to take the advantage.

"I know why you're here," she said. "And he can't have her. Arthur was distraught the night she was born, I know that. I've lived my entire life ruminating about what I might have done differently, and I always come up with the same answer: nothing. It was out of my hands. I did everything I could from the beginning of Serena's term until the very moment of delivery. It was tragic, mournful, awful. But I could not have prevented it. God moved in that room." She caught her breath, slowed. "He is her natural father and I waited, giving Arthur weeks, months, years, to come to his senses. I know there was grief. But now it's too late. I'll not put Polly through such a reversal that returning to a father she's never known would mean. I'll fight him in the court, I will. I'll mortgage this farm, sell my cows, whatever it takes to keep that child with me."

She'd moved closer to the man and towered over him in his slanted chair. She took a deep breath, stepped back. Color had drained from his narrow face. The arched eyebrow made him look confused.

"Am I to understand that you have the care of a child given to you at the time of her birth?"

"Arthur didn't tell you that detail?"

"My good woman, I have no idea who this Arthur is. Nor this Polly. But am I to understand this all occurred as a result of your handling the infant's delivery?"

"I'm a midwife," Adele told him. "But what happened wasn't

anyone's fault." She sat down, exhausted from remembering that night.

"It's your midwife status, your record of success—or failure—that interests me."

"You're not here to take Polly away?"

"I'm here for a midwife. Or, rather, for my sister, who needs one. She's alone, recently widowed, and we are all that's left of our family, the two of us and now her unborn child. I've insisted she move here from North Carolina, but she is still grieving the death of her husband. She wants to be sure she'll have proper care. She prefers a midwife, though I advised her there was a doctor here."

"Doc Pederson. Very good man."

"Caroline doesn't trust doctors. They didn't save her husband after his accident. They bled him, which she felt made him weaker. You don't do any bleeding, do you?"

"Certainly not." What a fool she'd made of herself rambling on about the worst midwife case she'd ever had, the worst and yet the one that had eventually given her the greatest joy. Adele's tongue often wagged when it should have waned. "We're not physicians but rather women trained to be with women in our God-given commission to bring life into being. I work with physicians," she assured him. "I can give you references."

Mr. Schmidt frowned, adjusted himself on the chair.

He won't want my services now. And I'll have to face him when I need my next farm loan, too. "I should have waited to see what you needed before burdening you with my personal concerns."

He cleared his throat, paused, and awkwardly moved his

legs as he pitched forward on the slanted chair. "I asked around regarding competent midwives. Your name came up often. My sister is quite. . .high-strung. She's forty years old, and this will be her first child."

"When is the baby due?"

He paused. "I'm not sure if we should continue this conversation. If you have drama involved in your deliveries—"

"I don't. Polly's mother's death was a tragic loss. I was barely twenty. It's the only death I've faced in all my years as a midwife. I like to be involved at the very beginning, helping prepare the mother and encouraging her confidence in being able to bring the infant safely into the world."

"The woman who died, had you been involved from the beginning?"

Adele swallowed. "Yes. Serena was a good friend. I might have known of her pregnancy even before her husband did. I would have given my own life to save hers, but she. . .the doctor said it was the way of things." Adele took a deep breath. "I've delivered dozens since. Polly has been my helper these last three years. The baby is due when?"

"Winter," he said. He tugged at his watch bob, and Adele couldn't tell if he was anxious to leave because of another appointment or if her grandmother's chair was taking its toll.

"Whatever your sister wishes will be honored. It's a mother's choice, and when she knows she's in control, the delivery goes much more smoothly."

"Oh, Caroline will definitely be in control."

"There are things that experience teaches," Adele told him.

"Hopefully your sister is willing to consider those occasions of imparted wisdom from others."

"What my sister is willing to consider is anyone's guess." He fidgeted then, and Adele was about to suggest he move to another chair when he stood, turned, and looked at where he'd been sitting. "I suspect you'll be able to handle my sister, if this chair is any indication." He grinned at her. "I assume it wasn't inadvertently cut off in front?"

Adele felt her face grow warm. "It was my grandmother's chair." She stood, too. "She found it...useful with certain visitors."

"I might confiscate the idea," he told her. "It would limit some of the bores who take up my time at the bank."

"I'm happy to have assisted your banking operations." She curtsied and smiled.

"Indeed," Mr. Schmidt said. He stared at her longer than necessary she thought, a small smile creeping onto his rather handsome face. He chewed that lip again. "I'll send you notice when my sister arrives, and you may come and meet her, see if you're willing to take her on."

They discussed her fee, and Adele ushered him out. She stood on the porch, her hand shading the afternoon sun as he mounted his horse. He tipped his hat and rode down the lane, sitting the horse quite well. Mr. Schmidt had taken her slanted chair well, too. It was a good sign that he could adapt and might even have a sense of humor. Well, why should she care about that? He was a client's brother; nothing more. But she did like the arch of his eyebrows and the curl of his mouth as he sat on that chair and realized why he was sliding toward her.

Chapter 3

MEMORY PUSHING TO WISDOM

Sixteen-year-old Polly Schultz dismounted the old mule, letting the reins drop where she stood, her bare feet pushing up dust, her bonnet dangling down her back, threatening to tangle with her now-loosened chocolate-brown braid. Polly reminded Adele of a deer: light on her feet, fine-boned, and well, beautiful. "Who was that?"

"A gentleman seeking a midwife for his sister."

"He's handsome."

"Not that you could see much of him as you rattled on past him." Adele motioned with her hand. "Pick up those reins, and put Beulah away before she runs off."

"She hasn't done that in months, Mamadele." Polly used the affectionate name Adele's husband had suggested when Polly first began to talk. It was different than what her friends would eventually call their mothers, yet somehow alike. Polly knew of her mother and her father and that tragic night.

"Mules, like people, can forget good habits if they're not

reinforced. That speaks of midwifery, too, you know. There are good practices, consistently attended to, that make all the difference when the birthing comes."

"I thought you said each birth is unique," Polly countered. She picked up the reins and held them loosely while the mule ripped at grass.

"Each is. But it's the usual practices that make one able to honor that uniqueness while sticking to things that are likely to ensure a good delivery."

Maybe that was why there'd been that terrible night with Serena. Adele simply hadn't had the years of experience she needed to know what to do. Adele and John were newly married, with no children of their own. The doctor said it might have been a blood-clotting problem or an aneurysm and that it wasn't Adele's fault. Still, forgiveness wisped away like morning fog on the pond, to return only when conditions were right.

"Mamadele?"

"What? I'm sorry. My mind went visiting. Your planting looks chirk. We should have peas and carrots and beets in no time."

"I'd rather do almost anything than plant seeds, Mamadele."

"How fortunate for you, then. You'll be weeding from now on."

Polly groaned.

"Pull that bonnet up. Your face will be as brown as a bean, and what will people say?" Adele shooed her toward the barn while the girl tugged on the calico bonnet. "After you've put Beulah up, I'll tell you what I know about this new client. It will be a challenge, I think; one that'll take both our good heads to handle."

The midwife would do, Jerome decided. He sat at his desk at the bank, the pale light of the lantern washing across his papers. He chuckled about the slanted chair. She was inventive. She'd need that to handle Caroline. His sister was a demanding woman who insisted on doing things her way. But he knew she suffered now or she wouldn't have agreed to come. He'd had his own losses and felt they'd help each other even if it inconvenienced him for a time.

Jerome finished notes made on a recent loan application. The owner of the flour mill along Mirror Pond wanted to buy a new grist stone. He was inclined to grant the loan with stipulations. A good banker always had stipulations. The village of Mondovi was growing. Still, he was reluctant to invest in the town himself, though he wasn't sure why. He'd left Milwaukee, unable to stay in the same city as the woman who had spurned him. She'd found a more "substantial man," she'd told him. The words still stung, echoing as they did the words of his father, charging he'd never amount to much.

Jerome took his timepiece from his vest pocket and looked it over. He ought to rid himself of it. A broken engagement should carry no baggage, especially not baggage associated with time. Maybe he hadn't given the relationship with Clarissa enough time before he proposed, but he'd so wanted a wife and family to share his future.

He stood. There was no sense in thinking about past agonies. His sister would be here within the month, and he'd be able to tell her he'd found a suitable midwife for her. His thoughts returned to Mrs. Marley and how she'd challenged him for not giving her ample time to prepare for a visit. Her blue eyes had sparkled with upset when she opened the door, her protectiveness for her daughter granting her substance. She bore wide shoulders and a high forehead; comely, too, she was, her hair the color of fading yellow roses, wisping around delicate ears.

He'd make another ride out to her farm within the month, he decided. She did have a loan with the bank, after all. A woman running her farm alone wasn't always the best risk. He needed to reassure himself about her abilities to manage his sister, too. Should he make it a surprise visit? No. He sat back down and wrote a note. He'd give her time. He could tell she was a woman who didn't like surprises, and if he'd learned one thing from his soured engagement with Clarissa, it was to figure out what a woman didn't like—and avoid it.

Chapter 4

Caroline's Command Performance

Adele had forgotten her bonnet and the sun beat on her face. The banker's visit flummoxed her, despite the week of preparation he'd given. He said he visited as part of her loan relationship with the bank, and he clearly evaluated the work she and Polly did. "I hire others to help with plowing and harvest," she assured him. "Most of the loan goes for labor." Polly walked behind them as robins chirped and hopped in the fields.

"One has to be a good judge of character to hire well, you being a widow and having a young girl around."

"Are you questioning my judgment?" She turned to look at him.

"Just a comment on managing risk. I wonder if you've thought about buying more land to pasture more cows, expand your herd."

"I'd have to go into greater debt for that. I've been cautious."

"Yes, yes, caution is important. But so is venturing into

something that might have greater return. One can't cross the continent to new adventures without leaving the security of home."

"I'm not the adventurous type," Adele said. Then, "Is there some problem with my loan?"

"Making periodic visits is something I thought the bank should do, not wait until the annual payoff. Head off any problems that way."

"So you're visiting all the people with whom the bank has loans."

"Eventually."

"Do you anticipate problems with mine?"

"It might be good if I continued to check. A good businessman—or -woman—needs a fine lawyer, a skilled book-keeper, and a future-thinking banker to be successful."

"I do my own bookkeeping. I've never had need of a lawyer, and until now, I didn't think I'd see my banker more than once a year."

"Times change."

Adele tripped then, stumbling on a rock. He quickly reached for her elbow to keep her from falling, and the warmth of his hand spread through her arm, causing alarm. It had been a long time since she'd felt such warmth.

"Now, see, you might have fallen if I hadn't been here." He continued to hold her elbow.

"I wouldn't be walking around the field if you weren't here. I'd be working in it. I'm just a little clumsy is all."

"Nonsense," he said. "You're as agile as a deer."

She thought of herself more like a bear, rounder than need be for someone not hibernating in winter. A deer was a lithe animal, and. . .beautiful, like Polly. John had never called her beautiful or agile or compared her to anyone but his mother, whom he adored. He'd called Adele "handsome," a word she associated with men.

Jerome smiled at her when he said the words, and she felt the heat of his fingers even after she'd regained her physical balance and he'd stepped appropriately away.

"I hope you won't mind my monitoring the bank's interests. It's my calling, after all, to assist orphans and widows with their needs. A woman alone doesn't make the best decisions, it's been my experience."

Adele bristled. "I've kept this farm going on my own for three years. And as a midwife, I've made dozens of decisions on behalf of a mother and child. That's *my* calling."

"What women do for each other. A natural thing. Hardly a calling."

"You're mistaken." She stopped, hands on her hips. "If you lack confidence in my skills, perhaps you should simply have Doc Pederson attend the birth."

"No, no. My sister wants a midwife, that's certain. Please. I've upset you, and I didn't intend that." He wasn't looking at her with a banker's eyes now.

Adele wished she'd worn that bonnet to hide the confused stirrings caused by a man who demeaned her work, yet looked at her with pleading eyes.

Mrs. Waste attended the church service. She expected her fourth child in October. "I love those experienced mothers," Adele said as she and Polly walked home from the circuit rider's monthly visit at the nearby school. As they walked, Adele noted that summer was in full bloom. "They bring their own methods to the lying-in and aren't as frightened as new mothers. We midwives can learn from them."

"More for your journal." Polly tugged on her shawl then looked back, waved a final good-bye to someone.

They finished the evening milking together. Adele looked forward to winter, when most of the cows dried up and had to be fed but not milked, when she and Polly could curl a little deeper beneath the feather comforter and wait for the sun to come up before stepping out onto the cold floor, dressing then heading outside to place the harvests of summer in the barn mangers. In spring and summer, the work was twice as much, tending to new calves and getting their mothers back into the routine of milking once the weaning (and bawling of mothers and their calves) was accomplished; cutting and putting up grass hay for winter; planting the garden, harvesting, picking berries; pulling porcupine quills from a calf's nose; whatever it took to tend the farm consumed summer. In between there would be babies to deliver, giving them both challenge and exquisite joy. She still followed up with the Bentz family, whose baby, Luke, was now a year old. That delivery had been a long, hard one, but both child and mother were doing fine.

"Could we have more lilac scent when we make soap next?" Polly asked as she washed her face before bed.

"Of course." It was the first time the girl had asked for something related to her grooming. *Is she thinking about boys?*

"Did you see someone special at church today?" Adele finished a stitch as she let the hem down on one of Polly's dresses in the waning evening light.

"Sam." She was always direct, a quality Adele admired. "He's smart in his schoolwork and not afraid to show it like some of the boys. I want to marry a smart boy."

"You'll need a smart one to keep up with you."

Polly dried her face, undid her braid. Before long Adele would gift her with the pearl cluster hair clip that Serena had given Adele as a birthday present one year. Adele had never worn it after Serena died, saving it for Polly to have on the day she married.

"Do you think Mr. Schmidt is smart?" Polly asked.

Adele felt a tug at her heart with the mention of Jerome Schmidt's name. That wasn't good.

"I suppose. He's a lawyer and a banker. A very good one, I think. He follows up on his clients at least. What made you think of Mr. Schmidt?"

"Your face got red when he was here last, Mamadele."

"Did it? Just the sun."

"He must have flummoxed you."

"Anytime a banker wants to talk about money I get flustered. But it's nothing more than business." They put out the candlelight then went upstairs together. Polly brushed her hair one hundred times and so did Adele, who was always thoughtful after the circuit rider preached. He wasn't a fear-raising man as some she'd heard but rather spoke often of forgiveness. The subject made her think of Serena and Arthur. Polly made Adele's life complete, Polly and the farm, her clients, her faith. She didn't need the complication of someone making her feel giddy, even if he did think of her as being as lovely as a deer. She blew out the candle. She also didn't need to jump to conclusions. The man was just doing his job.

Adele reread the letter Caroline Bevel sent requesting her presence the very next day. She smiled to herself. The tone was very much like her brother's, setting the date and assuming Adele would show up when told.

Adele had planned to go to town that day. She considered posing an alternate time, to exert control over this possibly difficult woman. But it was her duty as a midwife to give the future mother as much control as possible. Uncertainty tended to increase worry in some women, who then became rigid in their demands of others and on themselves. Caroline was a first-time mother at the age of forty, a grieving widow who had just moved halfway across the continent, all facts that could complicate a birth. Adele would give her as much power as she could.

Caroline shared her brother's height but lacked similar warmth in her brown eyes. One eyebrow arched higher than the other.

She was almost too slender, Adele thought, as she stood on the landing of the Schmidt home, wondering if the woman ate little or if she was one of those naturally thin souls who could eat their menfolk under the table and still not gain an ounce. This wasn't Adele's problem.

"Please. Do come in. My brother hasn't yet secured a maid and I did not bring my own, so I am forced to welcome you myself." The lilt to her words reminded Adele of singing. "But he says such informalities are part of the Western experience and I will come to appreciate them, something I truly doubt." Caroline sniffed the air, and Adele wondered if she'd stepped into cow manure without realizing it. "I believe my lilac-scented candle has burned out," Caroline said.

"I love lilacs."

"Do you? I prefer orchids or magnolia. But the candle was a leaving gift, and I burned it to rid the place of my brother's smelly socks, which I believe are making my stomach truly uncomfortable." She sighed. "Now then, follow me, and we'll find as pleasant a place to sit as possible."

The move to the parlor allowed Adele to glance at the ephemera in the cherrywood china cabinet—a collection of salt dishes with tiny spoons, small Indian baskets, a pitcher that looked like Dresden. The walls held framed paintings of likely ancestors bearing that same arched eyebrow. Flowers made of hair and silk splayed out from a Chinese vase. Adele wondered if the furnishings were Jerome's or his sister's.

"It's quite lovely."

The woman turned. "No, it's not. It is replete with my

brother's pedestrian choices. When my things arrive, by wagon I suppose, since we're in this outpost so far from civilization, I fully intend to have a housecleaning." She swirled in her hoop dress, an attire few women in western Wisconsin considered for daily wear because of the hoop's impracticality when milking, gardening, or fixing meals in small kitchens. "Now, let's sit, shall we? I have questions to ask you."

Adele sat. Today she'd listen and learn. Later she'd help prepare and advise, even though she wasn't sure Caroline had the temperament for either.

Adele had her fill of tea and of Caroline's opinions, which she freely gave on everything from dress shields to slavery. And they hadn't yet gotten to the issues of Caroline's pregnancy. The woman talked nonstop, and Adele wondered who Jerome would get to be Caroline's maid and how long she might stay. She'd have to strategize with Polly about how to approach this difficult woman who, while never being pregnant before, assumed a doctor's level of knowledge. "I am well read on this subject and am fully prepared to contest anything I deem as inappropriate."

"As is your right." Adele set her teacup down. "The most important thing for a mother-to-be is to feel secure in her own strength and in the abilities and intentions of those she permits to assist her."

"Indeed." Caroline looked over the tops of her glasses into Adele's eyes then wagged her finger. "My brother was duly impressed with you, but of course I've done my own checking. You've not been here long."

"Five years, but I assisted with many mothers back in Milwaukee and even before that was my grandmother's aide. She delivered hundreds of babies."

"You've had no complications?"

"Those can happen to any woman, anytime," Adele said. "But I have done my best to adapt as the circumstances needed."

"You've lost no child?"

"None, praise God."

Oddly, the woman didn't pursue the next logical question, to ask of the mothers' fates. But Adele knew that people sometimes intuitively don't ask a question when they fear the answer.

"I'll want to be certain you're able to manage any number of possibilities," Caroline summarized. "I'm an older mother."

Adele nodded. "When did your former midwife determine the birth time will be?"

"It's to be a Christmas baby." Her eyes watered then, and Adele saw for the first time the woman's vulnerability, her fears cloaked inside that wagging finger of control. "My husband's birthday was December 24." Caroline dabbed her eyes as she looked away. "I believe I've taken enough of your time. Thank you for coming." She stood and brushed at her breast. As she did, she cried out in pain and knocked loose a cameo pin, the clasp's sharp needle springing out as her hand brushed past the pin.

"Are you all right?" Adele asked. It looked like a nasty scratch.

Blood poured from the wound as Adele pressed her handkerchief into the woman's palm. "I'll get the doctor."

"It's so...debilitating," Caroline said, looking up into Adele's eyes, worry mixed with wonder. "Jerome did tell you, didn't he? I'm a bleeder. There's nothing to be done about it."

Chapter 5

GAINING KNOWLEDGE, SEEKING FAITH

O nce, Adele remembered, Serena cut her hand gutting a deer, and she said it bled a long time, but it stopped eventually. Adele should have been wary and sought advice beyond her own skills during Serena's delivery. She did know that most women were advised not to get pregnant if they learned they had blood that didn't clot. As Polly slept, Adele pawed through her grandmother's journal, seeking notes on blood clotting. She'd done this before but did it again. The book wasn't organized by any subject, something Adele did in her half of the book she intended one day to hand down to Polly. Her grandmother's book was a hodgepodge of recipes, reminiscences, and rules such as *Always wash your hands before adding oil to woman parts,* or *If the labor stalls, consider baking bread. The aroma of it will comfort the mother and allow the process to proceed.*

The doctors Adele worked with usually scoffed at such practices, but what woman wanted someone with dirt beneath their nails to be touching her, and who was to say that the familiar aroma of bread couldn't bring comfort enough to help a mother deliver her infant? Adele knew music sped a stalled delivery, too, and she often sang softly, learning the mother's favorite hymns as part of becoming familiar with each mother-to-be.

Spend ample time before the birth getting to know your patient, Adele read. *She must trust that you will be there for her no matter your own circumstances. Your own family, too, must be advised that the calling of the midwife means another's needs will take precedence over theirs. Trust is essential.*

Adele turned to her own section of the book and wrote the word *Trust.* What behaviors build such trust? She wrote: *Be honest, always. Be an even, stable influence, never cheery one day and morose the next. Be reliable. Arrive when you say you will. Remember preferences in food or concerns and help address them. Finally, you must accept the mother no matter your personal judgments about her decisions. If she wants her other children in the room with her during the delivery, accept this. If she wants to squat or lie down, accept this. Accept her.*

Adele closed the book.

She could do all those things except the last. Caroline never should have gotten pregnant. Adele wasn't sure her judgment of this woman's behavior could be set aside, especially when it reminded her of Adele's greatest disaster. Accepting another's choices wasn't easy for Adele. She still blamed Arthur for abandoning Polly, even though Adele had gained so much from it.

She must decline this patient. Besides, Jerome Schmidt had

said nothing of his sister's blood condition. He'd misled her. She had every reason to cancel their verbal contract. It made her sad, but it must be done. She would tell Jerome Schmidt in the morning.

"I am so sorry." The midwife sat before him in his bank office, his desk cleared of papers as he leaned back in his banker's chair and gazed at her pleasant face. Her bonnet had a small brim, which he liked because he could see her eyes, though they were in slight shadow. Jerome had agreed to see her without an appointment, without even advance notice as she'd insisted he give her. The woman continued, "I have met your sister, and—"

"She's pleased with you." He'd been so grateful to come home from the bank to his sister's first smile since she'd arrived. "She said you were both accommodating and competent, in that order, which is important for Caroline. Now, what are you sorry about?"

"I. . . She told me she is a bleeder." The midwife swallowed. "I don't think I'm skilled enough to care for her should something go wrong. She's already met Doc Pederson, due to her cut."

"A bleeder. Yes, I should have remembered that. Surely there are others with this malady."

"I've spoken with other midwives in the past. I've conferred with the doctor. I'm not the one to assist her."

"But she likes you!" She jerked back, and he lowered his voice. Caroline could be such a trial, and if he could not find someone willing to help, he wasn't sure he could endure the next three months of her lying-in. He needed a midwife as much as Caroline did. "I mean, she has confidence in you. Women still become with child despite these maladies. There must be someone who knows how to assist a bleeder. Please, contact other midwives, see if there isn't something to build your confidence—"

"It's not my confidence I'm worried about." She twisted the strings of her reticule. "It's your sister's health and that of her child."

"All the more reason it should be you doing the delivery. You care about her, even after so short a visit. Please. Look for answers before deciding. Trust yourself."

"I'll look. But you need to look, too, for another midwife."

He wanted to frighten her, intimidate her, maybe even suggest that her loan renewal was dependent upon her helping his sister. But he wasn't that kind of man.

⸸

Imagine his suggesting that she lacked confidence, Adele thought as she walked to the dry goods store to pick up supplies. Telling her to trust herself. Hadn't she just yesterday written of trust in her journal? But Adele would see what she could find out about helping a bleeder.

Back at the farm, she and Polly dug in the garden. Adele wielded the fork, and Polly bent to pick the carrots and brush the dirt from them. She rubbed a long carrot with her apron then bit it. "I love the taste of carrots," she said. "Even with dirt on them."

"A little carrot dirt never hurt anyone." The thought made Adele wonder if what the mother ate had something to do with blood clotting. Perhaps potions or elixirs helped. That evening, after Adele had prayed, she decided to discuss her decision not to assist Mr. Schmidt's sister. It would be good for Polly to understand the difficulties and how sometimes a midwife simply couldn't be there for her charge. Midwifery meant being honest with the mother and, even more, with oneself.

"It's something in their blood." Adele explained the bleeding problem as best she could. "No one seems to know what would make it better. It's. . .part of why your mother died, I believe. The blood refused to clot. You remember my telling you that."

Polly looked thoughtful. "But doesn't that mean even more that you should be there for Mr. Schmidt's sister? Who else will take on such a difficult case?"

"She'll have to accept a doctor's assistance," Adele said.

"But if what you were told is true, then even a doctor won't be able to help. You have to be her midwife, Mamadele. You'd never forgive yourself if something bad happened to her and you weren't there."

Could she walk away? Maybe she didn't trust herself. Maybe she'd never forgiven herself for not helping Serena. The child could be right.

"Someone at a college might know new things that would help." Polly took another bite of carrot, cleaned now and lying in the dry sink. "Sam's going to a medical college in Louisville next year. They might answer your questions."

"That's a grand idea, Polly. Let's write the letter together."

When they finished she wrote in her journal under the section she'd titled *INSIGHTS*:

Polly is such a comfort to me, and she is also a good partner in midwifery. She's not afraid to ask for help, something I must remember. Or perhaps I taught her that. I struggled today with whether to take on this difficult patient because of a fear that I am not wise enough. And yet, I feel called. I must remember the midwives of Exodus who together defied the Pharaoh when he instructed them to kill the Hebrew babies. Together, they resisted. My pharaoh is fear. I must pray to let God be my guide, to trust that if this is a calling, then like the Exodus midwives, I will not be alone. A midwife must always be willing to learn more, for we are intricately and wonderfully made, with complexities wrapped inside worries that only knowledge and faith can relieve.

Chapter 6

WHEN NEEDED

Jerome sighed. What he wouldn't give for a good newspaper to read. Surely he could manage better than this local rag. It only came out when it wanted to, so it was useless as advertising and rarely printed notice of events such as the Fourth of July picnic or the Harvest Festival with enough lead time for someone to actually plan to attend. Word of mouth was still the best way to get information to the people of Mondovi—that and pinning posters up at Olson's store. If he ever made it to Oregon, he'd start a newspaper and commit to getting it out on a regular basis so people could count on it.

He tossed the two-page paper in the trash basket and checked his watch. It was time to gird himself to address his sister's needs. "I need a fresh peach, Jerome." Or "I need these sheets ironed, and I haven't the strength." He couldn't get her the fresh peach, but the ironing he could do. He'd had two girls hired, but they left after Caroline's constant criticism of their efforts. He didn't mind ironing, because Caroline left him alone in the heat of the kitchen. He did wonder how she'd ever manage her "needs" over those of the child once it arrived. Hopefully maternal instincts appeared with birth. Maybe that little midwife would prepare her.

He was growing fond of time with Adele. He'd admired her concern about being the best midwife for his sister, and when she'd come to him later saying she'd had a change of heart, he'd been delighted. She'd found new information, she told him, and was ready to assist if Caroline would agree to her requests. She also said she'd prayed for guidance and decided he'd been right to suggest she might lack confidence in her own abilities. He couldn't have been more touched by her disclosure and her decision. He'd never told his sister Adele's service was questionable, instead telling Caroline that Adele's farm demanded much attention from her, but he was certain she'd be more attentive as her time drew near.

The biggest changes were the foods his sister now consumed. He hadn't realized midwives dealt with such things. She'd convinced Caroline to consume mounds of sauerkraut. The house reeked of it, and she said if mustard greens were in season, Caroline would be green from eating them at every meal. Stuffed bullock's heart was a regular, served with Caroline's southern corn pone. Adele came by every week now to talk with Caroline about this and that, fixing bran coffee with molasses, enough to last a week or more. Somehow Adele had gotten his sister to listen, even agreeing to allow the big Swedish doctor to attend the birth—if needed.

He checked his watch again. Adele usually came by at

midday. With the days shortening, and cold settling on dusk's shoulder, Adele liked to be home before dark, and her farm was three miles out. He donned his hat and locked his office door, telling Miss Piggins he'd be back by two. He set his own time here; he really didn't have much to do at all. He needed challenges. He wondered if Adele would mind some suggestions for her farm.

As he walked, he considered how to broach the subject of Adele's staying with them as Caroline's delivery approached. He didn't want Adele to say no, but he didn't have any suggestions for how she could tend to the farm while she was gone. He assumed that would be the primary reason she'd refuse. He'd also begun considering another question for this woman he'd grown fond of. When he saw her mule tied up at his home, he felt his steps quicken. When he walked around the village, he noticed women's things in the window of the dry goods store. *Women things and baby things.* If Caroline could have a child at forty, surely Adele wasn't too old to bear a child. He was certain she was younger than Caroline.

Caroline. Would she stay with him after the baby was born? If Adele might one day marry him—he knew that was thinking awfully far ahead—would she want to share a house with Caroline? If he proposed to Adele and she accepted, was he ready to leave the village and move to her farm, leaving his sister and her baby alone in the house? He'd have to hire a cook and housekeeper for Caroline. If he didn't marry and Caroline remained, there'd be a houseful of women surrounding his time, and the cries of an infant to wake to. He'd have to get a maid to help. Caroline would be relentless in her demands.

He watched squirrels chatter and sprint up an oak tree along the path to his house. What kind of mother would his sister be? It worried him, he realized. A successful birth was only the beginning. Only thinking of Adele's intervention gave him ease. He'd have to seek her advice about what would happen after the baby arrived. He didn't know when midwives finished their work, but he hoped it wasn't on the night of the delivery.

"It's not time to push yet, Melinda," Adele told the laboring woman.

"My body is riding that familiar crest, and I'm not sure I can stay in the boat."

"Polly, why don't you massage Melinda's back."

"I haven't had one like this before," Melinda Waste panted. "All the others came before I was even ready. My water broke, and before my husband could find the towel, it seemed like I was—oh, oh, oh, oh."

"That's right. Breathe just like that."

"I ain't breathing 'like that' for a reason," Melinda snapped. "It's 'cuz it hurts!"

"I know it does. But in a short while, you'll be pressing that baby to your breast and be the proudest mama around." Adele checked the woman's intimate parts, counted between the rise of her body and breath, squatted. "I see the baby's head. Nice black hair."

"Let me sit up. No, let me walk. Oh, oh, oh, I have to push,

Adele, I have to."

"Polly, take her hand." With oiled fingers, Adele soothed the skin that formed a stretching halo around the infant's head then broke into song. "Hark! the herald angels sing—"

"Glory to the newborn king," Polly chimed in, and then Adele heard Melinda singing, too, in gasping breaths that groaned out this new life inside of her. Adele stopped singing to concentrate fully on the little head, little shoulder, body, and soul, slippery as an eel, willing itself into life and this family.

"It's a boy! Bigger than a pork ham. I bet he weighs close to ten pounds."

"No wonder he took so much time." Melinda cried now, tears of joy. "Charley!" She called for her husband. "You've got your boy at last."

Her husband rushed into the room, three little girls with wide eyes behind him. Charley bent to look at his son. "I knew he was coming when I heard you start to sing."

Adele turned her attention to Melinda. "Everything is fine. You did amazing work." She wiped the woman's forehead of perspiration and her cheeks of tears. "Polly, get a cold rag and we'll ease that pain."

"What's that?" Charley pointed to a patch of wrinkly skin on his son's tiny wrist.

"A sucking blister. He's been practicing in the womb."

"Well, I'll be...," Charley said.

The room was filled with the spirit of hopefulness, of joy, of the mystery of life, and the cycle of birthing repeating itself. Adele felt a part of a larger gathering, of all women who had brought a child into the world, who see the work of creation nurtured within their bodies then brought forth to hear the voices of angels.

"May we speak a prayer of thanksgiving for you all?" Adele asked them.

"Oh, please do," Melinda said, and the little girls bowed their heads as Adele expressed gratitude for this new life, a safe journey, and God's blessings on the family for the years ahead.

November 5, 1858. Young Harold Waste has left behind the gentle waters and peaceful floating tethered to the life raft of placenta. He's on his own now, but he has many hands to help him become the man God intends for him to be. A loving father and mother, sisters who will spoil him, a home of sturdy logs with wood piled to the rafters, a faith to sustain them. Polly hummed "Hark! the Herald Angels Sing" all the way home beneath a star-filled sky. Note to Polly when you read this: Always remember to ask the mother if you may pray for her at the beginning and at the end. It is like a psalm and a benediction, assuring all that God is the center of the circle of this new life.

Chapter 7

PRESSING THE CASE

May I court you?" Jerome Schmidt surprised her as she donned her shawl and bonnet. They'd had a midday meal, and even Doc Pederson had stayed for sauerkraut sandwiches, making Caroline laugh her tinkling tones. Adele and Jerome were alone in the foyer of his home.

"What? Why?"

"Because I enjoy your company," Jerome said. "And because you're kind, of sound mind, and beautiful."

Adele laughed. "I'm not so sure about the sound mind part. Or the beautiful part, either."

Adele's husband—God rest his soul—had never called her beautiful. He often used words like "sturdy," "good-boned," and once even "comely" to describe her form. His word of choice— "handsome"—caused her the most distress. It was a word meant to describe a horse or a finely apportioned man, but a handsome woman? Who would find attraction in that? Jerome was kind and gracious, but he always greeted her with either "Mrs. Marley" or

48

"How's the little midwife today?" The latter with a jocular tone, as though he diminished the work she did. *Little midwife, indeed.* But now he wanted to court her? The words were not romantic, and she realized she wished they were.

She also knew she liked his company, and there was no reason not to agree to his request. And so they'd taken a number of walkabouts together, past Mirror Pond where geese gathered, flying south. He drove out to join her and Polly on Sunday afternoons to attend the evening services. Caroline was always invited, but she preferred to be "at home" as she called it, saying Southern women wouldn't be seen in public in her "condition." Adele tried to tell her that she didn't have an illness. Her pregnancy could be concealed beneath her hoops so no one even need know, and the exercise would be good for her. But Caroline declined.

After Christmas, there'd be no circuit rider until spring, and Adele realized she'd miss both the pastor's messages and Jerome's presence on Sundays. He had an easy banter about most subjects, but he had opinions, oh yes, he did. Adele could see his sister in his thoughts at times, that certainty and demand, and both could carry on quite fascinating arguments. Those times Adele left their house feeling grateful she didn't have to live with the two of them, both as certain as rocks are hard.

And yet when she rode her mule into her yard a few days before Thanksgiving and saw that he was there, reading a gazette on the porch, the paper expanded between gloved hands and just the top of his fur hat visible, she sat a little straighter on the mule.

"Is everything all right, Mamadele?" Polly said. The girl rode beside her on her own mule.

"What? Of course everything's fine. This corset just pokes a bit after a three-mile ride."

"Doesn't it do the same thing when we're in the wagon? You never jerk up straight then."

Adele looked at her and saw the tease in her eyes.

"Yes. No. Never mind," Adele said, annoyed at being flustered by the man's presence and having Polly catch her in it. "You take these mules to the barn. Soon as you're finished, come change and we'll get started milking. At least there's only one to milk now."

A soft snow fell as Polly led the mules away.

"Has Caroline gone into labor?" Adele motioned for them to go inside.

"No, nothing like that, but it seemed time to discuss yet another stage in Caroline's condition with you. Might you have one of your hard rolls with peach jam to ease a man's stomach as we talk?"

"Here I thought it was my sweet disposition that brought you out in the cold."

"Oh it is, it is," he said. "Hard rolls and peach jam are just added value."

"Spoken like a banker." She took the bread from the oven where she stored it, gave him a jug of jam. "I have cows to tend to, and then we'd be pleased if you stayed for supper."

"I'd be a fool to say no to that." He grinned. Adele hoped it wasn't just the food that made him look delighted. She headed up the stairs to change her clothes, aware of his presence on the first floor of her house. She wondered if he scanned the room, seeing what he could about who she was by what she surrounded herself with. She came back downstairs about the time that Polly entered. The girl said hello then climbed the stairs to change her clothes, too.

Adele tied her kerchief around her head and donned John's warm barn coat. She felt comforted in it. "We shouldn't be too long," she said as she sat to pull on rubber boots.

"May I help?"

Surprised, Adele looked up. "Well, yes, that could be arranged, but you're not dressed for the occasion. I could offer you a pair of my husband's pants, but they'd come high above your ankles." The thought made her smile. "And I'm not sure if his boots will fit you."

"I've brought my own change of clothes," he said. "I thought I might meet up with you about chore time. Of course, you're most always at work, aren't you? It's part of what I admire about you, that sense of purpose and determination. May I call you Adele?" He looked straight at her when he said it.

Adele blinked, stopped pulling on her rubber boots. Sometimes he seemed to read her mind about things she hadn't ever shared with him. He made her name sound melodious. And his compliment about her commitment to her work warmed her perhaps more than his use of her name.

"Why, yes. I mean, maybe; few do. I—"

"Perhaps Miss Adele would lend a little formality to the occasion."

"And what occasion would that be?" Adele stood.

"The first time you've let me milk one of your cows," he said, moving closer to her. She could feel her face grow warm, her mouth turn dry. He plucked an errant piece of hay stuck on her kerchief. "That is, the occasion when you actually allow me to participate in your work. I believe such work is your greatest love."

"Polly is my greatest love. Then midwifery."

He was so close to her now that she could see the follicles of his beard like tiny pinpricks against his chin. Her heart pounded in her ears—or was that his heart she could hear? "I do like the work I do. Don't you? I mean, work is—"

He bent down to kiss her, and the warmth of his lips spread like sweet honey against hers, swirling emotion down her arms, her legs, tingling her toes. He stepped back and placed his hands on her shoulders. "Miss Adele," he whispered, "how beautiful you are." He touched her cheeks with both hands, smooth hands. "So beautiful," he repeated.

She wanted to let herself unfold like a flower onto his chest, but she was aware of Polly upstairs and of the cows waiting to be milked and fed, how warm the room had become, and how astonished she was to have been called beautiful while her hair was mashed by a hay-streaked kerchief, and she stood in rubber boots beneath an old dress and John's tattered coat.

"Work is. . . What were you saying about my name?"

"I wondered if I might call you Adele."

She cleared her throat. She needed to regain control. "I think your calling me Miss Adele while we're in the company of others will be just fine. But. . ." She didn't know how to say what she felt. "But you can call me that. . .other, anytime we're alone."

"Which I'm hoping will be often," he told her.

They heard Polly clumping down the stairs, and Jerome excused himself to get his boots and coat. Polly joined them, and the three walked to the barn swinging buckets they picked up from the porch. Adele was certain Polly would ask why her face had turned crimson, but she didn't. The three went on about their work. Jerome was a good learner, Adele decided, and when they finished milking, he helped put the evening feed in the cows' mangers. It was nice to have a man to do some of the heavy lifting. She watched his arms, strong though lean in appearance. It took half the time to finish up and head into the house for supper. Adele smiled. She couldn't be more grateful, and Thanksgiving was just around the corner.

"There is one more thing we need to discuss before I go, Miss Adele," Jerome said. He liked looking at her and would be as proper as Adele wished with what he called her. Polly sat at the table and sketched in the lamplight. She had talent, though Jerome suspected that needlework would be a more practical avenue for a girl to pursue.

"And what would that be?" Adele asked. She put away the dishes Polly had washed that sat drying by the sink.

"It's Caroline. Her time will be soon, and I think it valuable for you to consider staying with us at the house."

"Of course I'll stay," Adele told him. "Once she goes into

labor, I'll be there day and night, as soon as you come to get me to let me know it's her time."

"Yes. Well, that's the problem. I think you should consider staying beginning in December. In case there are storms and I can't come to get you. Planning ahead," he said. "As you did by writing to that college to get information about certain foods that might help Caroline. It seems like planning to be there in advance of labor would be wise."

"I can't be away from the farm that long," Adele said. "I have other clients, too. Besides, I still have a cow that isn't dry so needs milking, and the others to feed."

"I could do it, Mamadele."

"I can't leave you alone here, Polly. I'll need you to help. No, we'll feed heavy, give them extra, and then we'll go when Mr. Schmidt comes to get us."

"Maybe I could stay here and tend to the cows," he offered, "or you could bring the milk cow along. We have a small barn behind the house."

"And the feed?"

"Yes. Well, it might be best if I came here and milked and fed."

"If you can come to milk them, then you can get through storms to reach me and let me know Caroline's in labor and take us back with you when it's time."

"The baby could come sooner than mid-December. Caroline's not good with dates or timing."

"What does Caroline say about my staying for a longer time?"

"She doesn't know what she wants." Jerome pulled at his vest, straightened in his chair. "So I've made the decision for her. A man often has to do that." He could hear the frustration in his own voice.

"Such decisions aren't always the wisest." Adele began skimming the milk for the cream and putting it into the butter churn. Soon the rhythm of the plunger filled the room. He wondered if he should offer some new argument, but he couldn't think of one. He just wanted Adele to come sooner and not only for Caroline. He looked forward to the time with Adele in his own home. It would give him time to ask her the question he'd been harboring for weeks now, without the distraction of Polly or the farm.

"I'll talk with Caroline." Adele wiped her hands on her apron. "A midwife always listens to the mother-to-be and not the uncle-to-be, no matter how well intentioned."

He should have remembered that being the proper midwife trumped even the farm. He was in competition with that part of her life, and he wasn't certain he could come out on top.

Chapter 8

CONCENTRATE ON MIDWIFERY

Caroline leaned in toward Adele and whispered, "I don't think Jerome does well in a crisis, and I'm not at all certain he will be up to doing what is necessary unless someone wise is here to tell him what to do. He hasn't kept a maid, so please, come and stay as soon as you can. The laundry is in piles."

Adele had enough of her own laundry to tend to without doing Caroline's and Jerome's, too. That wasn't the activity she'd hired on for. Cooking, yes, and keeping the lying-in area spotless, those were part of her duties, but Jerome would have to find someone else to wash sheets.

"My work is to be available for your delivery, to assure your success in bringing this infant into your family. Laundry isn't on the list of things a midwife does."

"Not even if it would make me feel more secure?" Caroline lay on a fainting couch covered in a rose brocade, the evidence of her pregnancy mounding up like a half-moon rising over the treetops.

"I want you to feel safe, Caroline, so if not having the laundry done becomes an issue, we'll discuss it. But I'll ask your brother to persist in finding you domestic help." Then she thought to ask, "Who does it now?"

"Jerome. He's quite handy that way, but of course it's unseemly for a man to be doing such woman's work."

Adele rather liked the idea that Jerome was willing to do woman's work when needed. It added a pleasant dimension to him.

"I think he avoids hiring another maid just to save money. But my husband left me well-off."

"Not a bad reason," Adele said, wondering why Caroline whispered. "Maybe he just doesn't want any more females gathering in his house."

"Oh, my brother loves the company of women," Caroline said. "He so enjoys your visits. A man needs a good filler at the end of his day, don't you think?"

Adele stepped over the affront and hoped this new baby would be a boy so Jerome would have a comrade-in-arms. Caroline had put on quite a bit of weight in her pregnancy, and the lower position of the baby suggested to Adele that it just might be a boy. Caroline didn't seem to have a preference. She just wanted a healthy baby she could "love forever."

"Have you made plans for what you'll do after the baby arrives?" Adele asked.

"I'll stay right here. Jerome is engaged, you know, to a woman from Milwaukee. He's quite smitten with her and she him. She gave him that timepiece he carries so proudly, and apparently she didn't resist too much when he moved to this little outpost of a village. I'm sure she'll be joining him in the spring. He doesn't say much, of course. Men never do. But I think that's why he hasn't wanted to hire another domestic. He knows that in the spring his Clarissa will arrive, and then I'll have help and the baby will have a family. It'll be a lovely arrangement, don't you think?"

Adele felt like a cow had just swatted her face with its wet tail. Her eyes watered; her face stung. "I hope they'll be very happy."

"They would have married by now, but of course my brother's opening his home to me set their plans back several months. He's so thoughtful, and Clarissa must be as well to have postponed a wedding. Goodness. A woman who would do that must have a heart of kindness."

"A heart of kindness, yes."

"So you'll come next week with plans to stay?"

Adele controlled her voice, which threatened to falter, and prevented a rush of tears down her cheeks. "If that's what you want, Caroline. I'll speak with Polly, and we'll see what can be done. I need to go now. I'll—"

"But my brother so likes it when you're here when he gets home. He enjoys your company. Please stay."

"He'll have plenty of my company for the next few weeks then, won't he?"

"I'll ask Roy—I mean, the doctor—to come for supper on Tuesday next. We'll have a happy foursome or five with Polly. Six, should Clarissa arrive at last. Oh, this will be such a fun time for us all!"

She'd been so foolish, thinking that kiss was something special, that Mr. Schmidt thought she was beautiful even. The mule slipped on the icy road but kept his feet beneath him as he carried Adele back to the farm. A cold wind bit her cheeks, freezing the tears. It was better to find this out now about Jerome's—Mr. Schmidt's—entanglements before she did something foolish while staying in his home to help his sister, like letting him steal another kiss or expressing care for him. She was there to assist Caroline, that was all. She'd gotten distracted. Her joy should have been wrapped in the mother's joy. She had Polly. She had her farm. She'd had love once, and that was more than many had in a lifetime. The one great joy that had eluded her was to bear a child herself, but God had blessed her with so many other babies whose lives she was a part of, so how could she complain?

Jerome Schmidt had caused her to dream again. But she was awake now and would stay that way.

At the farm she discussed with Polly what might be done about her being with Caroline longer than intended.

"I'll be fine here, Mamadele. I'd love to help you, and if the weather holds, I can come in when Mr. Schmidt comes to tell me that Mrs. Bevel is in labor. We'll feed the cows heavy before we join you, and I can come back and milk, even if it is later in the evening."

"You're a good girl," Adele told her, patting her hand. Polly sketched at the table. "I just hate to leave you alone with the responsibilities. There's wood to chop, butter to churn, the chickens cooped and fed. All the work the two of us do, you'll have to do alone. Just keeping the fireplace going will take time."

"It'll make me feel like a grown-up."

Adele brushed maple crystals from her daughter's cheeks. "You've been at the maple cone, I see."

"I love sweets."

"As do I. Unfortunately, sweets migrate from my stomach to my hips."

"You have nice hips, Mamadele." Polly grinned. "I think Mr. Schmidt likes them. I've seen him watch you when he's been here and you're at the dry sink peeling potatoes."

Adele stiffened. "What Mr. Schmidt does or doesn't like is no concern of mine."

"I'm. . . I'm sorry."

"I didn't mean to snap at you," Adele said. "It's just. . .men. John was such a dear, forthright and honest. I miss him so much."

"Isn't Mr. Schmidt forthright and honest? He's a banker."

"And I suspect a good one. He plays his cards quite close to his chest so his clients might never see it coming that he intends to foreclose. But charming has its shadows."

"We don't have to worry about a foreclosure, do we?" Polly looked alarmed.

"Not at all." Adele patted Polly's hand. "We have a good herd, and with our harvest I paid the previous note. Come spring I'll borrow for operating expenses again. No, we're fine."

"And you have the midwife fees."

"Yes, though the Wastes paid in bacon and hams. But that's nothing to complain about. We'll have one of those hams for Christmas dinner. Maybe invite the Bentzes and their little Luke. You could invite your friend Sam and his family."

"Mr. Schmidt and his sister, too?"

"Once the baby comes, our paths aren't likely to cross with theirs again."

Adele checked her midwife satchel. Oil, forceps—which she hoped she wouldn't need—needles and thread, special candles she'd scented with mint, clean rags, other sundries. Caroline would provide the cues for this delivery, for her and her baby. At least by staying at Jerome's, Adele would be able to see that Caroline consumed good portions of sauerkraut and onions, steaming even the old tops for breakfast. Eggs were good, too, the doctor from the college had written. Adele reread the letter before putting it into the journal. *It is good to remember that physicians often find that in delivery, clotting improves for a hemophiliac, perhaps as a natural protection for both mother and baby, even when bleeding is an issue prior to pregnancy. We are all fearfully and wonderfully made, are we not?*

Adele wished that had been so with Serena. She stuffed the letter then halted. Maybe Serena had died of something else! A torn artery, perhaps, or any of a dozen things that could go wrong. She'd settled on Serena being a bleeder because of what the doctor had said and because there'd been so much blood. But maybe she was wrong. She'd make note of that in her journal, something to encourage Polly one day and remind her that what she thought was so might not always be the case and to trust beyond herself, trust in the intricacies of creation, of the human body and its desire to bring new life safely into the world.

Her confidence increased with the doctor's reminder that God manages details like having blood clot as it should when needed for safe birthing.

Chapter 9

THERE WHEN NEEDED

I'm leaving," Adele called upstairs to Polly. It was December 15, and the wind swirled around the outside of the house, pushing late-falling leaves across the three inches of packed snow that covered the rolling hills, dusted the woods. Adele had baked and baked. She'd made hardtack, brought in a smoked ham Polly could slice off for a week or more. The two of them steeped chicken soup, and Polly was reminded to put leftovers on the porch high up so no marauding wolves or bears would come by and snatch them. The girl had plenty of powder for the musket and knew how to keep it dry. She'd picked up new paper for Polly to sketch with and told her if she ran out of books to read, she could open up one—just one—of the wrapped boxes they'd placed under the Christmas tree. Polly was the most important person in her life, and she'd done what she could to attend to her. Now her thoughts would go to Caroline.

And Jerome Schmidt.

Fortunately, she had not encountered him since the news of his impending marriage so blithely shared by his sister. Adele wondered when he planned to tell her—or if he ever did. But of course now that she'd be staying with them, she'd have to listen to his baritone voice, be required to serve him. Maybe that was why he'd wanted her to come earlier—so he wouldn't have to cook anymore or hire a girl. She hoped that when he told her of his marriage, she could look happy for him, the scoundrel.

God had placed Jerome Schmidt in her way to give her a pleasant summer, and God had taken him away. She put her knitted scarf over her head and stuffed the wool around her neck for more warmth. Her hair would look like a flatiron had pressed it, but she didn't care. She just prayed she'd make it safely, that the baby would come and all would go well, and that in the meantime Polly would feel grown-up without having a crisis.

She didn't want any crisis of her own, either, facing Mr. Schmidt.

"Miss Adele." He couldn't believe how pleased he was to see her safely arrived. He'd missed her. "Here, let me take your bag." He bent toward her as though to kiss her cheek.

She swept by him like a wolf pup spurting out of its den. "Just tend to the mule, if you would, Mr. Schmidt. And it's Mrs. Marley to you."

"What?" The word bounced off her back.

He returned to the house and heard the women chattering

in the small bedroom that had been his since Caroline's lying-in. He'd given her the largest bedroom. He'd already moved most of his things into the loft area so that Adele could be close to Caroline in the night.

"Adele's brought me a mint-scented candle." Caroline held it up. "See how thoughtful she is?"

"Indeed. May I help you get settled in any way?"

"I'll be preparing hot meals for us, so if you'll see to the filling of the wood box, I'd be grateful. I have bean soup with ham. That should be good for us all. Caroline, would you like a back rub?"

"I would, I would." Caroline pushed her burgeoning body so she lay on her side on the fainting couch. She was nearly too large for it.

"I believe we need privacy now." Adele's eyes told him to leave.

Jerome started to back out of the room when Adele reached across then handed him his timepiece, the gift from Clarissa. "I believe this belongs to you?"

"Won't you need it?"

"I have my own timepiece." Her words dismissed him.

He backed out of the room, stung by her words. His hands shook. What had he done to upset her? He hadn't even had an occasion to press his case with her, and from the frost of her words and her physical avoidance of him, he had to assume something happened to turn her against him. Could Caroline have upset her? His sister loved Adele as much as she seemed able to love anyone other than herself. What had he done wrong?

The next week bumped along. Adele made certain she was never alone with Jerome, who fortunately was there only in the evening or at midday, and that there were no lengthy conversations around the table. Caroline chattered about herself so easily there was really no need to speak, except to say, "Really?" or "How interesting."

Once Jerome had looked at her with piercing eyes while his sister told a family story, something about her husband's buying her a horse. His eyes were troubled with such hurt, Adele looked away. And later she nearly succumbed when he reached his hand out to her as she passed behind him in the kitchen. But she did not. Usually direct, she realized she had nothing to confront him about. He hadn't promised her anything; she'd merely let him into her heart and assumed it was where he wanted to be. His wounded look was just a shade of his charm, a way of "filling time" with Adele while he waited for his Clarissa. Adele would work to forgive herself for having been so naive as to think that if a man calls you beautiful it means he's in love.

At night, Adele read alone in her room, but she could hear Jerome moving above her in his loft. Once she thought she heard soft snoring. When she turned her face into her pillow, she imagined she could smell his cologne there even though she'd washed the pillow slip herself. She had to expel him. *I can do all things through Him who strengthens me*, she wrote in her journal, this time for her own delivery from longing.

In the second week of her stay, Adele told Caroline she was

going to go home for a day to make sure all was well with Polly. Caroline worked herself into a frenzy about what she'd do if the baby started to come and Adele was back at the farm, caught in a snowstorm, eaten by wolves. "The possibilities of danger are endless," Caroline wailed.

"There aren't that many wolves around here. And the sky is clear and blue, no snow clouds in sight. And Doc Pederson makes his way here easily."

Caroline began a silent crying. Adele could see her shoulders shake. Maybe she wasn't being dramatic; maybe she really was frightened of what could go wrong if Adele wasn't there to tend the birth. *A midwife does what she must to comfort and give assurance to the mother.* Adele stroked Caroline's hair. "I'll stay." Her obedience to her calling proved providential, for on December 24 the sky darkened, folded like a deep-blue blanket over the treetops and houses of the village, and buried the skyline, dropping snow so heavily and for so long that Adele could barely see the shed where her mule and Jerome's horse stayed. On Christmas morning, snow pushed up to the windows and stood two feet on top of the woodpile. And of course, Caroline went into labor.

"Let's walk." Adele urged her to stand.

"I can't walk," Caroline whined. "I don't like to walk."

"It will be good for the baby. You ate cabbage you didn't like either, remember? But you did it for your child."

The labor had stalled well into Christmas night, and Adele

had decided she needed to get Caroline to move, despite her bulk. But Adele was so short she didn't offer much assurance to an unsteady Caroline. She'd have to ask for help.

"Mr. Schmidt," Adele called. "Can you assist?"

He appeared as though he sat right outside the room, and maybe he did. If he'd been listening, he would have heard Adele ask if Caroline minded if she prayed for her and her baby before they began to walk; and he would have heard her asking God to bless this child and this mother and then Caroline telling her which song was her favorite. But all that was past and the labor hadn't started up.

"What, what can I do?" Jerome's arched eyebrow expressed his eagerness.

"Get on the other side of Caroline and help support her. We're going to walk."

"Is that wise? What if she falls?"

"There, you see? What if I fall?" Caroline's eyes grew large.

Adele glared at Jerome. To Caroline she said, "You have to trust me, Caroline. I wouldn't ask you to do a single thing that might hurt the baby. Walking helps. Mothers often walk, and if it's a spring birth where they can get outside, smell the apple blossoms, feel warm air on their arms, it speeds up the delivery. The baby wants to be here now. He broke the water. Your body is contracting as it should to help move him out."

"How do you know it's a him?"

"I don't. I'm just saying *him*, Caroline. Now he's a little tired, too, maybe, so let's help him or her arrive."

Caroline groaned, but Jerome said, "Sister, you can do this."

The three walked then from the bedroom to the kitchen table to the horsehair couch with a log cabin quilt hung over the side and then walked back again. Once or twice Adele felt Jerome's hand brush hers as they steadied Caroline. A tingle of desire ran up her arm, and she wished it would linger. She urged Caroline to talk about her childhood, speak of pleasant memories. Jerome chimed in a time or two when Caroline gasped for breath. "Good memories are important," Adele told them. "You're telling your baby what family he—or she—is being born into. Tell me about your parents, Caroline. Tell me what you loved about growing up in Milwaukee. Tell me about meeting the baby's father, all of that."

Caroline stopped to take a deep breath. The lamplight flickered with the howl of the wind, and Adele looked out the window. Snow fell again, the kind of snow that drifted up against the barns and made feeding animals difficult. She hoped Polly was all right, that she had plenty of wood in the wood box. Would she remember to tie a rope to the porch railing if the snow got too deep or the wind blew so she could always find her way back to the house from the barn? Assuming she could make it to the barn. She hoped Polly wouldn't try to feed the animals if the snow drifted deep and wet. The cows would have to fend for themselves. She prayed that the girl would be safe.

Adele was keeping one ear to the sound of Caroline's breathing and the other to the chatter between the brother and sister when Caroline arched her back and cried out: "Oh, that was horribly, horribly painful. Just horribly! You didn't tell me it would hurt so much."

Adele didn't argue with her. "You can endure this. You're strong enough to do this hard work of birthing." Adele broke into "Jingle Bells" then "Ain't Got Time to Tarry," with Caroline saying she'd heard that in the slave quarters and hadn't realized how fitting it could be for a woman walking toward motherhood. She laughed. "I want to sing 'Can Can.'" Can you imagine me doing that dance?"

Adele looked at Jerome, and both grinned. "I do believe I am no longer of good use here," he said.

But Adele told him he was. "Keep her walking and singing and laughing. What better home for a child to come into?"

Adele heard Doc Pederson arrive with Jerome late in the night, but before she could greet him, Caroline succumbed to Adele's encouragement that she squat, even though Caroline protested that only "Cherokee and slaves" gave birth that way. "I've put a hole in the wicker chair so you can sit and push against the arms, so it's not exactly the same." Within minutes of the position, Caroline cried out, and Adele was there to reach down and catch the baby. She held it while Caroline leaned back, sobbing, but this time with relief. "It's a girl." Adele watched for excess bleeding. She saw none.

Doc Pederson nodded. "Everything looks fine."

What the college doctor had written to Adele was true. This was nothing like Serena's birth, and there was no sign of blood refusing to clot.

The baby cried when Adele cleared her tiny mouth and

rubbed her slippery limbs. Caroline shouted for Jerome to enter, and Adele looked up to see tears in his eyes as he bent for his niece. Adele asked if she could offer a prayer of thanksgiving and Caroline nodded, but it was Jerome who spoke the words. "Our gratitude is beyond words, dear Lord." He turned to Adele. "My gratitude to you is beyond words as well."

Adele placed the baby on Caroline's breast and stood. Jerome reached out to Adele and she allowed it, a warm squeeze of a hand between two people who had worked together to make another's life better and to bring a new life into the fold. Adele freed herself then bent to attend to Caroline and her baby while Doc Pederson and Jerome left for cigars, Adele imagined, though she'd never seen Jerome smoke. Jerome would make a good father one day. Adele hoped this Clarissa person knew what she was getting.

Jerome's help and kindness at the delivery were a compress to Adele's hurt and disappointment over severed hopes. She could see that he was a good brother and he was a good banker. He was just a rotten fiancé. He should have told her he was engaged, and he never should have kissed her or called her beautiful.

Adele stayed two more days. The snow had stopped for a time at least, when she indicated she'd be leaving.

"I did find a girl to come in," Jerome told her. "She'll look after Caroline while I'm at work."

Until your fiancée arrives.

"I've asked her to come over today, as I know you're anxious to go. I want to go with you to make sure you're safely back at the farm."

"That's not necessary," Adele said. "I think we both know what wagon rolls ahead for each of us, and we are in separate carriages."

"I had hoped that—"

"Don't. I understand, I do. I have my responsibilities as well. I wish you well, Mr. Schmidt. I will see you at the bank in the spring. Until then, enjoy your new status as uncle. It's a very important role."

"But what's happened? We had such pleasant conversations together. I. . .wanted more of—"

"You must know that I am not the kind of woman who would interfere with a man's plans," she said. "I regret allowing myself to. . .care. So much. I have my duties. My Polly and my farm and my life delivering babies. For a short time I thought it might not be enough, but now I know it is. Thank you for allowing me to find that out. Good-bye."

"I have to go with you. I have to," he insisted. "The drifts—"

She left the porch and his words. She lifted herself onto the mule Jerome had saddled and brought to the front. Once outside of town, she would give the mule his lead and let his chest break the drifts as she trudged along behind, hanging on to his tail. She didn't want to need Jerome's presence. She could live well on her own.

The sky was as blue as her Willow plates, the sun so bright she pulled her hat to shade her eyes, to prevent burning. It took several hours to make the three-mile trek, but finally she saw the smoke rising from her chimney. When she stomped on the steps, Polly stepped out. "I knew you'd come home today," she said, her arms going around Adele.

"How did you guess?"

"I was just about to run out of sketching paper. I knew you wouldn't let me go very long without that or anything else I really needed."

"Like a good midwife."

"Like a good mother."

Chapter 10

FINAL DECISIONS

The winter of 1859–60 was harsh. Winds and cold kept Adele and Polly pushing hay from stacks while cows bawled and stood chest deep in snow. Narrow trails through the deep drifts marked the paths of deer and cows to the creek, and a smaller trail showed paths between house and barn that left both women exhausted from daily chores. By February, with only hours instead of days between light snowfall, Adele wondered out loud if they had hay enough to feed until green sprouts signaled spring.

"What will we do if we run out?" Polly wiped grease on her cheeks, so chapped and red. "No one else has hay to spare, either."

"No, they don't. We'll trust the Lord; that's all we can do." Adele stitched on a quilt face by the fireplace while Polly tried her hand at knitting. Adele didn't get much rest of late, and when she did fall into a deep sleep, she dreamed of Jerome Schmidt, much to her annoyance, in one of the dreams seeing him at the bank again to negotiate her loan. She'd have to seek a higher loan if they ran out of hay or had to replace stock that died in this thieving cold. At least she had the land. She read in the gazette that a Homestead Act was working its way through Congress that would allow land in the West to be had for twenty-five cents an acre. They could buy quite a spread if she sold the farm here in Buffalo County. And she wouldn't have to worry about begging Mr. Schmidt for money or running into his new wife, either. At least she guessed he had a new wife by now. She really didn't have any local news, since her last visit with Caroline occurred in late January when there'd been a slight break in the cold. Adele had donned snowshoes and made her way to town, sure to time it so she didn't see Jerome, and he wouldn't see her.

In late February, when the temperature dropped well below zero and stayed there, they broke ice from the creek for the cows to drink and one morning woke to discover four calves frozen to the cold earth, not able to survive their delivery during the cold night.

When March revealed a thaw, Polly's friend Sam trudged through the melting snow to give word of the preacher's plan to be at the schoolhouse later in the month. He brought other news as well, that the Bentzes were planning to head west along with several other families from the village. "Fed up with this cold," he told them, holding a cup of warm coffee in his hands. "Figure by the time they arrive in Oregon, Congress will have passed the Homestead Act, and they'll have cheap land to buy. A quarter an acre they say." Sam had thick dark hair and long slender fingers. *A surgeon's hands*, Adele thought.

"Is your family considering such a thing?" Adele asked. "Heading west?"

"Nope. We're staying put. My pa is hoping to buy up the farms of those taking leave of their senses, as he puts it. And I'm still heading east to Kentucky this fall, to start college. A man needs to be well educated in these times to take care of his family. That's what my Pa says." He smiled at Polly over his coffee cup. "I'm not sure how I'll do in school without Miss Polly here to help me with homework. I do fine with science and arithmetic, but my English, well, that's not so grand."

Polly blushed, and Adele wondered how her daughter would fare with this young man's company no longer a possibility on a summer afternoon.

"You'll have lots of girls willing to help you in Kentucky," Polly told him. "You really don't need my help. You never did." She looked directly at him, and Adele realized the girl was an encourager supporting a friend, not someone she wanted to give her heart to. "I hope you'll write now and again. I'd like to know how it is in college," she continued. "I want to go myself one day."

"Could you carry a message to a doctor there?" Adele refilled the boy's cup. "He was very helpful in giving us information about a difficult case I had as a midwife. That Polly and I had," she amended.

"I didn't even get to help with that one, Mamadele," Polly protested.

"You helped by suggesting we write to the college and by

staying here to keep things going. I'd have been lost if you hadn't. That's part of being a midwife, too, that your family keeps up their part of the bargain and allows the midwife to do her work."

"We're a team."

"That we are."

Adele hoped they always would be.

They celebrated Polly's birthday after the circuit rider's visit in March. She turned seventeen, and all the talk, aside from how lovely she looked, spun on Oregon. The Bentzes especially enthused about their plans to go west.

"You ought to come along." Idella held her toddler's hand as they sat on the ground at the schoolhouse, eating fried chicken. A spring wind caused Adele to pull her shawl tighter. "I know lots of women aren't excited about going, but I am. And Adele"—she leaned in to whisper—"I'm with child. You promised you'd be my midwife again."

"That was before I knew you wouldn't be a mile or two down the road."

Idella's voice got serious. "It is the only thing that worries me just a little. Gustaf says it'll take six months to cross, and that's after leaving from Council Bluffs in Iowa. We'll need a month to get there, and we have to be there no later than May 15. I'm already three months along. That means I will deliver somewhere between here and Oregon."

"You can do it," Adele told her.

"Aren't you ready for a new adventure? What do you have holding you here?"

Adele wasn't sure anymore. Surviving the winter had drained her, made her wonder if she could farm for the rest of her life. She didn't relish asking Jerome for another loan.

"It would be exciting, wouldn't it, Mamadele?" Polly said later. "All the talk about Oregon. And Idella does need help. A good midwife could be essential on a wagon train. You'd be well appreciated there."

"We can talk about it," Adele told her, wondering at the little stirring of interest that fidgeted in her breast. At least she'd never have to run into Jerome on a wagon train west, and she wouldn't ever have to worry about Polly's father catching up with them, either.

Jerome Schmidt's winter had been full of meeting Caroline's needs. He'd secured a young girl to come in to help. He'd hired three, in fact, as Caroline's demands sent the girls scurrying, one after the other. The latest—a Norwegian girl—said she could be as stubborn as an ox when he described Caroline's. . . ways. The girl stood up to her, and Caroline backed down. He realized what a gem Adele had been in being able to deal so well with his sister. Doc Pederson seemed to enjoy his sister's company, and Jerome didn't want to ask why. He appreciated the respite whenever the doctor took Caroline's attention. Meanwhile, little Emily grew fat and happy, and his time holding her was the joy of his life. The only joy in his life. He missed Adele and couldn't understand why she'd frozen him out so suddenly, just when he'd begun to believe she might have feelings for him. He hoped she'd be in soon for her interview about the loan. It was already mid-April, and several other farmers had come in so they could purchase seed and get planting as soon as the fields dried up. Adele was conscientious and should be coming in any day now. At least he might have a business relationship with her, and maybe in time...

He sighed then mumbled about the newspaper.

"What were you saying, Jerome?" Caroline rocked little Emily, smiling at the baby. Maybe Caroline would be an adequate mother after all, finding someone besides herself to truly care about.

"This rag," he said, folding the paper and tearing it into strips he'd use to start the fire. "It's a waste of good paper. Never says anything of import that I haven't already heard from the *Milwaukee Gazette*. I should start my own."

"There's little to be done about the news, anyway, so what does it matter if it's a month late?"

"Local news would be nice to get."

"You get that at the bank, don't you? Or Olson's store? Did you hear that a wagon train is starting out from the village with several from here joining up?"

"Yes, I heard the rumors, but there's nothing in the paper about it. And how did you learn of it?"

"Why, Adele came by for a final checkup with me and little Emily yesterday. She approves of your new hire, by the way, and she asked when Clarissa was going to arrive. I told her I didn't know. Any day, I suppose, though you certainly haven't said anything about the wedding date, dear brother. Not that I've asked. I'm not a meddler, you know."

"Clarissa?" he said. "Why on earth would Miss Adele mention Clarissa?"

"She knows she's your fiancée. I told her myself."

"What? When did you tell her?"

"Why, about the time she stayed here to help with Emily's birth. Was it a secret?"

"No secret, Caroline. But it also isn't true. I'm not marrying Clarissa. She isn't joining me here in Mondovi. She's already married someone else by now."

"How was I to know? You never said, and you always look at your timepiece with such longing. You said Clarissa gave it to you, and you told me you were engaged. I just assumed—"

"Wrongly. Quite wrongly." He stood, looked at his timepiece, sat down, then stood again. He could be at Adele's farm in less than an hour.

"Should we take the cast-iron spider with us?" Polly shouted to Adele, who bent over a barrel in the bedroom, folding quilts into the bottom.

"Just one skillet, that's all we'll need. And the Dutch oven. Gustaf says enough is as good as a feast, so just take enough." Adele walked back out into the main room where Polly sat like a frog on a lily pad surrounded by sifters, dishes, ladles, and pans. "We'll bury the Willow dishes in the cornmeal barrel."

She lifted a plate. The dishes would remind her of John, who had bought them as a wedding gift, although the color would always make her think of Jerome's deep-blue eyes. "Yes, just one skillet, but we'll try for the entire set of dishes."

Adele's heart fluttered at the speed with which she'd made this decision. Polly had danced with joy when they'd discussed going west well into the night. She'd already sold the farm to Sam's dad, cows included. Idella was almost as happy as Polly about their decision. "I'll have two midwives, just like last time."

"And I can look after Luke in the meantime," Polly said.

With the purchase money, Adele bought a wagon and hired a mule skinner to drive it, a cousin of Gustaf's. The two wagons would join three others rumbling out from Mondovi by week's end, the high water from the snowmelt having peaked. She felt excited, full of possibilities. She was thirty-seven years old but not too old to start a new adventure. She could farm in Oregon—or who knew what she might do there? The choices were endless.

"Will we be ready by Friday, Mamadele?"

"We'd better be."

Adele found herself nostalgic, running her hands across furniture they'd have to leave, memories flooding over her like rivers over rocks. "Are you all right, Mamadele?"

Adele wiped her eyes with her apron. "Just saying good-bye," she said. "It's the right thing to do, I know it is. But change is still hard, isn't it?"

"I guess," Polly said, and Adele envied the girl's youth and flexibility. She'd have to mine some of that from her own past.

"Rider coming." Polly squinted, looking down the lane. "He sits a horse like Mr. Schmidt, all tall and lean in the saddle."

Adele stopped her reminiscing, looked out the window.

"What could he want? I paid the loan."

The man barely pulled up his horse before he dismounted. "Adele. Miss Adele." He looked at Polly, who had moved in behind Adele on the porch.

"Is Caroline all right?"

"Yes, yes. How good of you to think of her. She's fine. Wonderful. In fact, she told me something that I have to confirm with you—" He looked around at the barrels and wooden boxes on the porch. "Confirm with you before you go? Are you going somewhere?"

"To Oregon. It's going to be wonderful. Mamadele and I are teaming up with the Bentzes. She's having a baby, and Mamadele and I are her midwives. She gets two."

"Oregon? But—"

"There was really nothing holding us here. And Polly was ready for a new adventure. So was I," Adele said. "I found I longed for. . .something more."

"Listen, please, before you go. Caroline told me—" He was gasping for breath. He swallowed and started again.

"Can I get you water?"

"Yes, please, Polly. Adele, Miss Adele, please stay."

"I'll get it." Polly disappeared to the pump with a ladle in hand.

"Caroline told me this morning that she told you about Clarissa."

"Such news should have come from you." Adele's shoulders were straight as a wagon tongue.

"Yes, but it wasn't any news at all. I was engaged to Clarissa—"

"Which you should have told me."

"But the engagement was broken long before I even came to Mondovi. Clarissa broke it off, and when I met you, I knew it was the best thing that ever happened to me. I love you, Adele."

It was what she'd longed to hear, but now?

"If there is even the slightest hope that you might find it possible to love me, too, I'll go to the ends of the earth to wait until you tell me yes."

"Yes to what?"

"To my proposal of marriage. Will you marry me, Adele Marley?"

"What have I missed?" Polly asked, returning.

"Mr. Schmidt, Jerome, has just asked me to marry him." She was laughing, the joy bubbling up inside of her like steam in a pot.

"Will you?"

"I—I don't know." She looked into his blue eyes the color of her Willow blue and said, "Yes. I will. Yes."

Jerome whooped and lifted her, spinning her around, and he kissed her right there in front of Polly.

"What. . .what does this mean for Oregon?" Polly said.

Adele stopped. "I don't know."

"The Bentzes are counting on us, Mamadele. And you've sold the farm."

"Yes, they are counting on us." She looked at Jerome.

"I'm not known for making quick decisions," he said. "But the wagon can probably use another man to help, and if my intended wife is heading west, then I'm going to be right there with her."

"What about Caroline?"

He paused, thoughtful then. "She has resources, and Doc Pederson to manage them, it seems."

"But what will you do there?"

"Maybe I'll farm." Adele frowned. "Or I'll. . .start a newspaper or work for one. Whatever it takes. We'll find a way."

"And you'll not object to my being 'the little midwife'?"

"Object? How can a man object to a woman's clear calling?"

Adele laughed, and then she cried in joy.

"I guess we'll have a wedding first," Polly said.

"I guess we will," Adele and Jerome said together, and he swung Adele one more time around the porch.

It was during that second swing that Jerome lost his balance and, still holding Adele, fell against the wobbly porch post, which gave way. The two of them landed just a short distance in the rocky dirt, but enough distance for Jerome to groan in pain when they hit the dust. The horse sidestepped out of their way. When Adele lifted herself from him and he rolled, she saw the rock that had broken their fall. And she saw his leg askew.

"I—I think it's broken."

"I think you're right."

Chapter 11

New Beginnings

After the doctor set the bone and Jerome lay resting, with Caroline hovering, Adele led Polly to the Schmidt porch. Adele sat with her arm around the girl, struggling with the greatest difficulty in her life.

"You can't leave him, Mamadele."

"I know. But I can't disappoint Idella either."

Polly took a deep breath. "You don't have to. Idella needs one of us, and that can be me."

"Oh, Polly. I'm not sure—"

"You can send your journal with me so I'll have your wisdom and God's help. You'll still be a midwife for Idella, in spirit and through me. You know I'm responsible. And I really, really want to go west."

Adele swallowed. "We could all wait until next year and go maybe, when Jerome's leg is healed."

"A midwife keeps her commitments. Isn't that what you said?"

"Yes, it is." Adele ached as though she were ripped apart.

"I might never see you again." Polly's eyes pooled with tears. "But either both of us stay here to help him heal or we sacrifice being together for another family." Polly tugged at her braid, adding, "One day I'll marry, and we'd part then, too."

Adele's voice caught at the truth of that. "You'd sacrifice having your Mamadele by your side?"

"Not just my Mamadele," Polly said. "But my mama. That's what you are." Adele hugged the girl, unable to speak. "I can do this, Mama, because you've taught me. I'll be strong, and you and Mr. Schmidt can have a new life here and come after, maybe."

"You did manage for two weeks on your own. A girl who can do that can travel west without her mother and help bring a new baby safely into this world."

Polly wiped away Adele's tears, pushing back her braid.

"You just have one last duty to perform before you leave."

"What's that?"

"To be my witness at our wedding."

The members of the wagon train stood ready to drive away from the schoolhouse as soon as the 6:00 a.m. vows were spoken and they'd feasted at the wedding breakfast.

Jerome sat with his braced leg straight out from the chair, resting on a cassock. Adele stood next to him in her best gingham dress. There'd been no time to make a new dress or even alter the one Caroline offered. This church dress would do. Polly waited behind Adele, and Caroline stood to the side as a witness for her brother, Doc Pederson holding Emily. The women held a few tulips as the circuit rider led them in prayer.

They could have waited to marry until Jerome could stand, but Adele wanted Polly to be a part of this important day and Polly was heading west. The girl wore the pearl hair clip that had been her mother's. Adele had given it to her with the story that accompanied it that morning as they'd dressed. "Your mother gave me this, and I know she would want you to have it."

"It's beautiful." Polly rubbed her fingers on the pearls. "Smooth as a baby's bottom."

Adele smiled. "Wear it knowing you have always been loved and always will be."

Jerome had surprised them both just before several men helped carry him out by insisting that Polly take his timepiece with her. "You might need it for that counting thing you midwives do."

Adele couldn't remember when she'd been so happy and so sad at the same time. It was a little like being a midwife— the joy of a birth and the sadness of leaving this new family to their own ways and routines. This second chance at love was the greatest gift Adele had ever been given—save her Polly—and yet waving good-bye to Polly because of it would be the hardest thing she'd ever do.

But it is what she did after the ceremony, handing Polly the old journal and pulling her close. "You remember to say your prayers." Adele patted the girl's back. "Nothing is impossible with God."

"I know, Mamade—" Polly stopped. "I know, Mama. I'll do my best to make you proud."

"You already have."

"I have something for you, too." Polly rushed to the back of the Bentz wagon and opened one of the boxes. "It's a self-portrait." She handed Adele the sketch paper. "I worked on it looking in a mirror while you were delivering Mr. Schmidt's niece. I think it looks like me."

"It does, oh, it does indeed." She would frame it and hang it. . .somewhere in a house that she and Jerome would share.

Gustaf Bentz stood beside her then. "Is time to go."

"I know. I know. You take good care of my girl." Adele clung to Polly, one hand on the sketch.

"And she takes good care of my Idella."

Polly pulled her hand loose and, fighting back tears, walked to the front of the wagon. Sunlight glinted off the pearl clip as the party moved out, the women and children walking beside. Polly turned and blew a kiss, and then Adele was standing back beside Jerome.

"You write!" Adele shouted. Polly nodded then walked down the hill out of sight.

Jerome reached for her hand. "Mrs. Schmidt, you are beautiful, even when you're crying."

She squeezed his hand back, staring into the space Polly left. "Mothers do cry, you know. In sadness and in joy."

Epilogue

One year later

My dearest Polly,

I hope this letter finds you happy and well. I await details of your new life. We are fine here. The ink for Jerome's new paper arrived late for the latest edition, but the story did get out about the President's refusal to sign the 1860 Homestead Act. Perhaps there'll be another so the Bentzes will have their Oregon farm after all one day.

My time goes well, though it keeps us from joining you. In two more months you will have a brother or sister. I have found a midwife comfortable with assisting at the first birth of an older mother. I wish it was you being my midwife, but I know you will be here in spirit. We midwives belong to that circle that tends and befriends, "with woman," wherever women gather and are together, no matter the separation of time or distance. We defy the pharaohs of fear and uncertainty and replace

*them with hope and joy. Blessings on your days, dear
Polly. Keep writing in that journal. I seal this with tears
of joy.*

Your beloved mother

Award-winning author JANE KIRK-PATRICK is well known for her authentically portrayed historical fiction. She is also an acclaimed speaker and teacher with a lively presentation style. She and her husband live in Oregon and, until recently, lived and worked on a remote homestead for over twenty-five years.

THE MIDWIFE'S
APPRENTICE

by Rhonda Gibson

Dedication

To Aili Rae Gibson Tullis.
I love you, Miss Bell.

Chapter 1

Summer 1860

F orm up!"

The words snapped through the hot morning air. Sharper than a mule skinner's whip, the order was picked up and echoed around the camp. Polly took her place beside the wagon.

Mamadele had called the trip to Oregon a grand adventure. Polly frowned. Her grand adventure had turned into endless days of walking, choking on dirt from the wagons, and being lonely. Since she traveled with the Bentz family, she really wasn't alone, but Polly was the outsider, just the midwife's apprentice. Oh, Idella Bentz had never called her such, but Polly could see the worry in the soon-to-be mother's eyes.

At the end of each day, thanks to Mamadele's journal and the sketch paper she'd brought, Polly found relief from the endless travel. The soothing sounds of the oxen, cattle, and horses also gave her comfort as she read or sketched in her small tent at night. Thanks to her little mule, Beulah, Polly was able to ride some days. When she was walking, Beulah gently pushed her from behind, often with Luke Bentz sitting on Polly's hip. At first the men had protested the small mule being with her, but Mr. Bentz had put a stop to their grumbling. For that, Polly was thankful.

According to Mr. Bentz, they should arrive at the new Fort Kearney by nightfall. Polly prayed it would be so. Her feet hurt and she was tired. If Idella didn't need her so badly, Polly would have already turned around and ridden her little mule home.

"Polly, would you mind carrying Luke for a while?"

Polly stopped at the sound of Idella's voice. Just last night she'd read Mamadele's words: *Be an even, stable influence, never cheery one day and morose the next.* She forced her face to relax and smiled. Idella's face was thin and pale beneath the blond bangs that escaped from under the stiff brim of her brown bonnet. She wasn't that much older than Polly but already had one child and another on the way. That she was in discomfort was plain in her taut face and posture. "Of course. You shouldn't be lugging him about." She offered a smile to take the sting out of her words.

"I know. But he's restless, and I can't continue to struggle with him in this heat up on the seat. I'm fearful he will fall under the wheels of the wagon like the Smith boy did last week." Tears filled Idella's tired eyes.

Again the words from the journal filled Polly's mind. *Be reliable. Your patient must know you will be there fully when needed, so be faithful in the small things.* She placed Luke on her hip and then reached with her free hand to pat Idella's shoulder. "Don't fret, Idella. I'll watch Luke as if he were my own. Go back to the wagon and rest."

"Thank you, child."

Child. The term angered Polly and at the same time reminded her that she'd only recently turned seventeen.

Idella waddled back to the wagon. Polly captured her lower lip between her teeth. Idella was larger than she should be at five months, and yesterday she'd confided that the baby seemed much more active than little Luke had been at this stage. Polly suspected that Idella carried more than one baby.

The sick, hollow feeling she'd been fighting for days filled her stomach. Could she be a midwife without Mamadele to help her? Why had she agreed to continue on with the Bentzes to Oregon? What if Idella died in childbirth, like her own mother had? If she did die, what would happen to Luke and the baby—or babies—should they live? Would Mr. Bentz abandon his children, like her father had her?

Polly took a deep breath. Her fate had been decided the moment Jerome Schmidt broke his leg and married her Mamadele. They'd sent her packing, never giving her the chance to think about what her new life would be like. Polly knew she was being unfair; it had been her own idea to continue on without them. Still, now, when she felt so alone, it was easy to blame them.

She blinked to clear her vision and focused her attention on the last-minute rush of activity to block out the hurt and fears. Women and children hurried to finish packing their wagons, men finished checking the yokes on their oxen, and whips snaked over the backs of the teams that were already prepared. The line began forming.

"Haw, Max! Haw, Ruby!"

The command drew her gaze from the rest of the camp. Mr. Bentz walked alongside his oxen. They leaned into their yokes and moved forward. Idella waved from the bench as their wagon fell into line with the others. Luke waved back.

Polly placed one foot in front of the other. After a little while the boy settled down and leaned his head on her shoulder. Within a few more minutes, he sucked his thumb and closed his eyes. Polly smiled, even though inside she felt like crying as dust and dirt coated their faces and her feet began to burn. Silently she prayed, *I can do all things through Christ who strengthens me.*

Gordon Baker stopped Rawhide at the edge of the knoll, rested his hands on the pommel, and studied the wagons rolling across the plain and toward the fort. The large mule under him brayed. He reached forward and patted her neck.

"What do you think, ole girl? Is that the one?" He eyed the wagons as they circled up near the fort.

The mule bobbed her head as if to say, "Sure, why not?" Gordon laughed. He closed his eyes and silently asked the Lord the same question. Deep in his soul he felt that familiar pull of direction. Yes, this was the correct wagon train. Gordon knew it was headed to Willamette Valley. He gently tapped Rawhide's side and started down the small incline toward the fort.

Halfway across the plain he noticed a woman with a little

boy settled on her hip. A small mule butted her back, and a purple bonnet shaded her face from his view. Her shoulders were slumped, and looking at her posture, he was sure she would drop at any moment.

He turned Rawhide and headed in her direction. When he came close enough, Gordon smiled and offered assistance. "Would you like some help, ma'am?"

The little boy hung on her much like pictures he'd seen of monkeys hanging on to their mothers. The boy giggled and tried to scramble free.

She raised her head. Tired hazel eyes looked up at him. A smile was painted on her full lips. She seemed much too young to have a child. "No, thank you. Luke's mother will be here in just a moment and she'll take him then."

Gordon enjoyed the silkiness of her honey-sweet voice and found himself offering more assistance. "What about your mule? Would you like some help with her?"

"No, thank you."

The smoothness was now gone from her voice, and a sting much like a honeybee's pierced through the silkiness, leaving no doubt she was annoyed. Gordon looked into her eyes. They no longer looked tired but hard and unrelenting. Her lips now were pulled into a thin line. "Then I will take my leave of you. Good day."

Gordon rode into the fort and sighed. It was too bad the woman's disposition didn't match her beauty.

Chapter 2

Gordon slid off the mule and turned it into the small fenced-in corral. He couldn't get the hazel-eyed woman off his mind. *Judge not, lest ye be judged,* circled through his thoughts. His first impression had been one of a bitter woman, but what did he know about her? Nothing.

Since they were going to be traveling with the same wagon train, he'd need to be more patient with her. After all, she was probably just tired from the long journey. The boy on her hip was a chubby little lad; toting him all the way from wherever their jumping-off point had been would certainly be wearisome for anyone. He made the decision to try harder not to judge others. *Thank You, Lord, for reminding me to watch my thoughts about my fellow brothers and sisters in Christ.*

"Hey, Reverend!" A young boy ran up to him. "Did you see the new wagon train that just pulled in?"

He ruffled the boy's blond hair. "Sure did, Daniel."

Daniel climbed on the log fence and stood on the lowest

log. "Think you might join up with them?"

Gordon nodded. "I believe so, Daniel." He rested his arms on the top rail and looked out at the mules.

"Did the Lord tell you it was all right?"

Gordon looked down at the ten-year-old boy. "Yes, He did."

"Did He say I can come with you?"

Gordon had known the question was coming, and he really wanted to tell the boy yes. But the truth of the matter was God had been silent when he'd asked Him that very same question. "Not yet."

Daniel jumped down from the fence. He lifted sky-blue eyes and choked out, "I was hopin' He'd let me come with you." Shoulders slumped, he walked away.

During his three-month stay at the fort, Daniel had become Gordon's constant companion. The boy had shared his parents' dream of going to Oregon and starting a farm. He'd told Gordon how they'd been swept away by one of the many rivers they had passed through. But it was the commander of the fort who told how one of the families had taken the boy in and then abandoned him when their train left the next morning.

Gordon laid his forehead on his arms and prayed. "Lord, if it be Your will for me to take the boy with me, please supply a way." He looked up to find the fort commander standing beside him.

"So you're leaving in the morning with the wagon train, huh?" The commander chewed on the end of an unlit cigar.

"If they will have me." Gordon pushed away from the fence and stood a little taller. He respected the man in front of him.

The commander was an older man with a gray beard and

eyes the color of coal. His uniform was always crisp and clean, but what impressed Gordon was the man's esteem for his men. He never asked them to do something he wasn't willing to do himself.

"Will you be stopping by the hospital before you leave?" He chewed the cigar, and his eyes bored into Gordon's.

As far as Gordon knew, there were no sick men at the hospital right now. Had the wagon train brought in sick or injured folks? "I will if I'm needed."

"I asked Doc to make up a box of medical supplies for you to take along. If there is a doctor among the immigrants, you can give it to him. If not, you'll have to use them to the best of your abilities." The commander took the cigar from his mouth and tucked it into his front pocket. Then he extended his hand to Gordon.

Gordon smiled as he shook the commander's hand. "Thank you."

"You be careful on that trail, Reverend. I'll look you up as soon as my tour of duty is over."

Gordon pulled the man forward and pounded him on the back. "I'll be looking for you, John."

The men separated, and John nodded. "Don't worry about the boy. I'll see that he's taken care of, should the good Lord see fit for him to stay behind." He turned sharply on his heel and walked away.

Gordon sighed. He hadn't realized how hard it would be to leave the fort. His gaze moved to the hospital and Sutler's store. They were wooden buildings, not very pretty on the outside but much nicer on the inside than the mud buildings that housed the soldiers.

As he entered the hospital, he heard a lowered female voice. "So as long as things go right, it will be like a normal birth?" Her voice sounded familiar.

Gordon stopped just outside the doorway and waited. He didn't want to interrupt the doctor and his patient. For a brief moment, he considered leaving the hospital and waiting outside, but then the doctor spoke again, catching and holding his attention.

"Much the same. The second baby will come shortly after the first. Do you have someone you can pass the first baby off to?"

Her voice sounded uncertain. "I'll see if one of the other women can be present. Of course, I have no idea what the conditions will be on the trail when the babies come."

Was that the voice of the woman he'd spoken to earlier? The one with the chubby little boy? From the sound of things she was expecting twins. No wonder she'd been cross.

The doctor's voice grew louder, as if the two were walking toward him. "I'm sure you will do fine, Miss Schultz."

Miss Schultz? Was she an unwed mother? Surely the doctor had said *Mrs.* Schultz?

Polly rounded the corner and found herself stopping abruptly as she came face-to-face with the stranger who had offered her assistance earlier. What was he doing here?

"I'll be right with you, Reverend." The doctor placed his

hand in the small of her back and said, "If you think of any more questions, feel free to stop by again before you leave."

Reverend? Reverend? The word screeched through her mind with the sound of a squeaky wheel.

Polly nodded, never taking her eyes off the cowboy who had moved aside to let her pass. What reverend wore a Stetson hat, had eyes the color of sapphires and a firm jaw with short whiskers that gave him a hardened criminal look?

Just before stepping through the door, Polly remembered her manners. "Thank you, Doctor, for your advice." She turned and her gaze connected with the reverend's over the doctor's shoulder.

"You are most welcome, Miss Schultz." The doctor smiled at her and nodded before closing the door.

She'd thought the reverend was a scoundrel when he'd offered help earlier. The man had been riding a mule and had been covered in trail dust. What must he think of her? She'd been rude. Polly shook her head. It didn't matter what he thought. They'd be leaving in the morning, and she'd never see the man again.

Chapter 3

Polly set her sketch paper on the blanket beside her. She ignored the face that looked up at her from the paper. To keep her mind off him, she focused on the fort that bustled with activity. Men, women, children, Indians, and soldiers entered and exited the stronghold. What was it about the reverend that had her sketching his face and looking for him in the hustle and bustle of the fort?

She shoved the paper into the tent and then stood to go check on Beulah. The Bentzes had gone to the store, leaving Polly to sketch to her heart's content. She'd already written in the journal about the fort and had even sketched it.

Polly's heart ached with longing for Mamadele. Reading the journal today didn't ease the loss of the only mother she'd ever known. She smiled at the young man keeping watch over the horses and mules. Beulah came running to her.

"Are you going to take her for a ride, Miss Polly?" He

brushed dark-brown hair off his brow; then his gaze darted to the ground.

Mark Calhoun was nice enough, but Polly couldn't see herself with the shy young man. He reminded her of Sam, the boy back home who had been her friend. "No, but I will take her for a stroll, if that's all right."

"I'm sure it is, as long as you stay close to camp." At her nod he continued, "It still amazes me that that mule will follow you around like a dog." He offered Polly the rope that he'd slipped over Beulah's neck.

The rope wasn't needed, but Polly understood the young man's use of it. Most mules were cantankerous, but not Beulah. Polly smiled at him. "Thank you." She scratched Beulah's ears and patted her neck.

As she walked away, Mark called, "See you."

Polly waved at him and continued walking. A path led to the river, and she followed it. She could still see the fort, so she felt safe in leaving the camp behind. The sound of water running greeted her as she drew closer to the river.

The little mule gave her a nudge in the back. "I hear it, too." Beulah gave her another push. "Stop shoving—I'm going." She smiled over her shoulder at her companion, the only breathing connection she had to home and Mamadele. *Lord, please keep Beulah safe as we journey to Oregon. I need her.*

Beulah drank deeply from the river. Polly sat down, pulled her knees up, and sighed. After several long moments of listening to the water run over the rocks, she laid her head on her knees. What had the reverend been doing at the doctor's? Was he sick?

Did he know and care about someone who was sick?

"Do you mind if I throw rocks into the water?"

She looked up to find a young boy with blue eyes, crooked teeth, and wheat-colored hair looking down on her. "No, go ahead."

"I'm Daniel Carter." He tossed a stone into the water.

"Is that the best you can do, Daniel Carter?"

"What do you mean?"

Polly stood, picked up a smooth stone, and weighed it in her hand. "I mean, is that your best attempt at skipping a stone across the water?" She walked to the river's edge, and with a sidearm toss and a flick of her wrist, she sent the rock skipping across the water.

Daniel gasped. "That's amazing."

"Haven't you ever skipped stones before?" Polly picked up another stone.

"Sure. But mine never go that far." He stared at her as if she were a three-eyed frog.

Polly couldn't help giggling at his awestruck face. "Want me to teach you the trick?" she asked, once she'd stopped laughing.

"Oh yes." He scooped up more rocks and came to stand beside her.

She showed him how to stand, pull his arm back at a twenty-degree angle, flick his wrist, and release the stone. Soon Daniel was skipping stones almost as well as she could.

"You're with the new wagon train, huh?"

Polly smiled as she rubbed Beulah's shoulders and back. She heard the sadness in his voice and turned to face him, but he was looking out over the water. "Yes, I am."

"I wish I could go with you."

Polly walked over to him and dropped her arm around his shoulder. "I wish you could, too, but I'm traveling with the Bentz family, and we don't have the extra room."

Daniel looked up at her with soulful eyes. "I don't take up much room."

"You would miss your family."

He shook his head. "Ma and Pa are in heaven."

Her heart twisted. "I see."

Daniel pulled away from her. "No, you don't. I've been cast aside like a dirty rag. No one wants me."

Didn't she feel the same way? Hadn't her father abandoned her, and hadn't Mamadele chosen to go on with her new life with her new husband? Sending Polly to travel to Oregon alone?

She touched his arm. "You would be surprised how much I understand."

Gordon searched everywhere for Daniel. He'd finished his business with the wagon master and wanted to tell the boy he'd be leaving first thing in the morning. When he couldn't find him within the fort, he decided to go down to the riverbank. Daniel often went there to think and play.

He spotted Daniel and the Schultz woman coming back from the river. The little mule followed them. The boy smiled at something she said, and his grin grew when he saw Gordon.

Daniel ran to meet him. "Reverend! Miss Polly said she

might be able to get me on the wagon train with you all."

"She did?" Why had she told Daniel such a thing? Why would she build his hopes and then have them dashed on the morrow?

"Yep, but I'll have to work hard because the family she has in mind needs help taking care of their team and the other stock they have with them. Isn't that right, Miss Polly?" Daniel turned toward Miss Schultz.

"That's right, Daniel, but I can't promise you that the Smiths will let you come. I'll have to ask them." She came to stand beside them. Her hazel eyes looked into Gordon's, and a light pink filled her cheeks.

"Isn't that great, Reverend?" Daniel beamed up at him.

"It is, son. Why don't you run on ahead? I'd like to talk to Miss Polly in private." He placed his hand on the boy's shoulder and silently prayed he would not be too bitterly disappointed.

"All right. I'll go pack. The Smiths might want me to come to the wagon tonight, and I want to be ready."

Before Gordon could answer, Daniel ran toward the fort.

Fury built in Gordon's chest at the woman. Didn't she realize how crushed the boy would be if this Smith family turned him down? Words forced their way between his clenched teeth. "Woman! Have you lost your mind?"

"No, I believe it is still here." She raised her head and continued walking.

"How could you make such a promise to that boy? He has been through so much already, and for you to build his hopes up, without knowing what the Smiths will say, is just cruel."

Gordon felt the rise of heat in his face and clenched his teeth to stop the anger that would soon spew all over the inconsiderate woman if he didn't get control of himself.

She spun on her heels and punched a finger into his chest. "Now you see here, Reverend. I did not build up the boy's hopes. We talked at length about this, and I can assure you, I did not make any promises." She poked him again before pressing on. "But, for good measure, I know for a fact that Daniel will be welcome in the Smiths' wagon. I just need to talk to the family and tell them his story." She stepped back and placed her hands on her hips. The color in her cheeks flamed. Dark-brown hair with auburn highlights escaped the confines of her bonnet. "And furthermore, that little boy loves you, and his only desire is to go with you to Oregon. So don't judge me. You are the one who is going to leave him behind like an overused shoe." With that, Polly Schultz turned around and stomped off to the wagon train. Her little mule hurried after her.

Gordon stood perfectly still. Her finger had branded his chest when she'd touched him. Her forthrightness had prevented him from any speech, and her anger could burn a hole through the toughest metal. That was one irate woman. He hated to admit to himself that she was right. He'd have to apologize to her.

He exhaled and followed Daniel into the fort. How would he take care of Daniel once they'd made it to Oregon? He figured he'd have to cross that mountain when he came to it. Gordon found the wagon master and let him know that Daniel would be traveling with him. He then went to the store to purchase more food supplies.

An hour later, Gordon found Daniel sitting on his small cot sorting through his few belongings. The boy smiled when he saw Gordon standing in the doorway. "I was just trying to decide if I'll have room for my slingshot in the Smiths' wagon."

"I don't think so, son." Gordon sat down beside him. "But there is plenty of room in mine, if you'd still be interested in riding with me."

Gordon felt a tug at his heart as the boy turned hopeful eyes on him.

His voice quivered. "Ya mean it?"

Gordon stood. "I do."

Daniel jumped up and hugged him tight around the waist. Sobs shook his young shoulders.

Until that moment, Gordon hadn't realized how much this trip meant to the boy. He gently pulled him away and knelt down in front of him. He pulled a handkerchief from his back pocket and wiped Daniel's face. "Here, blow." When Daniel did as he was told, Gordon continued, "I'm not your father, and I would never pretend I am, but on this trip you have to listen to what I say and do as I ask. Can you do that?"

Daniel nodded. "Yes sir."

"And that's another thing. I'll no longer have you calling me Reverend; that's too formal." Gordon rubbed his chin. Would it be all right for the boy to simply call him Gordon?

Daniel mimicked his actions. "Miss Polly told me her mama died and now she has a Mamadele. Maybe I could call you Papa Gordon?"

Gordon pretended to be in deep thought. He stroked

his chin and looked heavenward. "Hmm, Papa Gordon." He lowered his head and looked the boy straight in the eyes. "Kind of has a nice ring to it, at that. Are you sure that's what you want to call me?"

Daniel nodded and said, "Papa Gordon sounds right to me."

"Then Papa Gordon it is." Gordon stood and dusted off the knees of his pants. "Come along, Daniel. You can help me finish loading the wagon."

As Daniel gathered up his pillow, blanket, bag of clothes, and slingshot, Gordon's thoughts turned to Miss Polly. What was she going to say when she learned that he was now a papa?

Chapter 4

Polly stomped back to the wagon train. What was it about that man that set her on edge and caused her to lose her temper like that? His tone, and the way he acted all high and mighty. She shoved her bonnet back on and tied the stings as she walked.

Would he do as she suggested and take the boy on? Or should she approach Mrs. Smith about Daniel riding with them?

"Did you have a nice walk, Miss Schultz?"

She'd forgotten all about Mark and Beulah. She was thankful the little mule trailed along behind her. "Yes, I did. Thank you."

He picked up the rope that hung limply around Beulah's neck and took it off before turning her into the corral. "Miss Schultz, may I ask you a question?"

Polly dreaded to hear his next words. She nodded and tried to think of a way to nicely let him down.

"As you know, there isn't a doctor on the wagon train, and my sister is with child." He took a deep breath and continued, "We were wondering, would you be a midwife to her?" Again he paused. "Like you are to Mrs. Bentz."

Polly swallowed hard. So he wasn't interested in her as a woman but as a midwife. Hadn't Mamadele always said that being a midwife came before everything else? She looked down at her shoes to hide her disappointment. Not that she would have allowed him to court her, but it would have been nice if he'd at least been interested.

He cleared his throat.

When she looked up, Polly saw that his neck and cheeks were red. "I'd have to talk to your sister about it, Mr. Calhoun. If she wants to talk to me, I'll be in my tent."

"Thank you, Miss Schultz. I'll tell her."

Polly nodded and then turned to go. She looked toward the fort and sighed. Did she want to take on another mother? She wasn't sure she could do the right thing by Mrs. Bentz if she took on another mother. *Lord, please give me wisdom as I decide what to do.*

She made her way to the Smiths' wagon. Mr. and Mrs. Smith were sitting beside their campfire. "May I join you?" She stopped on the edge of their camp.

Mrs. Smith waved for her to join them. "Please, do come on over. I just put a fresh pot of coffee on."

Sadness from the loss of her son still lingered in the woman's eyes. Polly wondered if asking them to take Daniel would be too hard on her. But then again, maybe the boy was just what the couple needed. She prayed silently as she sat down.

"What brings you our way?" Mr. Smith asked. He picked up his pocketknife and began whittling on a small piece of wood.

Mrs. Smith handed a tin cup to Polly, and she took a sip before answering. "A ten-year-old named Daniel."

Mr. Smith grunted. "What about him?"

"Mr. Smith, don't be rude," Mrs. Smith reprimanded softly. She turned an interested gaze on Polly. "Please go on, Miss Schultz."

"Daniel would like to go to Oregon with the wagon train. He's waiting for the reverend to decide if he will bring him along with him, but if the reverend decides he can't, I was wondering if he might travel with you?" Polly felt as if she were out of air, she'd talked so fast.

The couple exchanged looks. Mrs. Smith's eyes held hope. Mr. Smith's were filled with sorrow.

He lowered his knife. "Now, Harriet, you know we can't take on the lad."

"Why not? He could help you with the team and the cows." She poured fresh coffee into his mug.

Polly took another sip of her coffee. She prayed that they'd take the boy. It hadn't occurred to her that Mr. Smith would refuse.

He shook his head. "That's true, but he'll never replace our boy."

Mrs. Smith's eyes filled with tears. "No, but we have both been so lonesome. Wouldn't it be nice to have the lad around during the day?"

Mr. Smith turned to face Polly. "Where's he gonna sleep?"

She sat up straighter. "I had thought he could stay with you, in your wagon." Polly knew Daniel could sleep under the wagon, but she hated the thought of him sleeping there alone at night. Even though he was ten years old, Daniel seemed small for his age.

Mr. Smith spit on the ground to show his disapproval. "I'll not have a half-grown boy sleeping in our wagon with us."

"If I can find him another place to sleep, would you be willing to keep an eye on him during the day?" Polly asked.

He nodded. "We'll feed him breakfast and lunch, but someone else will need to feed him supper." He sliced off another piece of wood with the knife.

Polly stood. What had she done? Polly had been sure Mr. Smith would be happy, even grateful for Daniel's help. Had the reverend been correct in his scolding? Who would take on feeding the little boy in the evenings and give him a place to sleep? Since she was traveling with the Bentzes, Polly couldn't very well offer to feed the boy. And, as Mr. Smith said, he was half grown. Would people talk if she allowed him to stay with her? Surely not. After all, he was only a child. She stepped out of the circle of light and started to walk toward her tent.

"You seem deep in thought."

Polly groaned inwardly. She recognized the reverend's voice. "I am."

"Anything I can help you with?"

She looked out of the corner of her eye and saw his knowing grin. "I don't think so."

"You never know until you ask."

Polly stopped and turned toward him. She took a deep breath and confessed. "You were right. I shouldn't have gotten Daniel's hopes up."

"It didn't go like you expected back there, did it?" He placed his hands in his pockets and leaned back on his boot heels.

She wanted to be angry at him but knew it was her own fault that she'd spoken before she should have. "No, it didn't. And now I have to tell Daniel he can't go." Tears filled her eyes. She hated being wrong, and she hated that she was going to have to break that little boy's heart.

The sight of impending tears caused Gordon's throat to grow dry. He hated to see a woman cry. "Miss Schultz, I've asked Daniel to come along with me."

Her head snapped back, and the purple bonnet slid off her head. "You asked him?"

Gordon nodded. He took his hands out of his pockets and gave her what he hoped was one of his reassuring smiles.

Her eyes flashed under the rising moon. "Why didn't you tell me you were going to take him? I wouldn't have made the mistake of talking to the Smiths." Blame and renewed anger dripped from her lips.

His own anger flared. He'd done what he thought was right and asked the boy. Who did she think she was to question him? Crickets chirped around them as the silence lingered. "I'm not in the habit of answering to you, Miss Schultz."

"It would have been simple common courtesy to tell me earlier today." She ground the words through her clenched teeth. Then she spun around and started walking again.

"Oh no, not this time. You will not get the last word here." He followed her. "I hadn't decided to bring Daniel earlier."

"Uh-huh."

She didn't believe him. Gordon looked up to the stars. What did it matter? What was it about this woman that drove him insane? He ran right into her back when she was stopped by a figure that had materialized out of the darkness.

"Hello, Miss Schultz. I hope I'm not disturbing you, but my brother, Mark, said you were a midwife who might help me."

Gordon stared from the very pregnant woman to Miss Schultz. She was a midwife? But she was so young. And stubborn. Weren't midwives supposed to be patient and kind?

Miss Schultz extended her hand. "Please, call me Polly."

"It's nice to meet you, Polly. I'm Margaret Fitzgerald." She turned her gaze on Gordon.

He heard Polly's soft sigh. "This is the reverend." A frown marred her features. Did she just realize she didn't know his full name?

Gordon stepped forward and offered his hand. "Gordon Baker. It's nice to meet you, Mrs. Fitzgerald."

"I'm so glad you are here, Reverend. My mother told me to make sure that a preacher was with me when my time came. Up until now, we haven't had one on the train." She turned her cornflower eyes on Polly. "I hope you don't mind if the reverend is there when I deliver. That is, if you will be my midwife."

Miss Schultz looked as if she wanted to refuse his presence. Instead, she said, "You are in charge, Margaret. I will be there to assist. You can have anyone you want with you. Although, I must say, having a man in the room other than your husband is most unusual."

Margaret laughed. "I'm sure it is, but Mama can't be here, and that was her request. I'll honor my mother in doing what she asks."

Gordon turned to leave.

"Please stay, Reverend," Margaret called after him.

He turned and smiled. "I would love to, Mrs. Fitzgerald, but I have a young man waiting for me at our wagon. I'll come around and visit you and your husband tomorrow. Is that acceptable to you?"

At her nod, Gordon turned his grin on Miss Schultz. "Good night, ladies."

Chapter 5

Rain hammered the canvas with deafening force. Polly shivered within her tent. She'd piled all her blankets under her to sleep on but now sat huddled in the center of them as the storm that had arrived in the middle of the night raged.

Thankfully, Jerome had made sure the tent had been sealed with tar to waterproof it before she'd left him and Mamadele behind. She gasped as the yellow brightness of lightning flashed its brilliance through the small space. Thunder crashed, its fury vibrating under her as the ground shook.

That strike was close! She snagged her lower lip with her teeth and pulled herself upright. Should she go to the wagon and check on Idella? No, her husband was sure to be there, comforting her. If Idella needed her, he would come.

Her next thought was of Beulah. Was the little mule all right? She reached for her green day dress and favorite purple shawl. She pulled them over her nightgown. Her thoughts on the mule, she opened the flap of the tent and was immediately peppered with rain.

She turned away from the wind and slipped and slid to the area where the horses and mules were kept. Lightning sizzled and snapped around her. Thunder clapped and rumbled. She flinched and followed the sounds of bawling, braying, and neighing. She forced her sodden feet forward, toward the wall of stone that offered the animals little protection from the storm.

Beulah brayed to her. A cry broke from her throat as she hurried to the little mule's side. "I'm so sorry you have to be out here." The sky darkened even further, and Polly could no longer see through the pouring rain; it drummed against the earth and stone. Polly wrapped her arms around the animal's neck and buried her face against its wet hide. It was as if she were alone in the watery world around her. Lightning and thunder continued to torment her and the miserable animals around her. Polly looked out into the darkness. A new fear gripped her heart. Would she be able to find her way back to the wagons?

Suddenly, Gordon Baker appeared like an apparition from the watery depths. "Miss Schultz, what are you doing out here?"

Polly looked up into his face. Rain dripped from his hat. She said the only thing that came to mind. "I had to check on Beulah."

He nodded as if he understood. Rainwater splashed her head and back, making her shiver even harder. His warm hand wrapped around one of her cold arms, and he pulled her with him under a deep ledge jutting out from the rocky cliff. The beating of the rain on her soaked body ceased. She shot a grateful glance at the ledge of rock that now formed a covering over her and the reverend. "Thank you, Reverend Baker."

"You're welcome." A few moments later, the lantern he held flickered to life. He took his hat off and shook the rain from its brim. "As soon as this rain lets up, I'll walk you back to your tent."

She wanted to argue and say she could return on her own, but she was simply too emotionally drained to argue. Her gaze met his and held. Rain continued to fall outside the small sheltered area. Lightning flashed and the thunder rolled, but those things no longer mattered. Something in his eyes made her feel safe.

He took a step toward her. "Polly? Are you all right? You're not hurt, are you?" He reached out and touched her arm.

His eyes darkened to the color of blue smoke as his gaze ran over her. His touch scorched her skin. She caught her breath. Her voice shook as she answered, "No, I'm not hurt."

Something flickered in the depths of his eyes, and he sucked in air. He released her arm. "Good. We seem to have time to talk a bit. Would you mind telling me why you are headed to Oregon?" He moved to a large stone and sat down.

Obviously, his touching her hadn't affected him as it had her. She wrapped her arms around her waist and pressed on her stomach to stop its quivering. "I came to midwife Mrs. Bentz."

He tilted his head to the side. "That's the only reason?"

Polly nodded. Mamadele and Jerome had sent her with plenty of money to buy a farm and start a new life as a midwife, but for now, she didn't look any further than getting Mrs. Bentz's babies born. Gordon's confused look prompted her to say, "The first rule of being a midwife is to put the mother-to-be above all else, and that's what I am doing."

"Surely you have dreams of your own." Gordon replaced the hat on his head. His eyes bored into hers.

Polly's hands began to shake. She clasped them together to hide how his gaze affected her. "No. Not at this time. Why are you going to Oregon?"

"I have three reasons." He raised his hand and counted on his fingers. "One, to preach the Word of God; two, to raise Daniel in the great outdoors, as his parents intended; and three, to farm a piece of land." He looked up at her and grinned.

She noted that he'd not mentioned marrying or settling down with a family. But, in a way, Daniel was now his family. Maybe, thanks to her meddling, he'd decided the young boy was all the family he needed. "Those are very good reasons. Will Daniel go with you when you travel to preach?"

"I believe so. God willing, we'll settle in a small town that needs a regular preacher and won't have to travel much." Gordon walked to the edge of their shelter.

Her gaze followed his out into the darkness. The storm still raged around them, but its intensity had lessened. What would it be like to know what path you were to take in life? Mamadele had laid out the path for her, but was it the path she wanted to follow? Being a midwife was a great calling, but was it her calling? All her life, Mamadele had trained her to be a midwife. Her journal encouraged Polly to press on with the same drive and love for midwifery that Mamadele had, but was this truly to be her path?

Polly looked up and found the reverend studying her. His blue eyes searched her face. Could he see into her soul? She lifted her chin. Did he know of the inner turmoil that she dealt with every day? Could he see the feelings of abandonment, aloneness, and sorrow?

Gordon searched Polly's troubled eyes. Protectiveness and something more welled in his gut. Various emotions washed over her face. Tears filled her hazel eyes. But the moment she noticed him watching her, she seemed to lift an invisible defensive wall.

"Where is Daniel?" she demanded, crossing her arms over her chest.

He sighed. "In the wagon."

Her voice rose above the rain. "Alone in this storm?" She wrapped her shawl around her slender shoulders and proceeded to walk around him. "We need to get back. You need to get back." Gordon grabbed her arm to stop her from entering the inky darkness of the storm. "He's not alone, and we are not going back yet." Lightning illuminated their shelter.

She swirled to face him. Her wet dress slapped his legs. "You cannot hold me here." She jerked her arm from his hand.

He felt his temper begin to rise. "It's too dangerous for you to go out in this lightning." A loud crashing boom filled the air between them.

Polly jumped. Her frightened eyes searched his face. Her voice sounded small as she admitted, "I shouldn't have come out into the storm."

Gordon looked up at the craggy roof over their heads and silently prayed, *Thank You, Lord.* The sound of her wet skirt dragging on the dirt floor alerted him that she was on the move again.

She flopped down on the rock he'd recently vacated. He'd been thankful earlier when his knees had gone weak and the stone had been there to support him. Did Polly feel the same way now? Was the storm affecting her, or was it his presence? She wrapped her arms around her waist once more and rocked herself. He wanted to envelop her in his arms, hold her close to his chest, and smooth the wet hair from her wide forehead. He wanted to assure her everything would be fine. His gaze moved to her full lips. The desire to kiss away her fear urged him to move toward her.

He took a step, and then the minister in Gordon came to his rescue. "No, probably not, but I understand your need to check on the mule."

"Her name is Beulah." A flush filled Polly's cheeks, and she ducked her head.

"Beulah. I like that name. My mule has a name, too." He knelt in front of her.

Her eyes rose once more to meet his. "What is it?"

"Rawhide." Gordon waited for her to voice the question that sprang into her eyes.

"Why Rawhide?"

He felt the smile tug at his lips. "Because my hide was raw after riding her for a few days."

Polly's laughter filled the small shelter. It reminded him of butterflies landing on pretty pink flowers, graceful and soft. He laughed with her. Maybe this young woman wasn't all salt and vinegar. Could she be another reason God sent him to Oregon? He'd always wanted a family, and this trip had already provided him with a son. Was Polly Schultz God's idea of wife material?

At this moment, with her lips spread into a soft smile that touched her beautiful hazel eyes, he hoped so.

Chapter 6

I'm here, Idella!" Polly put her foot on the step but stopped as Idella shoved aside the canvas flaps over the tailgate of her wagon. "What's wrong? Are you. . ."

"I'm fine. It's—"

A woman's moan came from the wagon's interior. Polly looked toward the sound then jerked her gaze back to Idella, who was climbing out of the wagon. Idella turned and held out her arms. "Come on, Luke."

The toddler scrambled into his mama's arms as another restrained groan came from the wagon.

Polly whispered, "Who is that?"

"Emma Edwards." Idella lowered her voice. "I thought it best to keep her here until you arrived."

Polly nodded, read all the things the woman left unsaid in her expression, and climbed in the wagon. Emma lay on a soft mattress to one side, clutching her swollen belly. Her face was pinched and pale, her mouth compressed into a thin line.

Polly made her way to the side of the bed. "When is your baby due?"

The young woman gave a soft hiss and rubbed her hands over the fabric that covered her stomach. "Next month."

Emma's eyes closed, and Polly noted how she clenched her jaw. "Is the pain constant? Or does it come and go like cramps?"

Emma released a breath and opened her eyes. "Like cramps. I think. . .think she doesn't know how to tell time." She tried to smile through the pain.

Polly nodded, kept her expression serene. "When did the cramps begin?"

"Not long ago. I was carrying the Johnson boy. The pain doubled me over, and I had to put him down. Idella saw me when their wagon came by and they stopped. She told me to lay on the mattress. I know you aren't my midwife, Polly, but Idella says you can help me." Emma's eyes filled with tears. "I don't want to lose my baby."

Polly reached out and squeezed her hand. How many times had she heard women in labor say those words? Too many to count. She answered as Mamadele would. "I cannot promise you that will not happen, Emma. But I will promise you that I will do everything I know how to keep it from happening."

"That's all I can ask. Thank you, Polly." Emma grunted in pain and closed her eyes again.

"You're welcome, Emma. What is your favorite song?" Polly moved to the end of the wagon and opened the box that held her midwife satchel. She pulled it to her and looked for the items she would need to assist Emma with the birth of her new baby. Oil, needles and thread, a special candle scented with mint, and clean rags. Everything was there, although she hadn't planned on using them until November when Idella's baby was due.

" 'What a Friend We Have in Jesus,'" Emma groaned. "Polly, can I stand up?"

Polly immediately moved to her side. "Of course, let me help you."

As soon as Emma was standing, she bent over at the waist. Polly stood by her side as the wave of pain passed. She tried to remember everything Adele had taught her. "Would you like me to rub your back, Emma? Sometimes that helps."

A midwife does what she must to comfort and give assurance to the mother. Mamadele's words drifted to her. At Emma's nod of approval, Polly began rubbing her lower back. "When the baby comes, we will sing your favorite song, Emma. How does that sound?"

"Heavenly."

Two hours later, Polly announced, "I can see the head." She did what she'd seen Adele do many times. She poured a little oil on her hands, worked to soothe the skin that formed a perfect halo around the infant's head, and said, "You can push now, Emma." While Emma pushed, Polly began singing: "What a friend we have in Jesus, all our sins and griefs to bear! What a privilege to carry everything to God in prayer!" She listened to Idella sing along outside the wagon.

Polly supported the baby as she slipped from Emma's body. First the little head, then the shoulders, body, and toes. *Thank*

You, Lord. Thank You, Lord. "It's a girl!" Polly announced for Emma and the small crowd waiting outside the wagon.

She smiled at Emma as they heard a loud whoop from outside. "Sounds like your husband is pleased."

"Lawrence! Did you hear that? We have a girl," Emma called to her husband.

His head came through the opening at the front of the wagon. "I sure did." He pushed his way into the cramped space and patted Emma's shoulder.

The young mother started to rise. "Wait for the placenta, Emma," Polly warned her just as she'd heard Mamadele do in the past. "You can hold her if you want to."

The baby took a huge gulp of air when Polly swatted her bottom. A tiny cry exited her young lungs, and then Polly laid the baby on her mother's stomach.

"She's so beautiful, Emma. You did good." Lawrence took a small hand into his. His eyes filled with wonder.

Polly gulped down the lump that had formed in her throat at this father's love for his daughter. Her own father had abandoned her shortly after she'd exited her mother's body. Pushing back the hurt, Polly turned her attention on Emma. "Everything is fine, Emma. You did wonderfully."

"I knew she was coming when I heard you start to sing. Idella told us to listen, and when the song started the baby would be entering the world." Moisture filled Mr. Edwards's big brown eyes. "Thank you, Miss Polly."

"I'm glad I could be here, Mr. Edwards. May I pray a prayer of thanksgiving for your family?"

"Oh yes." Emma smiled at her, and then she and her husband bowed their heads.

September 22, 1860. Thus far, I haven't written in this journal about being a midwife, but today I have something to write about. Little Laura Joy Edwards was born tonight at eight o'clock. She weighs six pounds and is about nineteen inches long. She has fine blond hair and big blue eyes. I've never seen a papa so proud of his little girl.

You may be afraid when called to help deliver a baby, but the joy you will feel afterward will wash away all those fears. Seeing God at work, creating life, fills me with a joy like no other. I now understand why Mamadele is a midwife.

Gordon stood off to the side of the camp. He'd just finished his round of guard duty and saw Polly duck into her tent. Her face appeared pale, and dark circles shadowed her eyes. Over the last month, it seemed every woman in the train either was expecting or thought she might be. Since she'd delivered the Edwards baby, the women called on her for constant assistance.

Polly pushed the flap back and stepped out into the evening air. She lifted her eyes to the heavens as if in prayer. He waited until she reached back inside and pulled out a water pail. For the past month, he'd wanted to spend time with her, but she always seemed to be surrounded by women, children, or both.

She started walking down to the river.

Gordon fell into step beside her. What was she doing? Didn't she realize the dangers of leaving the wagon train? He knew the wagon master had warned them all to stay close. He worked to keep the irritation out of his voice as he announced his presence: "It's kind of late to be going to the river alone."

Her jaw worked for a moment, and then she said, "I'm not alone, Reverend. You're with me."

"So I am." A breeze lifted the ties of her bonnet, and her sweet scent filled his nostrils. He inhaled deeply, enjoying the minty fragrance. Sensing she wanted silence, Gordon allowed himself to be content just to be with her. The trip to the river for water would be swift, and then they'd return to the safety of numbers, he assured himself.

She surprised him by stopping at the water's edge, sitting down, and slipping off her shoes. She unwrapped cloth from around her feet. They were swollen and red, and she dipped her toes into the water.

"I'm not sure this is a good idea, Miss Schultz." He moved to stand beside her.

Polly sighed. "Really, Reverend, I don't care if you think it's a good idea or not."

Patience, Gordon, use patience. He took a deep breath and tried to do as his inner voice said and find patience. "Miss Schultz. . ."

"And stop calling me Miss Schultz," she snapped. "Everyone calls me Miss Polly or just plain Polly. I don't know why you can't do the same."

Gordon took another deep breath. He kept his gaze on the hills around them. "Miss Polly. There is a reason the wagon master doesn't want women out at dusk, at the river, by themselves."

She wiggled her toes in the water. "I'm sure there is, Reverend. But you are with me now, so I'm not alone."

Why was she being so stubborn? Did she really not understand the dangers? Using the same steady tone he used with Daniel, Gordon tried again: "See the hills all around us?"

Polly nodded without looking up.

"They are full of Indians who are watching our every move right now." When she didn't answer, Gordon knelt on one knee beside her.

In a soft voice, Polly whispered, "Don't look now, Reverend, but we've been joined by the Indians."

"What?" Gordon moved to stand, but she held on to his arm.

"Lower your voice," she hissed and then in slow motion began pulling her feet from the water. She used one of the cloths she'd wrapped around them to dry off. "To our right, we have company." Polly slipped her feet into worn shoes, and slowly they stood.

Gordon felt the presence of the Indians now. He took her elbow and held his head high. With no gun, no horse, and a woman at his side, he knew they were in trouble.

As silent as shadows, Indians surrounded them.

Chapter 7

The scream welled up in Polly's throat, but no sound came out. Within moments of the arrival of the Indians, Gordon was on the ground. He'd wake up with a knot on the back of his head the size of a cantaloupe.

Her mouth had been stuffed with something soft and then bound so that she couldn't scream. Her hands were tied behind her back, causing her shoulders to begin a slow ache. She faced her captor. What were his plans?

The dark eyes returned her stare. He didn't seem angry—if anything, his expression appeared sad and almost hopeful. Then he picked her up and tossed her over his back, much like a sack of potatoes.

His shoulder blade in her stomach cut deep with every step he ran. But at least her feet were off the hard-packed ground. She'd been foolish and brought this upon herself and Gordon. Tears stung the back of her eyes, but Polly refused to allow even one to fall.

Would the wagon master send someone out for them? Or would their rush to get over the mountains cause him to leave them behind?

Polly twisted and raised her head to see where they were going. She counted six men running in the dark, the moonlight their only means of seeing. Gordon's head bounced against the back of the brave who carried him. His eyes were closed. Why hadn't they left him and just taken her? What evil plans did these men have for them? She shuddered at the thought.

Her head ached as blood continued to pound in her temples. They seemed to go on forever. Every part of her body began to protest, with the exception of her feet, she thought irrationally. She felt sick, the pounding in her head more than she could stand. She closed her eyes and tried to focus on Mamadele. What would she do in this situation? Would they ever see each other again?

Several times throughout the night, the braves stopped and set them down to rest. They never allowed Polly and Gordon to talk or communicate. She hated what was happening to them but could see no way to escape. Just when she felt as if her head might stop pounding, they would pick them up and move on.

When the sun peeked over the horizon, they stopped. The man set Polly down on the ground and held her arms to steady her.

Gordon's captor did the same. A small trickle of blood ran down the side of his face. "It's all right, Polly."

With her mouth gagged, Polly couldn't answer, so she nodded. The brave tears she'd held earlier slid down her face as she realized this was all her fault. The Indian took the gag out of her mouth and wiped her tears. She looked up to find his gaze also filled with sorrow.

She cleared her throat and then asked, "Why did you do this?"

He didn't answer but walked around behind her and untied her hands. She rubbed her wrists. They were in a small camp close to another stream of water. Polly counted ten tepees and saw there were about thirty horses in a corral off to the right of the camp. One tepee stood off by itself.

A woman's scream pierced the air.

Polly jerked as the horrors of what might be going on in the tepee rushed into her tired mind. The Indian began pulling her in that direction.

"Stop!" Gordon yelled and jerked against the two men who held him.

The Indian ignored Gordon and continued to pull Polly forward. She looked back and saw that Gordon had been forced to kneel on the ground. His panic-filled eyes followed her. Polly dug her heels into the hard ground and twisted against the hand that held her.

When he released her, she fell backward but caught herself before hitting the ground. She held up her hand to stop him from grabbing her again. She looked at Gordon. "I'm all right. Pray for God's protection."

He nodded.

Satisfied that Gordon would be praying, Polly turned back to the Indian.

Another scream tore through the air.

She held her head high and walked past him toward the tepee. Whatever fate awaited her, God would see her through. She stopped at the entrance and waited for the man to open the flap. Her hands shook, and she clasped them in front of her before bending to enter.

The flap closed behind her. It took a moment for her eyes to adjust. Two young women stood in the center of the enclosure, worry etched on their faces. Another very pregnant woman was squatting, holding on to two poles standing on each side of her. Sweat ran down her red, exhausted face. Then she arched her back and screamed.

Polly hurried to her. She waited until the girl withered against the poles and then captured her face between her hands. "How long?" she asked the woman.

The woman looked back at her, uncomprehending. Polly turned to the other two. "How long?"

They looked at each other and shrugged. Either they didn't know how long or they didn't understand her. Polly searched the room until she found a jug of water. She poured some into a bowl and washed the dirt from her hands. Then she returned her attention to the soon-to-be mother.

In a soft, reassuring voice, Polly spoke: "I want to help. So first, I'm going to pray."

Unsure if the laboring woman understood, Polly bowed her head and prayed: "Lord, please help me to assist this mother as she struggles to bring forth new life. Give me the wisdom to know what to do and her the courage to allow me to do it. Also, I ask for Your strength to sustain her. In Your name. Amen."

❦

As soon as Polly disappeared into the tepee, Gordon was yanked to his feet. He was pulled by his bound hands to another tepee, where the men sat down around a fire. He stayed just outside of their circle. They talked in low tones, and their eyes often moved to the tepee that Polly had disappeared into. When they didn't push him down or force him to sit, Gordon decided the best thing to do was join them. His thoughts moved to Daniel, and he prayed someone would look after the boy.

Once more a scream carried from the interior of the tepee. Gordon wanted to go to Polly, but when he started to rise, a young man shook his head at him.

The man who had taken Polly paced outside the tepee he'd shown her into. Gordon bowed his head and prayed. He asked for assistance, safety, and guidance.

It seemed like hours before a young Indian woman stepped outside the tepee. She handed the man a jug and said something to him, pointing to the stream. He immediately ran to fill the jug with water.

Once he delivered the jug to the woman, Polly's captor joined the rest of the men around the fire. His brown gaze moved over Gordon, and he jerked his head toward him, grunting what sounded like a command.

One of the men stood, pulled a knife, and walked behind Gordon. Gordon's insides quivered, but he refused to show fear.

To do so might mean his life and Polly's. Instead, he maintained eye contact with the first man.

At his nod, the knife swished through the air and Gordon's bonds fell to the ground behind him. Gordon swallowed. His shoulders ached as he pulled his hands around. He rubbed his wrists and rotated his sore shoulders.

The Indian in front of him nodded and motioned for Gordon to join them around the fire. Gordon followed and sat down beside him. He assumed this young man was the leader. The others seemed to follow him. One of the men went inside the nearby tepee and returned shortly with a bowl of dried fruit and jerky.

Gordon's stomach growled as the bowl was passed about the circle. Each man grabbed a handful of fruit and a piece of the dried meat. He didn't expect the bowl to be shoved into his hands but smiled gratefully at the man who handed it to him.

Like the others, he filled one hand with fruit and took a slice of meat. They nodded and grunted their pleasure. He'd always heard the Indians were savages and not to be trusted, but these men seemed pleasant enough. *If I don't take into account I'm their prisoner.*

He bowed his head and thanked the Lord for his food. When he looked up the others stared back at him. Gordon chose to try the fruit first, and as he chewed he nodded his approval.

Gordon sat and waited for hours, hoping Polly would return. He wasn't sure what was going on, and since he'd not heard her scream coming from the tepee, he continued to pray.

The other men worked on arrows and bows. They sharpened their knives, and after a few hours of waiting, one of the men left. When he returned he had a deer slung over his horse. The other men joined him, and they skinned the deer and cut the meat up. As time passed, the men's dark eyes darted between the tepee and their leader.

When Gordon thought he could no longer stand the waiting, another scream tore from the tepee.

Polly's captor stood. He hurried to the tepee that the scream came from.

Gordon stood and stretched. No one stopped him, so he decided to follow the leader. When the man arrived at the tepee entrance, he stopped and turned around.

Dark eyes filled with concern stared at Gordon. He'd seen the same troubled look in many men's eyes in his day. This man needed prayer. Gordon laid a hand on the Indian's shoulder, bowed his head, and prayed: "Lord, I don't know what is going on in there, but I ask You to give this man assurance and to give me strength to help him. Amen." He raised his head and found the dark eyes still studying him, but now they were filled with moisture and thanks.

Gordon patted his shoulder and nodded. He hoped the Indian would understand that he was there for him. His concern for Polly nagged at him, but he knew his place was with this man during his time of need.

Polly's sweet voice sounded through the hide of the tepee as she sang, "What a friend we have in Jesus, all our sins and griefs to bear! What a privilege to carry everything to God in prayer!"

Realization dawned. Polly was delivering a baby. A few minutes later the sound of its cry split the evening air.

Gordon pounded the Indian on the back and smiled. He called through the door, "What did you deliver?"

She laughed. "A baby."

"I know it's a baby! Boy or girl?" He continued to pat the brave on the shoulder.

"It's a boy! A big boy, maybe ten pounds or more." She laughed. "And the mama is going to be fine."

Gordon grabbed the man's hand and pumped. He smiled his widest grin and signed that the baby was a boy. The thought that the Indian man might not understand him never entered his mind.

The Indian gave a whoop and danced about. His friends ran over to join him. He spoke rapidly to them and then pointed at Gordon and made the same sign for boy that Gordon had made. They threw their heads back and laughed. He felt heat enter his face and neck.

A young woman pushed the flap back and exited the tepee. She held a small bundle wrapped in animal skins. The baby whimpered when she handed him over to his father.

The men all stared into the chubby little face. His father looked up at Gordon and then gently unwrapped the baby. He grinned when he looked upon his newborn son.

Caught up in the joy around him, Gordon still couldn't help but wonder. Now that the child had been born, what was to become of Polly and him?

Chapter 8

Polly was having the same thoughts. Mother and child were lying at the back of the tepee. Since this wasn't her normal approach to midwifery, Polly didn't know if she should pray over the family or not. The mother smiled at her over the little boy's head.

She bowed her head and prayed: "Lord, please bless this family and keep them safe. In Jesus' name. Amen." Polly raised her head and returned the woman's grin.

One of the other ladies motioned for Polly to follow her outside. Polly stepped into the cool night air and inhaled. Her back ached from the bent-over position she had maintained most of the day. The stars twinkled down upon her, and she marveled that a full day had passed. How had Gordon passed the time? She glanced around.

Gordon sat beside a fire. He stood and walked over to her with a smile. "You did well."

Polly returned his smile. "Thank you." She rubbed her lower

back. "It was a hard labor, but the mother is doing fine."

He nodded and looked up into the star-filled sky. His handsome features were reflected within the light. Light-brown hair fell across his forehead. Dried blood caked his temple. She wondered if his head still hurt from the blow that had knocked him out.

An Indian man exited one of the tepees and knelt beside the campfire. One of the women who had been with Polly throughout the day entered another tepee with an armload of skins. The camp seemed alive with activity, and at the moment the Indians didn't seem to be paying any attention to her and Gordon. For that, she was thankful.

Polly gulped. "I'm sorry I got you into this, Reverend. I should have listened to you."

"It's all right, Miss Polly. God knew what was going to happen, even though I didn't. I think it's a good thing you were here to deliver the baby."

Why did he have to be so kind and understanding? She rotated her shoulders and looked up into the heavens with him. "What do you think they are going to do with us now?"

He sighed. "I'm not sure. We need to put our faith and hope in God that all will go well. Something that helps me is remembering Philippians, chapter 4 verse 13: 'I can do all things through Christ who strengthens me.'"

She smiled. "That is one of my favorite scriptures."

"Mine, too."

Polly frowned. "Do you think there is a search party looking for us?"

Gordon shook his head. "They have to get over the mountains, and I don't believe the Indians were foolish enough to leave a trail to follow."

Tears stung the back of her eyes. "So they left us behind?" Her voice cracked.

"I promise I'll do everything I can to get you to Oregon." The strength in his voice gave her hope.

Silence hung about them. Crickets sang and frogs croaked. If only they weren't in danger, it could have been a peaceful time.

The Indian by the fire stood and walked toward them. Gordon straightened his shoulders and stood a little taller, placing himself between the man and her. Polly felt a moment of pride and fear. She'd grown to care about Gordon and prayed the Indians wouldn't harm him.

He motioned for them to follow him. Gordon reached back and took her hand in his. Even in their dire situation, Polly couldn't ignore the tingly feel of his warm palm against hers. They followed the Indian to a tepee. The man pulled the entrance open and motioned for them to enter.

Gordon led the way inside, pulling Polly in behind him. A fire burned in the center of the room, casting dancing shadows against the hide. Skins were piled against one wall. Polly wondered if they were as soft as they looked.

The man entered after her. A few moments later, one of the women who had assisted Polly during the birthing entered also. She carried two bowls of steaming stew.

The smell of rich meats and spices caused Polly's stomach

to growl. When was the last time she'd eaten? Yesterday noon? Time seemed to have sped by, and in its passing she'd had no chance to eat or sleep. Both actions were demanding her attention now.

Polly offered a wobbly smile and took one of the bowls. She moved to the fire pit and sank down onto a thick fur. Weariness seeped into her bones.

Gordon joined her but didn't sit. He took the bowl the woman held out for him.

Polly sensed his unease. It hung in the air as thick as the soup she scooped out with the spoon-shaped bone the woman supplied. Polly sipped at the delicious stew. Small bits of spicy meat and vegetables in a rich gravy washed over her tongue. "This is very good, thank you." She offered another weak smile.

The Indian woman returned the smile and then departed. Polly held her breath as the man stepped closer to them. Once more Gordon blocked her view by stepping in front of her. She leaned to the side and looked up at the Indian man.

He didn't seem to be a threat. His dark eyes studied both her and Gordon; then he motioned for them to eat. His hand moved in a sweep to indicate that the furs at the back of the room were intended for them to sleep upon.

Polly was surprised when Gordon shook his head. He motioned toward his bowl and then to the furs, shaking his head. The Indian man's expression showed signs of confusion.

Gordon tried again. He motioned that they would eat, and then he pointed to Polly and the furs. The other man nodded, but the look of confusion remained in his dark eyes.

Polly felt confused, too. She continued to watch as Gordon pointed to her and the furs and then at himself and the tent door.

"What are you saying?" Polly asked.

He spoke without turning to look at her. His eyes remained locked on the other man. "I can eat here with you, but we cannot stay the night alone in here."

Understanding dawned. "Oh, I see." A chill ran up her spine and into the hair at the back of her neck. How could he protect her if he left?

The Indian motioned for them to eat. At Gordon's nod, he turned and left.

"Where will you sleep?" Polly asked, once more wishing she'd not dragged him into this mess.

Gordon eased down beside her. He looked into his bowl. "Right outside the door. I won't leave you, but I can't sleep alone in the same room with you. We are going to have a hard enough time, when we return to the wagon train, convincing some people that this trip has not compromised your reputation."

Polly noted that he didn't say *if* they returned to the wagon train but *when*. His strong jaw worked as he chewed. Determination shone in his eyes, and she could see that his mind was searching for a way of escape.

Someone tapped the flap of the tepee. Gordon stood and pulled it open. Polly tried to see who their visitor was but couldn't see around Gordon. He returned with a jug of clear water. "It seems our every need is being considered. I don't believe they plan on harming us."

"It seems the only reason they took us was so that I could help deliver the baby. Do you think they've been watching our train long?" She yawned.

Gordon picked up his bone spoon again. "It's possible, but I think they just grabbed the first woman they could in hopes that she could help. This camp is small and filled with young adults. Other than the baby, I've not seen any children and no elders."

"Lucky for them, they found the midwife's apprentice." Polly finished the stew and set her bowl aside. She stood and looked in the pile of skins for a small, clean piece of soft rawhide.

She felt Gordon's puzzled gaze follow her as she found what she was looking for. She poured water into a bowl and dipped the hide into it. Would he allow her to clean his wound?

"What do you mean 'apprentice'?" He tilted his head to the side and allowed her to wash away the blood from his temple.

Polly chewed her lip. "I'm not a real midwife, Gordon. I'm just an assistant. My Mamadele is the real midwife."

Gordon enjoyed the sweet way she said his name, almost as much as the sensation of her light touch upon his brow. She reminded him of a butterfly unsure where to land. The tremble in her voice shook him. Was it insecurity that caused her to snap at him from time to time? He had to reassure her. "Polly, you have been a midwife since the night you delivered Laura Joy for Mrs. Edwards."

She gnawed at her bottom lip as she set the rag in the bowl.

"That's a nasty cut. I'm afraid it might scar." She rinsed out the small hide.

He hated that she moved away from him. A wide yawn escaped before she could cover it. Her bonnet hung down her back, and her hair had come loose sometime during the day.

Polly had proved that she was a strong woman. She'd not slept in thirty-six hours, and yet she'd stayed with the mother until she was sure both of her patients were safe. Gordon continued to admire her hair. He wanted to run his fingers through the silky-looking strands. The thought startled him, and he cleared his throat. "Well, I need to go so you can get some sleep."

Polly walked to the pile of hides. She scooped up an armload of skins and passed them to him. "I am pretty tired."

Her soft smile caused his heart to melt. The more he got to know Polly Schultz, the more he wanted to know her better.

She bent over once more and scooped up another armload of skins. "I am moving my bed closer to the door, to be closer to you." She walked to the left of the entryway and dropped her skins. "Why don't you take those out and come back in for more. There are plenty here, and I don't want you to get cold."

Gordon grinned while he did as she instructed. He dropped the skins on the right-hand side of the door so that they would only have the tepee wall between them and then reentered for another load.

For a brief moment, he couldn't find her. He turned in a complete circle looking for her. And then he saw her. She'd curled up on the furs and snuggled down. She resembled a kitten, purring away. So sweet and beautiful. Gordon knelt down and covered her with a soft skin. Her bonnet lay off to the side, and her hair was fanned out on the furs.

Polly smiled in her sleep. Gordon sat back on his heels and studied her face. What sweet dreams was she having? Was she reliving the birth of the Indian baby? Or perhaps another child's birth?

That simple smile melted another part of his heart. Gordon frowned. At the rate he was going, Polly would have his heart before they even got to Oregon.

Chapter 9

Polly awoke to the sun shining through the top of the tepee. She stretched and yawned, enjoying the sensation of soft furs under her body. Her feet hurt as she pushed up and stretched again. How long had she slept? She combed her fingers through her hair, pulled it up, and repinned it into a neat knot at the back of her head. Small tentacles of hair slipped free and brushed her cheeks. Since there was nothing that could be done about that, Polly picked up her bonnet and tied it under her chin. She then brushed off her dress and limped toward the door.

The scent of wood smoke filled her nostrils as she pushed back the flap. The two women from the day before were sitting outside the entrance sewing rawhide together into what looked like shoes. They smiled at her and indicated she pick up a bowl and scoop out whatever was in the pot over the fire. Polly's stomach growled. She looked in the pot and saw that it held some type of mush mixed with berries.

After scooping out the mush, Polly sat down beside one of the women. The sun was almost in the center of the sky. Her gaze scanned the camp in search of Gordon as she ate. When she didn't see him, she turned her attention to the women.

They smiled and chatted with each other. After she finished her breakfast, Polly stood to check on the new mother and her baby. When the women didn't try to stop her, she walked across to the birthing tepee. The flap had been tied back, and Polly realized that the woman inside could see her approaching. Still, out of politeness, Polly knocked on the hide wall as she'd seen the others do, and at the woman's answer, she entered the room.

The young woman sat at the back of the tepee. Like the other women, she seemed to be sewing something. Her son lay on a pile of furs beside her. His small chest rose and fell gently as he breathed. His big brown eyes watched as Polly approached. Polly smiled and motioned toward the child.

The woman picked up her son and held him out to Polly. Polly took the babe and cuddled him close. Black hair topped his little head and his eyes were alert and dark. She touched his toes and fingers. Would she ever have a child of her own? The question had floated to her every time she held another woman's baby. *God willing*, she told herself.

She handed the babe back to his mother, who laid him down on the furs and smiled. She indicated that Polly sit across from her. She picked up her sewing and continued working. Polly watched but wished she had something to do with her hands as well.

As if the woman could read her mind, she stopped sewing

and picked up two pieces of hide and handed them to Polly. Then she threaded a needle of bone with what Polly assumed was thin muscle from an animal. The other woman showed her how the two pieces fit together and then motioned for Polly to begin.

As her hands worked, questions ran through her mind. Where was Gordon this morning? When would they leave? Were they prisoners? It didn't feel like they were. They seemed to be able to move around at will. But then again, where would they go if they were free? They didn't know where they were—at least she didn't.

Her gaze met the woman's, who smiled and nodded, then went back to her sewing. The questions continued to circle in Polly's mind. Had they just been brought here to help with the birthing of the baby? Would she ever see the Bentzes again? Or the green hills of Oregon?

Gordon followed the brave to the corral to where the horses mingled. A black stallion reared back and neighed his greeting. The white strip down its forehead flashed in the morning sun. "Beautiful."

The brave nodded and said something in his language. For the hundredth time, Gordon wished he could understand him.

A teenage boy hurried toward them and said something to the Indian. Gordon listened to the low speech as they conversed for several minutes. The odor of horse dung and churned-up dirt filled the air. A flock of geese flew overhead, their honks filling the skies.

Soon the wagon train wouldn't be able to get over the mountains. The chill in the air felt good now, but within a few weeks, it would turn cold.

The boy ran toward the corral. Dread filled Gordon. What if he and Polly weren't able to catch up with the wagons? Then what would they do? He felt a surge of hope when the boy returned with three horses and handed the lead ropes to the brave.

In turn, the Indian man passed two of the ropes off to Gordon. He admired the sleek coats of the animals. Both were mares—one with a brown coat and the other black. A quick look at their teeth and legs confirmed they were both young—not yearlings, but not much older than five.

Gordon looked back to the man. He'd swung up on the black stallion's back. His dark eyes indicated that Gordon choose one of the mares and do the same.

Sitting bareback astride a mare felt much different than riding on a saddle. Gordon clutched his knees tightly around the brown horse's middle as they rode back to camp. The black mare followed easily behind him.

Once in camp, the women pointed to the birthing tent. They rode up to its entrance, and the brave called out words that Gordon didn't understand. His heart pounded as he waited to see what would happen next.

Polly stepped through the flap, a confused look on her face. She looked from him to the brave. He admired the way she held her voice steady as she said, "Good morning, Reverend."

The brave indicated she should mount the black mare.

Gordon offered what he hoped was a reassuring smile. "Good morning, Miss Polly. It seems we are about to take a trip." He slid off his horse and offered her his hands as a stirrup to help her onto the mare.

Polly nodded and slipped her small foot into his hands. He steadied her as soon as she was astride. A light pink filled her cheeks as she tried to pull her skirt over her exposed legs.

Gordon quickly looked away. Both of the Indian women were hurrying to Polly's side. He stepped back as they held up a large hide tied to look like a large sack. Polly took the bundle and smiled. They nodded and patted her leg.

The Indian man indicated it was time to go by leading the way. Gordon quickly swung onto his own horse. He turned to Polly. "You follow him, and I'll follow you."

"All right." She waved to the two women and gently touched her heels to the mare's sides. The bag sat in front of her, and she balanced it between her arms while holding on to the reins.

Two other braves joined the leader, spoke for a few moments as they walked their horses, and then veered off to the right and the left of them. Gordon stayed alert as they traveled.

"Where do you think he is guiding us?" Polly called back to him.

Gordon eased his horse up to ride along beside her. "I'm not sure, but I'm praying we're headed back to the wagon train."

"As am I." She shifted on the mare's back and the bag slid. She attempted to catch it and barely succeeded.

"Here, let me take that." Gordon reached across and took the sack.

Polly smiled. "Thank you. My arms were getting tired."

He placed the bag between his arms like he'd seen her do and wondered what could be in it. "You're welcome." It wasn't very heavy—perhaps it was simply several furs tied together. But why had they given them to Polly?

They continued to ride in silence most of the day, and Gordon spent much of it praying they were headed toward the wagon train. A breeze rustled through the drying grasses. When they were traveling with the wagon train, the constant wind blew sand into their eyes. This was much more pleasant. Gordon raised his head and inhaled the fresh air. They topped a rise, and the brave stopped.

Gordon motioned for Polly to wait as he moved his mount up beside the Indian's. Below them he could see the thin line of the wagon train. He breathed a prayer of thanks. The Indian motioned that they should ride side by side the rest of the way. Gordon nodded.

"The train is below, Miss Polly," Gordon called over his shoulder. "We are going to ride down together. Would you be so kind as to ride behind us and in the middle?"

"All right." Polly nudged her horse forward until her mount's head was between the two men.

They proceeded down the hill. The wagon master and scout broke ranks from the train and headed in their direction. When they came within calling distance, the wagon master asked, "Reverend, is all well?"

"Yes sir. It is."

The wagon master motioned to one of the men, and the

wagons began circling up for the evening. Then he and the scout continued toward them. "What happened?"

Gordon looked back at Polly. Her head was down, and she did not raise it to answer the wagon master's question. So he did. "We went to the river for water, and this gentleman and a few of his friends met us there."

"Did they harm you?" The Indian brave's and the wagon master's gazes were locked.

Gordon thought of the cut on his head and the headache he'd sustained from it. "Not enough to mention."

The scout moved forward and spoke to the Indian man in his native tongue. After several long moments, he then turned to the others: "He says his wife was having trouble bringing forth new life, and this woman helped her." He directed his question to Polly. "Is this true?"

She raised her head. "Yes, it's true."

The Indian began speaking again. The scout nodded.

"He is bringing in a couple of his men," he told them.

At the men's nods, the Indian motioned with his arm, and the two men who had left them earlier returned. A deer draped each of their horses' hindquarters. One of them dismounted and pulled the deer from his horse and shoved it onto the back of Gordon's.

The Indian spoke again, and the scout said, "He says thank you for bringing his son into the world. In payment you can keep the horses and the deer."

"Thank you," Gordon replied.

He looked to Polly, who nodded and said, "Yes, thank you."

The Indian men turned their horses and rode away. Gordon

sighed. The adventure was over. Polly watched them leave. Under the bill of her bonnet, her brown bangs and the hint of auburn in them shone under the fading sun. Was that the only adventure Polly and he would experience together? Or did God plan more in his future with the beautiful young woman?

Gordon silently lifted a prayer for the latter. He was in love with Polly Schultz and prayed she felt the same.

Chapter 10

Polly felt as if the air were being squeezed out of her every few minutes. The women of the wagon trail hugged her tight and long. She missed not being around Gordon but knew the men had whisked him away to hear the details of their capture.

"Polly, I don't know what I would have done had you not returned," Idella proclaimed again. "I told Gustaf that we had to bring your things with us, just in case you found your way back. Praise be to God that you did."

"Was it horrible, Polly?" Mrs. Edwards asked as she cradled Laura Joy close.

Mrs. Bentz indicated that Polly should sit down on one of the wooden crates that surrounded the campfire. She did as asked and then answered, "At first I was very afraid. I didn't know what they wanted, and then when we got to their camp, I could hear a woman screaming in one of the tepees. Honestly, I didn't know if she was being tortured or what."

"What happened next?" eight-year-old Christina York asked. She leaned against her mother's leg.

Polly offered her a smile. "Well, the reverend had to stay with the men, and I went into the tepee. There was a woman in there, and she was having a baby. So I helped her."

Christina smiled back. "You are so nice. When I have a baby, will you help me, too?" The last few days had been hard on Polly, but she knew to help the Indian woman have her baby, she'd do it all again. "If we are together, then I will be honored to help you, Miss Christina."

"Thanks." She pulled her rag doll to her chest and looked up at her mother. "Did you hear that, Ma? Miss Polly is going to help me have a baby when I get bigger."

The women laughed and smiled at one another.

"I'm glad to hear that, Chris. Now it's time for sweet little girls to be off to bed. Night everyone." Mrs. York took Christina's hand and led her back to their wagon.

The other ladies proceeded to leave as well. "Good night, all," Idella called after them.

Once they were alone, she turned to Polly. "You are all right, aren't you?"

"Yes, I am fine. But I am tired, and tomorrow we will be starting out bright and early." She stood, yawned, and stretched.

Idella cleared her throat to get her attention again. "Polly, please sit down. There is one other thing I wish to discuss with you."

Polly did as she was asked. She searched Idella's face.

"Are you all right? I'm sorry, I should have asked about your well-being sooner." She reached out and took Idella's hands in hers.

Idella smiled. "The baby and I both are fine. My question is about you."

"Oh, all right."

"When you were out there, alone with the reverend and those men, were you compromised in any way?" A deep red filled Idella's cheeks.

Polly jerked her hands back. "Of course not! He was a perfect gentleman." How could Idella ask such a thing of her?

Idella's voice hardened. "Please lower your voice," she hissed at Polly. "We are all thinking the same thing, and unless you hadn't noticed, young lady, you arrived not with just one man, but four." Idella softened her voice. "I'm not trying to be mean, but if I am to help you, you must tell me if your reputation was tarnished."

Polly's blood boiled. Her ears roared with anger. "I have nothing to be ashamed of, Mrs. Bentz." She stood. "Now, if you will excuse me, I'm going to pitch my tent and go to bed." Tears burned the back of her eyes.

The other woman sighed heavily. "Polly, we'll talk more about this tomorrow."

"No, ma'am, we won't." Polly pulled her tent and bag from the wagon and moved as far away as she dared from the Bentzes' wagon to pitch her tent.

I have lost track of the days so for now will leave the date off and fill it in at a later time: I'm not even sure if Mamadele would want this entry in here, but I must share with whoever comes behind me and reads this. Two days ago, I was taken, along with the good Reverend Gordon Baker, by Indians in need of a midwife. I'm not sure they knew they were getting a midwife, but they did. The baby was turned the wrong way. I'm so thankful I'd read Mamadele's tips on how to turn babies around that are coming into the world feet first. Thank You, Lord, for giving her the wisdom to put such things in this journal. So the second baby I've delivered was that of an Indian couple. I learned something from these people. We've been told to watch out for the Indians, that they are dangerous, and they probably are in the wrong situation, but I found them to be like everyone else. Kind, loving people, who are only different in the way they speak and dress. Yes, their skin is tanner, but their hearts beat the same as mine.

This is the part that Mamadele might not have wanted in this journal. Idella seems to think that I was compromised by either the good reverend or one of the Indian men I spent the last two days with. I'm not sure Idella or the other women believe me, but I am still pure in both body and spirit. Why do people feel the need to judge others? I'm praying no harm will come of this sort of talk, especially for the reverend. My heart softens more for him each day, and I don't think I could stand to be a part of his ruin, should it come to that.

Gordon looked at the men as if they'd grown two heads. "Are you mad? No! I'm not going to marry her." He crossed his arms. Yes, he cared for Polly—but marry her? Not like this he wouldn't.

"Our wives are very insistent, Reverend." John York took the same stance. "I for one do not want to hear mine grumble all the way to Oregon."

John York, Omar Masters, and Lawrence Edwards stood around him. "Look, I know it doesn't look good for either of us, but marriage? No, that's out of the question. Besides, who would carry out the ceremony? I'm the only preacher on this train. I'm not going to perform my own wedding and that's final." He appreciated the men taking care of Daniel and his wagon, but he couldn't tolerate them putting their noses in his business. Especially where Polly was concerned. Gordon prayed they'd return to their own wagons and forget the whole subject.

"My wife's not going to like this."

The other men grumbled similarly as they stomped off. Gordon sighed. "Thank You, Lord."

"Why don't you want to marry Miss Polly?" Daniel asked.

He'd thought the boy was asleep in the wagon. He was thankful the men hadn't heard Daniel's question. If they had, he felt sure they would have stuck around to hear the answer.

Daniel jumped out of the wagon. Gordon felt he had no choice but to answer. He turned to face the young boy and placed his hand on his thin shoulder. "Daniel, when two people get married, it should be for love. Both parties have to love each other—at least, for me that's the way it has to be, and that's not the way it is."

"Why don't you love her? She's pretty." He tilted his head to the side and searched Gordon's eyes.

Gordon didn't answer. He did love Polly. But she'd never indicated she had feelings for him, and if Gordon Baker was going to get married, his wife would have to love him with all her heart. He grinned. "She is very pretty, but pretty isn't love. Now, don't you have a couple of last-minute chores to do before we line up this morning?" He ruffled Daniel's hair.

"Yes sir." Daniel started to run around to the other side of the wagon.

Gordon called after him. "Hold up, son. I just thought of something." He moved to the wagon seat and pulled out the skin bag he'd been holding for Polly. She'd been enveloped by Mrs. Bentz and led away so fast the night before that he'd forgotten to return it to her. Under their present situation, Gordon decided maybe Daniel should be the one to give it to her. "I'll finish breaking camp if you will run this over to Miss Polly."

Daniel took the bundle with a smile on his lips. What boy didn't want to get out of his chores by going to see a pretty lady?

Chapter 11

Everything was back to normal. Well, as normal as it could be, Polly supposed. She packed up her tent and supplies and placed them in the corner of the Bentzes' wagon. Her feet stung, reminding her that another day of walking was ahead of her.

Idella had seemed a little cold in her attitude this morning, but Polly dismissed the behavior, praying it was due to her being tired from her pregnancy and the long trip. Little Luke had been fussier than normal, and Idella had cuddled him close while doing her normal chores.

Polly offered to help with Luke, but Idella told her she could manage. Sitting in the shade of the wagon, Polly worked on the sketch of the Indian mother and her newborn son. She wanted to remember them. The echo to form up the line traveled to them. Polly put her sketchbook with the rest of her belongings and went in search of Idella and little Luke.

She found them returning from the river. "Would you like

me to take Luke this morning?"

"No, thank you." Idella walked around her.

Polly reached out and stopped her. "Idella, what is wrong?"

Cold eyes bored into hers. "You've been gone for two days, doing who knows what with those men, and you've shown no remorse or regret at all. I don't want you taking care of Luke any longer, Polly. And if it were up to me, I'd ask you to find another wagon to travel with, but Gustaf says no, that you are to stay. So stay you shall, but I no longer need your help."

Tears filled Polly's eyes. "Idella, you can't mean that." The pleading in her own voice sickened her—never in Polly's life had she been accused so unjustly.

Idella jerked her arm away from her. "I do. Now, please, excuse me." She picked Luke up and walked away.

Polly followed at a slower pace. She stood off to the side and watched the train begin to form.

"Here, Miss Polly. Papa Gordon said to give this to you." Daniel thrust the animal skin bundle into her arms and then bent over and panted. "I've been looking all over for you."

Polly stroked the hair on the soft skin. "I'm sorry, Daniel."

"That's all right, Miss Polly." He looked up at her. "Are you crying, Miss Polly?"

She felt the moisture on her cheeks and wiped it away. "Yes. But I'm fine." She offered him a wobbly smile.

"Is it because Papa Gordon doesn't want to marry you?" he asked, still bent over and looking at the ground.

Had she heard him right? Gordon didn't want to marry her? "What?"

"I heard him tell Mr. York and some other men this morning that he wasn't going to marry you. Is that why you are crying?" He straightened up and looked at her.

Polly's head began to ache, and the tears flowed more freely. "No, Daniel." She touched her throbbing temples. "I just have a headache. Thank you for bringing me this." She hugged the bag to her.

"You're welcome. I'd better get back to Papa Gordon." Daniel ran back the way he'd come.

Polly felt as if all the air had been squeezed from her lungs. Why did it hurt so bad to know that Gordon had no feelings for her? The sharp pain in her heart confirmed to her that she had fallen in love with the reverend.

She dared not think why the men had demanded that he marry her. Did the whole train think they had been sinful? Dirt rose as the wagons pulled out. If she stayed where she was, no one would miss her. But if she stayed where she was, she'd also be disobeying Mamadele. How was she going to face everyone again?

Polly shook her head to clear her thoughts and opened the skins. Inside were two pairs of moccasins. She realized that the Indian women had noticed her discomfort and offered her shoes that would ease her pain. One pair was ankle high and the other looked as if they would go up to her knees. When winter hit, the moccasins would feel wonderful.

Give the mother as much control as possible, since there is only so much a new mother can control. Mamadele's words filtered through her tired mind.

If Idella didn't want her traveling with her family any longer, she'd ask and see if she could store her things in someone else's wagon.

New shoes, new circumstances, she thought. Polly took her shoes off and wrapped them in the animal skin. She slid her feet into the soft moccasins and sighed. They felt heavenly. Then she hurried to catch up with the wagon train.

Polly walked and thought about her situation all day. The Millers were an older couple and might have room in their wagon for her tent and few belongings. As soon as the train stopped for the evening, Polly walked to their campsite.

Mrs. Miller was pulling the camp together when she arrived. Polly cleared her throat. When the silver head rose, Polly asked, "May I speak to you for a moment, Mrs. Miller?"

"Of course, Polly." She tugged on a wooden box. "Come and help me get this crate out, won't you, dear?" She grunted as she pulled.

Polly hurried to her side and took the majority of the weight and lifted the crate down.

"Thank you. Normally Mr. Miller gets it down, but the men are having a meeting, and I wanted to start supper." She lifted the lid and began to work. "What did you want to ask me?"

Now that the time had come, Polly felt her palms get sticky. "Mrs. Bentz isn't happy that the reverend and I were off alone, with Indians really, and she's angry at me because...well, I'm not really sure why." She clasped her hands together and inwardly fretted. The words just weren't coming out right.

Mrs. Miller nodded. "Yes, I've heard. The ladies seem to

think the whole situation was improper. I'm sorry she is being so hard on you, dear."

Polly gulped down the knot in her throat. "There was nothing improper about it. We were kidnapped, asked to help with the birth of a baby, and then returned here. That's it, that's all that happened, Mrs. Miller. I promise." *So much for a new attitude,* she thought as she fought the tears that threatened to spill over at any moment.

The older woman walked over and embraced Polly. "It's all right, dear. Why don't you come and stay with Mr. Miller and me? I could use your help, and I've missed good company."

"Really?" Polly sobbed against her shoulder.

Mrs. Miller pulled back and lifted Polly's chin. "That was what you were going to ask me, wasn't it?"

Polly nodded. Mrs. Miller's eyes were a soft blue, surrounded by a halo of kindness.

"Good. Now before you say yes, I think you should know. I don't like gossip. I'm not above saying what I think, and I enjoy reading."

Why the older woman thought she needed to know that she enjoyed reading, Polly didn't know, but she smiled. "Then we should get along nicely, except I don't read a lot—well, other than my mother's journal. But I enjoy sketching."

Mrs. Miller nodded. "Good. Why don't you gather your things? I'll let Mr. Miller know we have a new wagon guest."

"Oh, I won't be any trouble at all. I only need a small space for my tent and other things." Polly was fearful Mrs. Miller would change her mind.

"I know, dear." The older woman waved Polly off and returned to her crate.

When she returned to the Bentzes' wagon, Idella was setting up camp also. She ignored Polly as she pulled her things from the back of the wagon.

Polly said to Idella's back, "I'm staying with the Millers now, Idella. Should you need me, please come and get me. I will still help you with birthing the baby."

Silence hung between them. Polly picked up her things and walked away. Her heart ached as she realized that another new chapter had started in her life. She prayed that within the next few months Idella would come around and that she would be allowed to deliver the Bentzes' baby.

Over the next few months, the wagon train made its way over the mountains. Gordon's heart ached for Polly. She kept her distance from him, and he missed her. He'd noticed that only a few of the women now befriended her, and the men seemed to hold him at bay also, at least when they were within seeing and hearing distance of their wives.

Polly grew thinner with each passing mile. Most evenings he found himself watching her from the shadows. She and Mrs. Miller had become friends. Polly huddled in front of her small tent, under the skins her Indian friends had given her, sketching, writing in her journal, or sewing.

One evening she looked up when Gustaf Bentz hurried up to her tent. He held little Luke in his arms. "Is time."

"Go get the reverend," Polly instructed. At his swift nod, she hurried into her tent.

Why did she want Gustaf to come get him? Gordon hurried back toward his wagon. If he hurried, he might beat the other man back. He had just stepped into the firelight of his own camp when Gustaf rushed toward him. "Is time," the man told him.

"Time for what?" Gordon asked. He didn't want Gustaf or anyone else suspecting he'd heard the man summon Polly.

"The babe. Time to go."

"Daniel!"

The boy stuck his head out the back of the wagon. "I heard."

"Take little Luke from Mr. Bentz; he can sleep in our wagon tonight." He watched as Gustaf handed a sleeping Luke up to Daniel. "I'll be back as soon as I can. Stay close to the wagon and get some sleep." He picked up his Bible and followed the father-to-be.

When Gordon arrived at the wagon, he stopped and asked, "What can I do to help?"

"You can get in here!" Idella yelled from the wagon.

He looked to Gustaf, who simply shrugged. Some help he was. Gordon wondered if all the men in the wagon train were afraid of their wives.

"Now!"

Gordon hurried over the wagon's tailgate and into the wagon. "I'm here," he announced unnecessarily.

Idella was sitting in a rocker rubbing her stomach. Polly sat on the floor beside her. Both of them ignored him as Idella rode out a wave of pain. Her pale, pinched face and the way she gritted her teeth told the story of her labor. When the pain passed, she looked up at him. "I want you here to pray."

"I can do that outside, ma'am." He'd never even been in a birthing room, much less this close to a woman about to give birth.

Pain flashed across her features again. She gritted her teeth and closed her eyes. Sweat broke out on her brow.

When the pain eased again, Polly wet a small rag and gently washed Idella's face. He looked to her for guidance. "Idella, the reverend is right. He shouldn't be in here just now. He'll stand outside the wagon and pray, while your husband comes in here and takes the first baby when it's born. How does that sound?"

Idella leaned forward in her chair. "That would be nice. Thank you, Reverend."

The two men exchanged places. Gustaf stepped to the side, looking confused.

Gordon turned just in time to see Polly indicate Gustaf should move behind his wife and watched as he began to slowly rub her back. He closed the flap and silently prayed for all those within the wagon.

"Lower, please," Idella groaned. "Are you praying, too, Gustaf?"

"Do you want me to pray out loud or silently?"

She answered, "I don't care; just pray. I want this baby to live."

Gordon heard Polly's sweet response. "I will do everything in my power to make sure this baby lives, Idella."

Gordon silently asked God to make this baby come fast.

He realized this probably was not what Idella meant when she'd said to pray, but he'd never felt so uneasy in his life.

Finally Idella said, "I know you will, Polly. I'm sorry I've been so cruel to you."

Gordon was glad he wasn't in the wagon. He was sure the tension was so thick you could stir it with a stick.

Polly answered, "It's all right, Idella." Her voice remained calm when she said, "I think it's time to start pushing. Would you like to squat to have the baby? With your husband here, that might be the most modest way, but as you know, the choice is yours." When Idella didn't answer, Polly pressed on: "Idella, you need to make a decision. This baby is entering the world. I can see the top of its head."

"I'll squat."

"Gustaf, would you continue to massage her back?"

"I'll be happy to."

A few minutes later, the sound of Polly's singing filled Gordon's ears. "Oh come, all ye faithful. . ."

Gordon joined her. "Joyful and triumphant. . ." He admired the way their voices blended. Idella panted out the song with them.

Polly stopped singing. Standing outside the wagon, Gordon had no idea what she was doing. A soft cry later, and he heard her say, "It's a girl, Idella. A girl!"

"Praise be to God," Idella cried.

Gordon held his breath and waited for more sounds. Soon he heard a soft smacking noise and then the baby cried. "Are we done?" he called.

"No, keep singing. I see another head," Polly instructed.

"Gustaf, come take your daughter."

Gordon began singing again.

"You are doing fine, Idella. One more push." Polly's voice sounded as sweet as honey to his ears. He admired the way her voice stayed calm as she delivered the second baby.

"And a son for Gustaf," Polly announced as she smacked the second baby's behind.

Gustaf's rich laughter of relief filled the air. And then he said, "They are beautiful, Idella."

The sound of soft panting came from the wagon. "Thank you."

"What are you going to name them?" Polly asked.

"We're going to name them Jesse and Bessie. Jesse after my father, Jess. Bessie after my grandmother."

"Those are sweet names," Polly said. In just a few minutes, Polly opened the flap and gestured to Gordon that he could come look at the babies.

Idella looked up at him. "Reverend, can I ask you a personal question?"

He leaned against the wagon and smiled. "Sure, I don't see why not."

Gustaf helped Idella settle both babies into her arms. He hugged all three members of his family before standing upright again.

Idella took a baby's hand in hers and counted the fingers and then asked, "Why don't you want to marry this young woman? She's smart, kind, and not bad to look at."

"She's too young for me, Mrs. Bentz. Let her grow up, and then we'll talk."

Idella's head snapped up. "I was talking about Polly, and you know it," she scolded.

Did he owe this woman an explanation? His gaze moved to Polly. She continued to clean up and pretended to ignore him. Gordon knew that he'd probably not get to talk to her again in a very long time, so he answered Idella's question honestly. "Well, ma'am, I do love Miss Polly, but she doesn't feel the same way."

Polly looked at him. Her cheeks turned pink, and her mouth opened and closed much like a baby bird's.

"How do you know she doesn't love you? Have you asked her?" Idella seemed focused on the baby.

Gordon searched Polly's face. "No, I guess I haven't. Do you love me, too, Miss Polly?"

Polly's gaze flashed to Idella and the babies.

Idella didn't look up as she continued examining her new children. "You'd better answer the young man, Polly. He may not ask twice."

He held his breath for her answer. Could she hear his heart pounding in his chest?

Her voice came out in a whisper: "I do."

"What did she say?" Gustaf grinned down at his wife.

Idella laughed. "She said yes!"

Gordon helped Polly down from the wagon, making sure the flaps were securely tied behind him.

He turned to Polly. "Did you mean it? You love me?"

She nodded. "I've loved you since the day I saw you ride up on Rawhide, but I've been afraid to admit it, even to myself."

Gordon pulled her to the dark side of the wagon and

enveloped her in his arms. She smelled sweet like mint. He hugged her close. "When we get to Oregon, will you marry me, Polly?"

She leaned back in his arms. "Will you ever leave me, Gordon?"

He shook his head. "Never."

"And do you understand that I'm a midwife, and my mothers will always come first in our lives?" Polly searched his face.

"I do. Now will you marry me?" Gordon prayed she'd not come up with another question. He wanted to kiss her but wouldn't until he had her promise of love and marriage.

Polly's full lips turned up, and her eyes sparkled. "I will."

Gordon did what he'd wanted to do since the first day he'd met her. As he kissed her, he felt her shove into his body. He opened his eyes then pulled away from her. Beulah stood behind Polly, head down, ready to push her again.

Polly laughed. "I think Beulah wants to be asked for her blessing." She stepped out of his arms and waited, a teasing glint in her eyes.

"What do you think, Beulah? Is it all right for me to marry Polly?"

The mule brayed and then pushed Polly back into his arms, where Gordon planned to keep her forever.

RHONDA GIBSON resides in New Mexico with her husband. She writes romance because she is eager to share her love of the Lord. Besides writing, her interests are reading and scrapbooking recipes. Rhonda loves hearing from her readers!

BIRTH OF A
DREAM

by Pamela Griffin

Dedication

A huge thanks to my critique partners and helpers—Theo, Mom, and Jane. And to my dad, remembering our tea parties of my childhood. To my Lord and Savior, always there for me as my source of strength when I feel so weak and unable. As always with every book I write, this is for You.

Let nothing be done through strife or vainglory;
but in lowliness of mind let each esteem other
better than themselves.
PHILIPPIANS 2:3

Chapter 1

A harsh pounding threatened to splinter the wood of the heavy front door.

Christiana's cheerful humming came to an abrupt halt, and she almost dropped her mother's good china. She spun around, her hands clutched around the plates, and wondered who could be visiting so late. Why hadn't they pulled the bell? It must be going on half past ten! No decent time for any caller.

In immediate response to her thought, the chimes rang—followed by more frantic knocking.

Pulling in a deep breath, she laid the stack of plates on the tablecloth. She wished her parents were home and that their housekeeper wasn't visiting her sister in Seattle.

"Stop borrowing trouble," Christiana scolded herself. "You're no helpless child."

Slightly encouraged, she moved to the entry hall, her hands going to her hair and smoothing whatever stray locks might have escaped their pins. She glanced at the umbrella in the stand, a possible weapon if the need should arise.

She hoped she appeared more confident than she felt.

Opening the door, she almost got her nose rapped on by an impatient masculine hand poised for another knock. Christiana blinked in surprise. The man standing there pulled back his arm in equal shock.

The gaslight from the entryway showed her visitor to be taller than her by a few inches, wearing a black hat and overcoat, lean in build. He had a nice face and rich coffee-brown eyes that looked anxious. Her mind picked up the details in the few seconds before he spoke.

"Please, miss, I need to speak with Mrs. Leonard at once," he explained in a rich, well-modulated tone.

"Mother isn't here at the moment. Would you like to leave your card? I can tell her you dropped by."

"No time for that. Have you any idea when she'll return?"

She shook her head. "I'm sorry. She went to deliver some papers to my father for the Exposition—the Lewis and Clark one that opens soon." She realized the inanity of elaborating; every member of the populace of Oregon and many from the entire nation, indeed, from around the world, knew of the Exposition.

"That's on the other side of town," he calculated aloud, "at least an hour to get there, even with taking the trolley. With all the traffic due to the Expo, double that."

She nodded, wondering the reason for his visit.

"I can't wait hours, not even one." He shoved his hands into his overcoat pockets. "Can you tell me the location of the nearest doctor?"

His gruff question triggered the alarm of comprehension in

her mind. "What did you say your name was?"

He blinked. "I didn't. Sorry. I'm Noah Cafferty."

She regarded him in surprise. "You're related to Lanie Cafferty."

"She's my stepmother. The reason I'm here. Her time has come, and no one else was home when I arrived at their house."

Instantly, Christiana's thoughts clicked into gear. "How long ago?"

He studied her as if debating whether he should share the information. He glanced at his pocket watch. "It's taken me twenty-six minutes to find your house with her bad directions. She, um, she wanted your mother to know..." His face turned a shade dark, and she sensed discussing such delicate matters was uncomfortable for him. For her, it was second nature.

"It's all right. You can tell me."

"She said her water broke." He cleared his throat. "That the baby was coming."

Christiana nodded. She could wait for Mother to arrive, though with evening traffic and the distance, it could take hours. Even with the information Noah Cafferty related, it was impossible to know how far along Lanie was without an examination. Christiana had learned that for every woman childbirth was different. Only one matter was certain: Lanie would be delivering a child soon. And Christiana was the sole person available to handle the job.

"We shouldn't linger. I'll just get my coat and hat."

"Wait—*what*?" He grabbed her arm. She stared at him with her brows raised in curious question. He shook his head and let go of her sleeve. "Sorry. Wasn't thinking. This whole thing has my brain coming unscrewed."

She smiled. "It's perfectly understandable. I won't be one moment." Again she moved to collect her things.

This time he took a step inside. "You can't mean. . .you don't plan to take your mother's place?"

At his clear alarm, she nodded while turning to the hat tree for her coat and hat. She hoped he couldn't tell that she was shaking in her shoes at the idea of assuming her mother's role in delivering a baby. *And* without assistance.

She felt uncertain she was ready for this, but she had no choice. Grandmother Polly had done it at her age—and all alone, on a wilderness trail, in the middle of nowhere.

Christiana could do it, too.

"You can't be serious." Noah eyed the young woman who looked little more than a girl. "What are you—seventeen?"

She winced at his guess, and he knew it must be dead-on.

"I assure you, Mr. Cafferty, age has little to do with skill. I've assisted my mother for the past two years. I know exactly what needs doing."

"Yes, but have you ever done it alone?"

Her anxious expression and the resounding silence gave him his answer.

"There must be a doctor somewhere close," he argued hopefully.

"Knowing Lanie as I do, I don't think she would care for the idea of one, but of course you must do whatever you feel is best."

That was just the problem. Noah had *no idea* what was best

for his father's young wife. He had only thought to drop in for a visit, since he rarely came by except for the occasional Sunday dinner. It wasn't that he disapproved of his father's choice of a bride any longer. The age difference had unsettled him at first, Lanie only five years older than himself. But lately he had made a concentrated effort to accept her as family. The knowledge that Lanie's well-being and that of his little half brother or sister rested solely in his hands was nerve-racking to say the least. If he made the wrong decision, his father might never forgive him. He might never forgive himself.

"Can you tell me where the doctor lives?"

"I'm sorry. I don't know."

"You *don't know*?" He regarded her in disbelief. "How could you not know?" He shook his head. "All right, then. Have you got a telephone?"

She motioned to a nearby table. "There've been problems with it. The connection is horrid, full of static. You're welcome to try, though."

He moved toward the candlestick phone and picked it up, bringing it to his mouth while clicking the hook and putting the receiver to his ear. A series of disturbing clicks followed.

"What's the doctor's name?" he asked.

She gave an apologetic shrug. "I don't know that either. Lanie mentioned it once. She and her husband use a different doctor than we do."

"Your family doctor, then."

"He's out of town. I remember him telling Papa at church that he was going to be absent for a week, to sort out things with his father's estate."

Noah's eyes shut in dismay. Of course. Why should he expect a doctor to be available with the way this evening had progressed so far?

"You could ask the operator to connect you with Lanie's doctor—she might know who he is."

He could, *if* he could get through. Frustrated, Noah set the earpiece on its hook and the phone back on the table.

"I might not be much in your estimation," the very-young-looking Miss Leonard said carefully. "But right now I'm all you have. Once there, you can ask Lanie the name of her family physician if you feel better about doing so. I won't take offense at your lack of confidence in my skills. I just want to make sure she's all right. Her health and that of the baby are what's important."

This time, *she* rested her hand on the forearm of *his* coat sleeve.

"I don't envy your position, Mr. Cafferty, and I do understand how upsetting this is to you, to find yourself so suddenly in charge of such a monumental decision." By the grim way she said it, she understood only too well. "But I have learned in my years of assisting at births that babies wait for no one. If you don't make a decision soon, it might be too late."

Her words sounded like a death knell; he felt the blood drain from his face. He didn't know if it was the fear of arriving too late to save them or the mature manner in which the young Miss Leonard presented herself or even the wisdom glowing steadily in her gray-blue eyes; but for whatever reason, Noah nodded his consent.

"Then we should go."

"I'll just grab Mother's bag. I'll need that, too."

Noah watched her hurry away, hoping he had not just signed Lanie and little Baby Cafferty's untimely death sentences.

Chapter 2

At first Lanie showed hesitance with the idea, but when another pain gripped her middle, she clutched Christiana's arm. "Help me," she begged between clenched teeth.

Christiana patted her friend's hand, which she'd been holding since she arrived. "I know what I'm doing, Lanie. I've assisted at more births than I can count on two hands."

Brave words for as apprehensive as she felt. Yet one of many important nuggets of truth she had learned from her ancestors' journal, passed down to her mother, was to never let anyone see her fear. As her great-grandmother Adele had written, *It's in how you act that others will react. If you're worried and doubtful, the mothers will know and likewise feel the same. Keep them calm. First-time mothers are the most fearful. In all things, put your hope in God, and He will give you the peace and assurance you need to carry out this great undertaking to which you've been called.*

The journal was filled with inspiring words that the original owner left to her granddaughter Adele, Christiana's great-grandmother, and which, in turn, Adele, her daughter, Polly, and Christiana's mother added to over the years. Soon, Christiana planned also to jot down words of wisdom to share with any descendants who might seek the journal's knowledge, should they decide to take up midwifery as at least six generations of her family had done.

Christiana looked toward the doorway where Lanie's step-son watched, his expression hesitant and more than a little anxious. Clearly he had no wish to be there, but his eyes were watchful of every action Christiana made, as if he felt he must oversee in his father's place. Mr. Cafferty also had shown reservations upon first meeting Christiana's mother but was soon reassured. Had he known Christiana was the only one present at the birth of his first child with Lanie, she felt he would have shown the same anxiety as Noah. But his shadowing her made *her* nervous, and she must keep calm.

"Would you please light the kitchen stove and set a kettle to boil?" she asked, more to busy his hands at a task than because of any need to have water at the moment. By her estimation, Lanie still had some time before the baby came. But even if he had to boil five kettles of water, she reasoned the activity would help him gain some peace of mind.

"Of course. Anything to help."

Quickly he left, clomping down the stairs in his haste. Lanie's contraction passed, and Christiana took the opportunity to examine her. With Lanie only eight years her senior, the two had become as devoted as sisters during Lanie's term. Christiana read the fear in Lanie's hazel eyes as she labored to bring her first child into the world.

"Have you decided on a name?" Christiana prodded in a soothing tone.

Her heartbeat skipped to realize Lanie was closer to delivery than she'd thought. She hoped her mother would see the note she had left and arrive soon, but she doubted it. Papa would insist he return with Mother, not wanting her traveling alone at night, and he likely wouldn't be happy that she had taken it on herself to bring him his forgotten briefcase. Nor would he wish to leave the impending exhibit until all was in order. With his meticulous ways, that could take hours. She forced a trouble-free smile, grateful to see Lanie's brow also smooth.

"Clarence and I spoke of it this week. Roderick, if it's a boy. Juliet, if it's a girl."

"Those are lovely names."

Sorrow filled Lanie's eyes. "We had a row. That's why he's not here."

Wishing to keep Lanie as serene as possible, Christiana doubted the wisdom of speaking of their altercation but needed to know. "Have you any idea where your husband went?"

"Likely the gentlemen's club, playing cards or talking politics. He goes there when he's upset."

The loud clatter of banging pots came to them from downstairs.

Christiana rose from the bed. Row or no row, the father should be told his child was entering the world. "I'll just see if your stepson needs help." She squeezed Lanie's hand before going. "Would you like something for your thirst?"

Lanie nodded against the pillow. "Please. I'm so grateful you're here, Christiana."

She smiled. "Where else would I be? I'm here as long as you need me. Don't worry. You'll be fine."

Another contraction hit, and Lanie tightened her hold painfully around Christiana's hand. Christiana again sank to the bed, gently reassuring, as Lanie's face turned as red as a tomato and she squeezed her eyes shut, desperately clutching the mound of her stomach.

"Breathe, Lanie. No—don't hold your breath!"

"I'm going to die, aren't I?"

"No, you're not."

Stark terror filled her friend's eyes. She had to calm her quickly. The idea that came was foolish, counting off seconds, but it was all she could think of.

"Say it with me, Lanie: one Exposition, two Exposition, come now. Three Exposition, four Exposition. . ."

Lanie looked at her oddly but obeyed. Somehow they slowly made it to "twenty Exposition" before Lanie again rested and Christiana retrieved her reddened, nail-marked hand from Lanie's relaxed hold. That pain had come longer and stronger. Christiana feared they didn't have much time before the final moments of labor, which could take minutes or hours. She wiped the damp hair from Lanie's forehead.

"You did well. If another pain comes, do what we just did and remember to *breathe*. I won't be long."

She hurried downstairs and found Noah standing amid pots and pans of all sizes, the cupboard doors and pantry flung wide open. He turned to look at her, his eyes frantic. "Would you believe there isn't one kettle in this entire blasted kitchen?"

At her home, the pots hung from hooks in the ceiling. Here,

they were stowed away on hidden shelves. If he couldn't find a kettle, she doubted she would have better success. Christiana grabbed the largest pot. "This will do. You'll have to make twice this amount and put all of it in a washbasin. Where is the linen closet? We'll need plenty of clean towels."

"I wish the doctor was here."

"If you feel it necessary, then you must call him. I'm not stopping you."

"I tried—but would you believe he's out on a call!"

His words reminded her of Lanie's husband. To send Noah out on a short errand, especially when he was at his wits' end, would be good for all of them. "Do you know the location of your father's club? He should be told."

Noah nodded brusquely. "Yes, yes, I thought of that earlier. The operator of the exchange couldn't connect me, so I went there myself—before coming to you—but Father wasn't there."

Calm. Calm. She must remain calm; she appeared the only one able to do so.

Christiana drew upon every nugget of training she'd received from her mother and the wisdom from her ancestors' journal.

Dear God, help me in my hour of need, to fight my own pharaoh of fear.

"All right. Let's just take this one step at a time. I'll start water to boil. And I'll need you to chip off some ice from the block in the icebox, small enough for Lanie to suck on." The ice would help cool her and worked better than drinking water while she was in labor. She grabbed the pot and put it under the pump as she instructed him, propelling the handle until water gushed out. Quickly she set the filled pot on the stove he'd lit and watched as he chiseled pieces of ice into a bowl. With the cupboards wide open and the glasses in plain sight, she grabbed one. "Watch the water while I take the ice to Lanie." She dropped chunks into a glass, hesitated, then said what must be addressed. There was no time for dillydallying. "If Mother doesn't get here in time, I'll need your assistance when the baby comes."

He stared at her as if she'd just told him to strike a match and set himself on fire.

"If you don't think you can do it, tell me now." She had always assisted her mother. She could not imagine accomplishing the task alone, though if she must, she would do her best.

He went a shade paler but nodded. "I'll do whatever needs to be done."

Chapter 3

Three hours later, Noah remembered his brave words, gravely telling himself, as he'd been doing all night, that he would *not* pass out. And to think, women had been doing this for centuries! After hearing Lanie's screams and witnessing her travail, he didn't see how.

No one had come, not his father, not Christiana's mother. Now Noah stood a discreet distance from Lanie, giving her what privacy he could offer while assisting Christiana by handing her whatever she asked for or giving Lanie yet more ice or his hand to squeeze to a pulp. Lanie had shown some expected awkwardness to have him there at first, but now she seemed oblivious to his presence in the room as she leaned forward, fisting her hand to the mattress, a determined look on her face as she struggled to bring her child into the world.

"Push, Lanie, push hard!" Christiana urged from beneath the tented sheet of Lanie's bent knees. "Once more should do it. I can see the head!"

The news had Noah grabbing the bed frame for support,

feeling dizzy, even as Lanie let out a determined, triumphant wail and seemed to crunch the bones of his other hand.

Minutes seemed like hours before Christiana gave a happy little giggle and delivered the news they had waited hours to receive.

"She's here, Lanie. You have a baby girl."

"A girl?" Lanie breathed softly, all smiles, no trace of pain remaining on her face. "Can I see her? Let me hold her."

"Yes, of course; just a minute while I take care of things."

"What things?"

"Normal things," the young Miss Leonard calmly assured. "Nothing to worry about. Just relax."

Within a short time she brought Lanie a writhing bundle swaddled in soft toweling.

"She's quiet," Lanie said, sitting up urgently. "Why's she so quiet?"

"It's all right," Christiana soothed. "She's fine. See?"

She bent to lay the bundle in Lanie's arms. Noah's heart seized with worry as he saw the dark-blue eyes of his new half sister stare wide and unblinking from a wrinkled red face that looked up at Lanie. Apparently the baby's appearance gave neither woman alarm, though the head was misshaped. Lanie cooed to her newborn, and Christiana straightened to stand upright. Her body swayed.

"Easy." Noah rested his hands at her waist to steady her. "Are you all right?" he whispered so only she could hear, though Lanie appeared so caught up in her baby he doubted she would notice a tidal wave break outside her window at the moment.

The young midwife nodded, but he felt her tremble.

"You should sit down."

"There are things I must attend to first." She glanced at him. "I won't be needing your help any longer if you'd like to wait downstairs."

Noah just prevented himself from running for the door. He was no coward but still felt ill at ease to be thrust in the middle of such a womanly situation, one entirely out of his element. "I'll make coffee."

"That sounds splendid. I'll be down straightaway."

He held eye contact with her. Their interaction felt oddly intimate, as if they'd known each other years instead of hours, and he nodded in affirmation at her easy smile.

In his exhaustion, he almost forgot his salutations before making his quick exit. "Lanie, congratulations. I'm happy for you and Father both."

"Thank you, Noah. For everything."

He nodded and glanced at Christiana once more before heading downstairs.

With everything accomplished, Christiana cleaned up while Lanie cuddled her baby. Twenty minutes had passed by the time she went downstairs to join Noah. On the landing she stopped, feeling a bit woozy. He appeared suddenly, coming from the parlor. She grabbed the banister, and he moved to her side, putting a hand to her waist to steady her.

"You all right?"

She offered a brief nod. "Yes, Mr. Cafferty, thank you. I only came down the stairs too fast."

"After all you've done, it's no small wonder that you're exhausted. And please, call me Noah. May I call you Christiana? Somehow, after tonight, formalities seem bizarre."

She felt the same way, as if she'd known this man much longer than one evening. With his hand supporting her waist, his words seemed more familiar than they actually were, but she nodded her consent.

"You should sit. I'll check to see if the coffee's ready." He steered her toward the parlor sofa, and obediently she sank to the cushion. She found it amusing that for the past few hours she had told him what to do, and now he was taking charge. She rather liked the difference.

He looked at her in concern as if she were the one who'd just given birth. "Sure you're okay?"

She wondered what her appearance must be for him to ask twice but again assured him she was fine.

Once he left for the kitchen, she sank her head back against the cushion. Her neck and shoulders ached from being held in one position too long. She felt she'd been awake for days instead of just one of them. . . .

The next thing she knew, a hand on her shoulder shook her gently awake.

"Christiana. . ."

The low, masculine voice was unfamiliar, but the soft way he spoke her name caused warm contentment to spread from the center of Christiana's being. Wearily, she opened her eyes. At the sight of Noah looking down at her with kindness, she came instantly awake and sat up.

"How long have I been asleep?" She patted her fingers at

the sides of her head in a futile attempt to sweep the thick, loose tendrils into some form of acceptability, finally giving up the notion as hopeless and letting her hands fall to her lap.

"Two hours."

"Two hours?"

He nodded and moved away from her. "I decided you needed rest more than you needed coffee."

Disconcerted that she'd fallen fast asleep on his family's sofa, she stood and smoothed the wrinkles from her skirt. "Has my mother come yet?"

"No, but my father did, fifteen minutes ago."

"Oh?" She regarded him in surprise.

"I thought you should know. That's why I woke you. He's upstairs with Lanie."

She hated to intrude on their privacy and deliberated what to do. Since no one had wakened her before this, mother and baby must be faring well. "I should go before my parents return home."

"I would think they are home already." He gestured to the mantel clock, and Christiana's jaw dropped.

"Twenty till six? I had no idea!" In confusion she wondered why Mother had not come; it wasn't like her to neglect her patients.

"I'll take you home," Noah offered.

Christiana nodded shyly. She didn't wish to put him out—he looked just as exhausted, but she had no desire to walk three miles home in the dark by herself either.

The brisk air did little to keep her awake. Several times she found herself nodding off, the sway of the buggy rocking her to sleep. She woke with a start to realize her head lay against Noah's strong shoulder. She straightened with a mumbled apology and moved the scant distance to the edge of the short seat.

"I believe this is where you wish to go?"

In the dusky lantern light, he smiled at her, and she realized that the buggy had stopped. She looked to see she was home. She had never been so happy to see the two-story blue and white building in her life.

He helped her down and walked her to the front door.

"It's been a pleasure and an experience, Christiana. One I will never forget."

His quiet farewell seemed to hold more than what rested on the surface. It warmed her all the way up the stairs of the dark, quiet house and to her bed. Her last waking thought was to hope she might see the helpful young Mr. Cafferty again.

Somehow, she would see to that.

Chapter 4

Christiana woke, disoriented and uncomfortable. Realizing she slept in her dress, she stripped down to her undergarments then fell back into the cool sheets. Sleep wouldn't return, but the memory of what occurred in the wee hours of morning did. And at the center was one man with whom she had shared a unique closeness while they worked as a team—more connected than she'd felt to some friends of years.

With sleep elusive, she performed her daily ablutions and dressed. While offering morning prayers, she said a special petition for Lanie and her baby, which led her to remember that her mother had never shown up at the Cafferty residence.

Curious and concerned, she went downstairs. Had something happened to Mother? Had she taken ill?

Her glance went to the entry table, bare except for a fresh vase of flowers. She then noticed the sheet of paper at the baseboard and gasped to recognize her note. She plucked it up and hurried toward the breakfast parlor.

Merciful heavens! Her mother had never seen the note! A gust of wind from the door opening must have knocked it off the table.

Looking healthy and as composed as ever, her mother

poured morning tea. Not a dark hair rested out of place. She looked up at Christiana, the laugh crinkles at her blue eyes deepening as she smiled.

"Christiana?" Her smile disappeared. "Whatever is the matter, dear?"

"Lanie had her baby!"

"What?" In clear shock, her mother set down the teapot.

"Last night. I left you a note before I went there." Christiana held up the paper.

"*You* delivered the child?" Mother's soft voice contained both awe and pride.

Christiana nodded. "Her stepson came to collect me."

"Oh my. . .I trust there were no complications."

"None. I *was* frightened, though I made certain not to show it." Again Christiana thanked God for His intervention during those anxious hours. "Once I arrived, she was far into her labor. If her stepson—Mr. Cafferty—had not come by to visit, she might have been alone at the end. He assisted me, and a little over four hours later, she gave birth to a girl."

"*Noah Cafferty* assisted you?" Her mother looked startled then slowly smiled. "Frankly, I'm stunned that he didn't insist on a doctor. Lanie told me he shares the views of those who believe midwifery should no longer exist in this day and age."

Recalling their initial conversation, Christiana wasn't surprised. But surely, after being a witness to the birth, Noah would have changed his opinions. Thankfully it had been an easy delivery; not all of them were.

"I never supposed I wouldn't be with you during your first time, dear, but I have long known you were ready for the next step and just needed a boost of confidence to get there." She reached to where Christiana had taken a seat and laid her hand over hers, squeezing it before pulling away. "After breakfast, we'll visit Lanie and her baby to ensure all is well."

Christiana smiled and reached for a muffin. Scrambled eggs were in a serving dish on the sideboard, as well as sausages, but she was famished and said a quick blessing, intending to collect more once she took the edge off her hunger.

She'd not yet taken a bite when the bell cord of the front door was pulled.

Remembering that their maid was on vacation, she rose from the table.

"I'll get that, Mother."

Once Christiana opened the front door, she blinked in surprise to see Noah there. This time, no concern tightened his relaxed features, and the morning sun brought a sparkle to his dark eyes, enhancing his good looks that the night had only hinted at. For a moment she stared before she remembered her manners.

"Mr. Cafferty, how nice to see you. Lanie and the baby are well?"

"Quite. And it's Noah."

At the reminder, she felt a blush but nodded.

"Forgive the intrusion at such an early hour. I thought you might need this." He offered her mother's bag of birthing items. She didn't know she'd forgotten it.

"Thank you, yes!" She held out her hand for the bag, not realizing she still held her muffin. Her face heated further. A smile teased the corner of his lips, causing her to smile at the amusing situation as well. The warmth in his eyes eased any lingering discomfort. Again she found it odd how connected she felt to this man on such short acquaintance.

"Mother and I were just having breakfast. Would you like to join us?"

"I wouldn't wish to intrude—"

"Oh, you're not intruding!" At her effusive reassurance and his clear surprise, she added quickly, "Mother will want to meet you. She's curious about Lanie, and there's plenty to eat. Mother doesn't often bake, but when she does she gives her utmost since she loves it so well." She took the bag and held the door open wider for him to enter.

He looked puzzled by her garbled explanation. Not wishing to demolish the English language further, she didn't add that in the mode of fitting in with society's expectations for their class, her parents had hired a maid who doubled as a cook.

"If you're sure it's no inconvenience. . ." He lifted his brows, and she nodded. "Then I accept."

He took off his hat as he entered and hung it on the hat tree. She smiled shyly, setting the bag on the table before leading him through to the breakfast parlor. Her mother looked up in curious surprise. Introductions were made, and Noah was invited to take breakfast with them a second time. Christiana fixed him a plate and then her own before taking her chair across the table from him.

As they ate, Mother brought the conversation around from pleasantries to the events of the previous evening.

"Christiana told me that you assisted in the delivery of the baby."

Noah looked as if he just managed not to strangle on his food. "Yes, well, that was an experience I wish never to repeat. Your daughter was amazing, though I wish I could have located a doctor."

"Is something wrong with Lanie or her baby?" Christiana asked in concern.

"No. The baby did look more like a baby this morning—not so red—though the top of her head still looks a bit squashed."

Christiana hid a smile, recalling his wince of barely veiled horror at his first sight of an infant newly born.

"That will change," Christiana's mother reassured. "She'll look better with each day that passes."

Noah nodded. "I'm glad I chose the field of journalism. I never could have been a doctor."

"Why do you wish a doctor had been there?"

"Christiana," her mother warned softly under her breath.

But Christiana couldn't let his earlier statement go and set down her fork. "You must admit everything went well. Neither Lanie nor her baby unduly suffered."

"Yes, as I said, you were a wonderful stand-in."

His praise had the opposite effect and spoiled her satisfaction in her accomplishment.

"Stand-in?"

"Since the doctor couldn't be there."

"Lanie chose to have a midwife. There's nothing wrong with that."

"It's just not natural."

"Not *natural*?" She straightened her spine in disbelieving shock and just managed to keep her tone at the same pleasant, conversational level. "Mr. Cafferty, midwives were in existence long before doctors took over. The pharaoh didn't order the physicians to kill the newborns; he told the *midwives* to do so."

His brow lifted at her formal use of his name, but even if she wasn't upset with him at the moment, she felt odd taking that liberty on such short acquaintance when they weren't alone.

"That's ancient history. We're now in a progressive era, and things must change."

"*Must* change?" she scoffed. "That seems a little dictatorial, doesn't it?"

Her mother softly cleared her throat in the manner she used to stem a rising argument. "Of course, everyone is entitled to their opinions; that's what makes life so much more interesting, don't you think?" She looked at Noah. "You mentioned you're a journalist. What paper do you write for?"

"The *Portland New Age*. They just started this year."

"And does your boss share your views on what is and what isn't natural?" Christiana asked sweetly, though she still seethed inside.

"Christiana!" This time her mother's warning whisper came more forcefully.

Noah regarded her in curious puzzlement. "As a matter of fact, he does. After all, doctors have had professional training. . ."

"Midwives are also trained."

". . .at an educational institution," Noah continued, as if she hadn't spoken. "He doesn't believe women should work outside the home in this day and age. In fact, I'm doing a story on one of those suffragist meetings this week."

"Oh?" She folded her napkin and laid it on the table. "In

favor of the movement or against it?"

He smiled, but his apparent ease didn't fool her. "Totally unbiased, of course."

She leaned forward, her smile deceptively sweet. "Your own views never cloud your work?"

"I don't write editorials, Miss Leonard. I just report the news."

"As seen through your eyes, of course."

His smile slipped, and his eyes grew a trifle hard. "How else? After all, I'm the one writing the story."

"Before your arrival, I told my daughter we should visit Lanie after breakfast," her mother put in quickly, rising to her feet and picking up her plate, half the food untouched. "Forgive me, Mr. Cafferty; I have much to accomplish today. Please feel free to finish your breakfast. Christiana, a word with you."

Noah took the napkin from his lap and dropped it to the table as he rose. "I should be leaving for the office. I've lingered far too long. Might I give you and your daughter a lift to my father's house?"

"We wouldn't wish to put you out of your way."

"Not at all. His house is in the direction of the newspaper office."

"In that case, we would be most grateful. Christiana, would you please help me put these things away, dear?"

Noah excused himself to wait outside. The moment he was out of earshot, Christiana moved with what was left of the eggs to take them to the sink, but her mother clasped her arm to stop her. Knowing her mother was upset, Christiana lowered her gaze to the serving dish she held.

"Christiana, you must learn to curb that tongue of yours, especially with guests present."

"But you heard what he said. He thinks nothing of our calling!"

"While perhaps you think too much of it?" her mother suggested softly.

Christiana blinked and looked up into her gentle eyes. "Are you saying midwifery isn't important?"

"No, of course not. But are you certain it isn't wounded pride that compels you to speak so vehemently? Mr. Cafferty shares the views of most men in our society and out of it, which is why the suffragist groups formed. He's only speaking what he was taught. As are you. A difference of opinion is no cause for contention. The Lord's Word says that where there is strife there is every evil work. You would do well to remember that, dear."

Christiana restrained a sigh and gave a brief nod. They finished their chore, collected their things, and left the house.

Mother was right; Christiana knew it. Still, she remained silent on the drive, in part not trusting herself to speak but also having nothing to say. Once Noah pulled his team of horses in front of his father's home, he helped her mother down from the carriage. Christiana felt half inclined to reject his aid, but not wishing to fall flat on her face, she laid her hand in his warm one. Before he let go she felt the gentle squeeze of his fingers, which shocked her enough that she looked at him for the first time since they'd left her house.

"I'll leave you both here and wish you well," he said, his eyes never straying from hers. "I must get to the office before my boss gives up on me." He smiled in mild amusement.

Christiana felt her lips curl in the slightest grin.

"Thank you, Mr. Cafferty," Mother said. "You've been most kind."

"It was a pleasure." He nodded to her, then to Christiana, fingering the brim of his hat and tipping it, then climbed back into the buggy.

"Christiana?"

At her mother's soft query from the front door where she waited, Christiana was discomfited to realize she still stood staring at Noah's departing carriage.

Noah had been unable to get Christiana out of his thoughts for days. Not that he particularly wanted to, but concentrating on the sometimes sweet, sometimes fiery young brunette did tend to interfere with his work.

Like now.

He licked the tip of his pencil and jotted notes on his pad as a speaker for the women's suffragist committee stood at the podium at the front of the public hall and decried their inability to vote. He had stayed tucked in a back corner but knew he'd been spotted. A few women looked over their shoulders at him, some with curious interest while others stared in open hostility. He had not failed to notice he was the only man within eyesight and not for the first time questioned his request for the assignment. He thrived on adventure, but the idea of what must amount to at least one hundred women ganging up on one man—at the moment, the opposite gender clearly the bane of their existence—amounted to certain massacre. He imagined from the unsettled mood generated by the speaker's words that many of these ladies would like the chance to take out their frustrations against all men, perhaps using him as a target with their reticules and parasols.

Relieved when the speaker concluded her oration, Noah slipped out the door. Two women who'd spotted him managed to catch up and practically demanded his reason for being there. His answer that he was a journalist sparked questions of his views, which he politely sidestepped with his convenient response that he only reported the happenings and preferred to keep his personal opinions to himself.

They weren't pleased with his answer, and the entire walk back to the newspaper office he remembered a similar conversation he'd had with Christiana. She also had not been pleased by his responses involving a similar matter of "rights" involving women in the workplace. For that reason alone, he'd kept his distance, though he would have liked to call on her.

At the office he doffed his coat and tossed his hat in the direction of his cluttered desk then took a seat behind it. He wasted no time in transferring notes to paper. Once he'd fashioned a rough draft, he loosened his necktie and leaned back on two legs of the chair, propping his heels on the edge of the desk. So engrossed was he in what he'd written, he didn't realize someone had approached until a figure blocked his light.

Ready to give the errand boy a mild reprimand, he snapped his head up—and gaped.

He must be mistaken. Thoughts of her surely conjured the lovely mirage.

When he realized Christiana really stood there, he brought the soles of his shoes back to the floor and his chair to its original position with lightning speed, almost falling out of it. He dropped his paper to the desk and hurriedly worked to straighten his tie as he stood to his feet. He cleared his throat in an effort to recover some stability.

"Miss Leonard, to what do I owe this honor?"

She blushed a shade of soft rose. "Please, it's Christiana, remember? When we're alone I don't mind dispensing with formalities."

He glanced around the drab room of six men, the air clouded with blue smoke from his editor's pipe. No one was currently within earshot, but they were hardly alone, and his guest was receiving her fair share of looks, much to Noah's irritation.

He hid his ire with a tight grin. "Christiana, then. Do you have a story you'd like reported?" He doubted that was why she was there but couldn't figure out a reason.

"No." She bowed her head, ill at ease with whatever she'd come to say, and fiddled with the strings of her reticule. "I came to apologize."

"Apologize?"

"With regard to our previous conversation. I shouldn't have judged you for your beliefs."

Amazed by her refreshing candor, he shook his head. "I wasn't completely without guilt in my responses. I could have been kinder."

"But I baited you. I was trying to influence you to approve my way of things and admit your error in judgment." She shrugged one shoulder delicately, lifting her eyes to his. "As

Mother said, there will always be differing views in all matters, neither considered truly wrong—unless of course they go against God's Word."

"Yes, that's true." He returned her smile, deciding to suggest the idea that had been brewing in his head since the night he'd met her. He leaned back and sat with one hip on the edge of the desk, casually crossing his arms over his middle. "Have you been to the Lewis and Clark Centennial Exposition yet?"

"The Exposition?" She stared at him in clear confusion.

"The night we met you mentioned your father had a part in it."

"Yes, he helped arrange one of the displays for the university. He's a professor of science and dabbles with his own inventions besides." She hesitated then seemed to realize she'd forgotten to answer. "I haven't been yet, but I have every intention of attending before it's over."

"Would you consider going with me?"

Chapter 5

For a moment, Christiana could only stare.

"Why, Mr. Cafferty, are you asking if you may court me?" She responded with all the flirtatious aplomb of an experienced coquette. In reality, she was new to courtship and astonished by his invitation.

He chuckled. "If you like, Miss Leonard, yes. May I call on you?"

His dark eyes gently teased back, but his tone was sincere. She wondered what her parents would think about such a shocking notion—her attending social functions in the company of a man she scarcely knew—and wondered if society would frown on her for accepting or think her fast or loose. Mother liked him, a point in Christiana's favor. But more than that, the connection she'd felt with Noah since the night Lanie gave birth never dispersed, though she had tried valiantly these two weeks *not* to think about him. It was the knowledge that she would like to know him better that prompted her response.

"I'll need to seek my parents' permission, but I can't see why they won't allow it."

Her words came shy and uncertain. His eyes flickered in surprise as if he thought she might have refused him.

"Of course. I wouldn't dream of asking you not to follow the mandates of propriety. I look forward to meeting your father."

She smiled, relieved that he was no wolf but ignorant of how this courting matter was carried out all the same.

"This Saturday, then?" he asked quickly, as if rushing to pinpoint a date before she could change her mind. "We can spend the afternoon there."

"Yes, I should love to attend the Exposition with you this Saturday." Suddenly feeling timid, she excused herself. "I must be going. Mother is expecting me."

"Of course. Until then. . .Christiana."

The softness of her name on his tongue warmed her. Still floating with the turn of events, she left his office and met her mother at the millinery shop down the street where she'd left her deliberating on two hats. She chose not to inform her of her plans until the purchase was made and they rode home. At first her mother seemed surprised and uncertain, then gently resigned, but she did not disagree.

Her father, however, was a different story.

"Absolutely not." He pushed his plate of pie crumbs aside. "Who is this cheeky young whippersnapper? Never heard of him."

"Actually," her mother put in, "you have. Noah Cafferty is a fine, responsible young man. I told you how he helped Christiana with Lanie Cafferty, dear."

"Yes, yes, of course. But who does he think he is to swoop

down on my little girl like some hungry vulture seeking a baby bird?"

"A baby bird? Really, Papa!" Christiana was accustomed to her father's overprotective attitude, but that didn't stem her indignant frustration at being thought of as a little girl. "And he's hardly a vulture."

"Christiana, would you please bring more coffee? Your father could use a refill."

She nodded, knowing her mother wished to speak to him privately. On her return to the dining room, before she could push the swinging door open, she heard her mother's voice:

"She's no longer a child, Isaiah. We knew this day would come."

"She's barely seventeen," he spluttered.

"The same age I was when I met you," she countered softly. "And I've had no regrets."

A pause ensued, and Christiana leaned closer to the door to hear, feeling only a minute twinge of guilt at eavesdropping. After all, her future was the topic at hand.

"Lanie and I have been friends for two years," her mother continued. "She's had nothing but nice things to say about Noah."

"He's a newspaperman, isn't he? They're the worst kind."

"The worst that can be said about a journalist of his caliber is that he might be a bit too inquisitive. He doesn't smoke. He doesn't drink or engage in lewd activity. His manners are impeccable."

"It's those young gents who appear to be contenders for sainthood that are the true devils in disguise!"

Her mother gave a scoffing laugh. "What poppycock! Is it the matter of his profession that gives you concern? Or is it because he's taken an interest in your little girl?" she asked more gently. "Meet with him. Judge for yourself what kind of man Noah is."

"I intend to. And I intend to find out just what this young scalawag's intentions are toward my daughter."

Christiana let out a sigh of relief and entered with the coffee. At least Papa had agreed to see Noah, but she didn't envy Noah his first meeting with her papa.

Noah stepped into the foyer of the Leonard home, removing his hat and following Christiana to the parlor. He had been in several unsettling, even dangerous situations in his short career as a reporter, but this afternoon he felt as if he were entering a proverbial lions' den, and he was the main course.

And the lion, with his curly brown beard and glaring topaz eyes, looked as if he might suddenly charge and tear him limb from limb.

Noah cleared his throat and stepped forward. "Mr. Leonard." He put out his hand. "A pleasure to meet you, sir."

His hand was ignored, and Noah dropped it limply back to his side.

"Christiana," the unsmiling master of the lair said, "please bring us some refreshment."

"Yes, Papa." Before hurrying away, she looked anxiously between them, and Noah remembered her hushed words of greeting. "Be careful what you say. He's not in a good temper."

He believed the man's order for refreshment had more to do with privacy and less to do with concern for their guest's thirst. But Christiana was worth whatever trial he must endure.

What followed resembled what Noah felt the Spanish Inquisition might exemplify sans the bizarre methods of torture. Where did he live? What did he do for a living? How much did he make a year? For what purpose had he come home to Portland? How long did he intend to stay? Did he believe in the church and in God? Endless questions, many of them personal and inquisitive.

And then the bearded lion leaned forward in his chair, his eyes intent, his mouth curled in what resembled a snarl—what reason did Noah have for wishing to court *his* daughter?

Why Christiana?

Did he realize she was little more than a child?

Mr. Leonard stated that Christiana had only just stopped playing with dolls, putting an end to his rapid-fire questions, all of which Noah had worked to answer with accuracy. At last given a chance to speak rather than respond, he said that Christiana was a beautiful, intriguing young woman for whom he held a great deal of respect and would like to know better.

The disgruntled professor sat back and crossed his legs, switching the topic to his elaborate gun collection and mentioning that he'd been an expert marksman in his youth.

Mrs. Leonard swept into the room with Christiana behind her bearing a tray of lemonade. "And not a one of those guns will fire," the lion's wife added, a lilt to her voice. "They're intended for show—a few of them my husband donated for display in Oregon's exhibit that he also helped put together.

One of his weapons not at the Exposition, a musket, dates back to the Revolutionary War, originally belonging to an ancestor who lived in the colonies. Isn't that what you told me, darling?"

Her husband gave a grumbled affirmation, stating that they *might* fire, clearly not happy with the outcome of his intended threat. Noah gratefully accepted a glass from the tray and took a few gulps of the sweetly sour drink, his clothes sticking to his perspiring skin from the verbal flaying he'd just received.

"I understand you're something of an inventor?" he offered, hoping the professor would warm to the subject and temporarily forget Noah's interest in his daughter.

A light entered the yellow-brown eyes. "Yes. Among other things, I'm working on an improvement to the automatic hat tipper of several years ago."

While away at college, Noah had seen the mechanical device that tipped the hat by squeezing a bulb in the pocket of one's coat. He gratefully relaxed in his chair as Mr. Leonard spoke of other unusual inventions.

"Many inventors have their items on display at the Exposition." His eyes narrowed on Noah. "I understand it's your intention to take my daughter there this afternoon." He didn't add "over my dead body," but his glare implied it.

"Actually, sir, I thought we might all attend if you're willing," Noah quickly stated. He wasn't afraid of Christiana's father but didn't want to persist being a villain in the man's eyes. "I would be interested to see the exhibit you helped to prepare."

For the first time the lion displayed his teeth in a smile. "Excellent idea! Anna, get your things." He rose from his chair.

Mrs. Leonard regarded him in disbelief. "Isaiah, really—I

just put a roast in the oven!"

"It'll keep until we return."

"Hardly. It will burn to a crisp by then and possibly take the house down with it. It takes at least an hour to reach Guild's Lake—and that was when there was little traffic, before the Exposition opened to the public. The trolleys are packed on a Saturday afternoon as it is, and traffic is horrendous. The *Oregonian* stated that visitors are coming from all over the nation—all over the *world* to attend!"

"Then since you just put the roast in the oven, it won't suffer being stowed away in the icebox and served for tomorrow's dinner."

"That's not how it works, dear. It can't be refroz—" She glanced toward Christiana, who gave her mother a pleading look, clearly of the same belief as Noah—that her father wouldn't let her attend if her parents didn't chaperone. Her mother faltered. "Oh, never mind. I won't be five minutes." She left for the kitchen.

Her father exuberantly clapped his hands together. "Excellent. Christiana, go and collect your things. We're going to the Exhibition!"

She shared a look of relief with Noah before hurrying to gather her hat and parasol.

Chapter 6

Welcome to the Lewis and Clark Centennial American Pacific Exposition and Oriental Fair." Noah stated the full title given to the festival with panache.

Christiana stared with wonder at the magnificent sight. "It's glorious," she breathed in awe.

Noah chuckled. "May I quote you on that?"

She looked away from the layout of buildings that ringed the shimmering lake and into his dark eyes. "You're writing a story on this?"

"I'm always looking for a story—that's the life of a reporter. My boss asked me to do a piece for next week's edition. A coworker has the main assignment, but as you can see, this exhibition is huge and would take a lot of ground to cover."

Noah handed the attendant two dollars for the entry fee for the four of them.

"I think since Papa helped, he has free admission," she whispered.

Noah shrugged with a smile and slipped his arm through hers as he accompanied her through the gates.

She looked over her shoulder at the attendant, who smiled and tipped his hat to her, then looked back at Noah. "You shouldn't have to pay," she insisted.

"It's all right, Christiana. I invited your parents; it's only right I should pay for their tickets, too."

"But Papa doesn't need—"

"Christiana, please don't concern yourself. It's only fifty cents. Look around you." He motioned to the buildings nearest them. "Enjoy your time here. This exhibit will someday mark a milestone in our nation's history, I guarantee it. You'll be telling your grandchildren about it, and they'll tell their grandchildren that their grandmother saw it firsthand."

She nodded with an uncertain smile. Clearly he wasn't bothered by the idea of paying for an unneeded ticket, so she shouldn't be concerned. She doubted he had shares in a gold mine, but she hoped he wasn't a wastrel.

With her parents a few steps behind, she strolled with Noah along one of many wide, paved paths. Those in charge had done a magnificent job in giving the impression of entering an exotic land of plenty.

The greater part of the buildings, as far as the eye could see, gave an intense flavor of Spanish influence, with graceful cupolas, arched doorways, and impressive domes. Red-tiled roofs created the perfect foil against a sky of cloudless blue, and the calm silver lake, with Mount St. Helens rising in snowy grandeur in the background, topped off the lovely vista. Above the entrance, a hot-air balloon hovered, while brightly colored pennants fluttered in the breeze at the pinnacles of some structures.

They walked amid myriad groups of other exhibit-goers of every race and nation, judging from the manner of their clothing and the varied languages and accents Christiana caught snatches of in conversations. She clung to Noah's arm, slightly anxious that she might become separated from him. What must have been hundreds of people strolled the pathways and entered exhibits—and those were the ones she could see. Judging by that knowledge alone, she realized there must be thousands here today, more people than she'd ever been among in her life!

"Don't you fret." Noah patted her hand. "I won't let you get lost."

That he could so aptly discern the source of her anxiety made her regard him in wonder. "How did you know?"

"It's in your eyes. They reveal your every emotion. I'll never let anything bad happen to you, Christiana. Not while I'm around to prevent it."

Would it always be this way between them? This closeness, as if they had known each other far longer than their short acquaintance? Yet what did she truly know about Noah Cafferty? She did know that he didn't approve of her calling. At the thought, she sobered.

They took their time at each exhibit they visited. Christiana assumed the fair covered miles of ground, and it would take days to observe each site.

Italy's contribution made Christiana's jaw drop as she viewed the many marble statues that covered a huge pavilion. Of supreme artistry and skill, the graceful representations depicted the Romans of a bygone century and their gods.

Noah scribbled in a small book he carried, also talking with an attendant in charge a short distance away, while Christiana stood beside her parents and studied a statue of a Roman maiden with flowers at her feet and entwined in her flowing hair.

"If the artist had had you for inspiration," Noah suddenly said beside her in sotto voce, "there wouldn't be enough pavilions to hold his works."

Heat flashed through her face at his outrageous compliment. She looked to where her parents were, only just realizing they had moved a short distance away and out of earshot.

"Noah, you mustn't say such things."

"Why not?"

"Because. . ." Flustered, she gave a little shrug. "Because I'm not the sort of girl whose head can be turned with flattery."

"That's good to know, but I was being sincere." His eyes mirrored his words. "Your features are ten times more beautiful than that statue. I say what I mean, Christiana, which is one reason I chose the profession I did. I don't get a chance to express my personal viewpoint in my articles, but I'm honest with what I write. And I don't think much of those gents who say what they don't mean, just to get a woman's approval."

"Then you *don't* seek my approval?" she teased mildly, her heart racing with his words.

He didn't smile. "I wish for your approval more than you could know. But I'm not going to play false with you to get it."

The more he spoke, the more time she spent with him, the

more she could see what an astounding man Noah was. She couldn't think how to answer but was saved the need when her father strode their way. Christiana suddenly realized how close they were standing.

"You should put that parasol of yours to use so your skin doesn't burn, my girl," her father said gruffly, narrowing his eyes at Noah.

Christiana obediently brought it from her shoulder and directly over her head, forcing Noah to step back or be impaled by the metal points.

‌⸺⸻❧⸻⸺

Throughout the afternoon they visited other exhibits and viewed countless items, including those by Claude Monet at the Smithsonian Institution's display. Christiana enthused over how the artist depicted light and color in his scenic paintings, finding them refreshing.

They drenched their palates with flavored ices, caught a show—one of many presented at the exhibition—and ate at an outdoor café. At each site Noah jotted notes and spoke with those in charge, and throughout the day Christiana's father continued his subtle insinuations to keep Noah and Christiana apart. Therefore it stunned Noah when he made reference to the Exposition at night while trying to explain it to Christiana, that her father, who was always one step close behind, spoke up:

"There's no use for idle words when she can see it for herself, is there?"

Noah stared at him then at Christiana in frank surprise. The same bewilderment shimmered in her eyes. He had thought her father would whisk them away as soon as the first hint of evening came, in order to separate him from Christiana—not choose to extend their visit.

At the Oregon exhibit, Professor Leonard was in his element, almost treating Noah as human as he explained to them the various objects on display dating back to the statehood of Oregon. Historical documents, geographical artwork, and elaborate inventions of technology filled the area.

"Twenty-one countries and nineteen states have exhibits here," he said. "And each state will be granted a day to publicize, with visiting dignitaries in attendance."

Noah nodded, already planning to attend on Portland Day, which the media had designated as their state's day.

"When is Oregon's day for the pageantry, Papa?" Christiana asked, putting a voice to Noah's thoughts.

"September 30th."

"So far away. . . ?"

A hint of longing in her tone prodded Noah to speak. "Would you like to come again? I'll be covering the story."

"Ahem." Her father loudly cleared his throat. "As I was saying, this display here shows how loggers felled the trees, when Portland was nothing more than forest. . . ."

Later they viewed a free motion picture, and Christiana was stunned to see people captured on film. "They were actually *moving*," she exclaimed later, as they again walked along the path. "Like numerous daguerreotypes all strung together!"

Noah grinned, catching on to her excitement. "One day you might be able to hear them speak."

Her eyes grew wider. "How?" She tried to imagine how

people's voices could be extracted and put into film.

"This is the age of progress. You've seen many marvels of technology presented here. I wouldn't be surprised if not too far in the future every home has one of those touring cars or something like it—self-contained motor cabs that travel on fuel—and will completely dispense with the need to harness a horse to a buggy for each outing or even the need to have to wait to catch a crowded trolley. I mean, think of it, Christiana— before the Wright Brothers flew from Kitty Hawk two years ago in their Flyer, did you believe men would one day be able to soar through the clouds? And they successfully did so with gliders years before that. The idea of getting off the ground has long appealed to mankind. Even da Vinci was known for more than his *Mona Lisa* or *The Last Supper*. He designed a human flying invention back in the Renaissance period."

She looked at him in curious awe. "I didn't realize you knew so much about art."

He grinned. "I learned more at college than journalism."

She gave a soft nod. "Have you ever ridden in one of those flying inventions?"

"No. But one day I will."

She smiled at his confidence. "I find it telling that mankind, as you say, has long wanted to tour the heavens and devised methods to do so. Like that, for instance." She pointed to the hot-air balloon held down by ropes and hovering over the Exposition. "Perhaps such desires arose from a deep-seated need to be close to their Creator, even an intuitive need to find God, for those who don't know Him."

He looked at her with approval. "That's a lovely thought,

Christiana. May I quote you on that?"

She laughed. "Is everything a story to you?"

"Life is made up of millions of individual stories, each worthy of notice."

She smiled. "I think I like you, Noah Cafferty." Her cheeks bloomed with warmth at her words, and her eyes sparkled shyly with expectation.

"I know I like you, Christiana," he said, low enough so only she could hear.

"Mrs. Leonard!" A young woman approached them. "Miss Leonard. How wonderful to run into both of you on this fine day."

"Jillian." Christiana's mother took her hands in greeting. "How are you feeling, dear? Is this hot sun not too much for you? Wherever is your parasol?"

"I broke it earlier—got it caught in a tree branch, and it tore. Dreadful affair."

"Then you must take mine."

"Oh no, I couldn't. Besides, it's nearing sunset."

"You really shouldn't be out in this hot July sun, dear."

"My husband is taking me to one of the shows indoors. I'll be fine."

At Noah's curiosity at such an outpouring of concern, Christiana whispered to him, "Mrs. Merriweather is one of our clients."

"Clients?" He looked at her.

"She is with child."

"Ah." Inadvertently Noah's gaze dropped to the woman's waist. Her gathered and flounced skirts hid her condition well.

Christiana sighed. "You still don't approve of midwives in this century, do you?"

He chose his words carefully. "Christiana, I don't want to argue with you and spoil our lovely outing. I can't help my personal views."

"No, I suppose not. Not when you've been led to believe that way." She seemed almost dejected then thoughtful. A sudden gleam lit her eyes. "From what little I know, you seem the adventurous sort. . . ."

"Yes. . ." He let his answer trail, wary of what was on her mind.

"And you said you're always on the lookout for a story. Life is a story to you. . . ."

"You listen well," he answered in curious amusement.

"Would you be willing to do the same? To listen?"

"Pardon?"

"Jillian Merriweather is an outgoing soul, the sort who's unafraid to say or do anything. If I were to seek her permission and that of another woman who might also agree, would you be willing to interview them, to hear their reasons they chose to employ a midwife? It would be a chance to see the issue from the other end of the spectrum."

Noah had long ago learned there were two sides to each story. With the woman suffragist movement so prevalent in the news, an article of human interest might appeal to the paper's readers, though there would certainly be those opposed. His editor, for instance.

"Let me think about it."

Christiana nodded at his answer. At least it wasn't an outright no.

If he did agree, she hoped the women would also.

Too excited with the idea to wait, she received her chance to ask when her father decided they would all attend the show. Before they entered through the double doors, Christiana urged Noah to go ahead, assuring him she would soon follow, and privately pulled Jillian aside to broach the question.

Jillian's eyes lit up like those of a child experiencing her first taste of candy. "A journalist, you say? Oh my, yes, that would be exciting, wouldn't it? Perhaps I can even sneak in a few points about why women should be allowed other rights, too."

"I don't see why not." Christiana grinned. She wasn't an active suffragist like Jillian but agreed that women should be given the right to vote in Oregon, since from what she'd read, a number of other states had acceded to the idea.

Christiana rejoined Noah, who stood at the back, waiting, her parents also standing nearby. He lifted his brow in concerned question, and she wondered what he would think of her views on the vote. She decided it best to remain silent on the matter, not wishing to begin another clash of wills and minds. The day had been too perfect to ruin it with opinionated drivel. She smiled and took the arm he held out to escort her to her seat.

The show was delightful, tasteful, the costumes from an earlier era, the singing in another language and superb, operatic in nature. Christiana enjoyed every moment sitting beside Noah in the darkened room and the respite from the day's heat.

She did wish, however, that her papa would stop glaring at

her escort and hoped that he would soon grow accustomed to the idea of having Noah around, since she anticipated seeing much more of him.

Once the show concluded and they left the building, she stared with wide eyes. The Exposition had become an exotic fairy tale against an evening sky!

Small electric lights covered the framework of every building in sight, near and far, and Christiana felt as if she'd been transported to a foreign world of splendor and mystery. The dark lake served to magnify the feeling of enchantment as it reflected the multitude of lights softly shimmering in the water.

Due to the amount of time it would take to reach home with the traffic, her father soon announced it was time to leave. They had spent all day there, but Christiana didn't feel as if they'd covered even a tenth of what the Exposition had to offer.

"If you should like to come again," Noah said, sotto voce, "I would love to bring you."

Eager to spend another day in his company, she nodded at his second invitation.

"I plan to come back in two months for Portland Day."

"Oh." She tried to stifle her disappointment. She didn't want to wait *that* long to see him again and wondered how her mother would feel if she invited Noah to Sunday dinner. Would that be too forward, especially since Sunday was tomorrow?

On the trip home, Christiana pondered how she might see Noah before September. He had not yet accepted her offer to do a story, and she wondered if he would.

The perfect gentleman, he helped her on and off the trolley, finding her a seat though he was forced to stand. He kept close, to protect her from the traffic of the crowds. And Christiana felt a little more of her heart open to him with every hour in his company. Somehow she would see to it that they met again—sooner rather than later.

Once they arrived at her house, Noah helped her alight from the hansom cab her father had hired to take them the rest of the way home.

She turned to him. "I've had a wonderful day, Noah. It's been a pleasure. Thank you for asking me."

"The pleasure has been all mine."

"Christiana, are you coming?" Her father turned from walking up the sidewalk with her mother and stared.

"Yes, I won't be a moment. I'd like to say good night if I may?"

"Of course." Her father didn't budge.

"Come along, dear." Her mother eased her arm around his sleeve and gently pulled him toward the house.

Christiana hid her embarrassment with a little laugh. "I'm his only daughter," she said by way of explanation. "His only child."

"If I had a daughter like you, I'd do the same."

The gaslight flickered on near the porch, causing them both to look that direction. Her father stood in the open doorway, watching them.

Christiana curbed a sigh. "Have you given any thought to writing the story?"

Noah looked away from her father, hesitated as if considering, then nodded. "I'll do it."

"You will?" She wasn't sure if the bulk of her delight was because he agreed or because she would be seeing him again sooner than expected.

He grinned. "Tell me when and where, and I'll be there."

"Would you like to come to Sunday dinner?" The words were out before she had a chance to think about what she was saying.

His surprise was apparent by the manner in which his brows lifted.

"I mean—" Christiana thought of a way to endorse her rash invitation, making the idea up as she went along, while knowing all she said was true. "Mother will want to speak with you first. . . ." And she would definitely need to speak to Mother about the whole affair tonight! "And it would be an opportune time to discuss things." It wasn't like he hadn't shared their table before.

"Are you sure my presence at your home would be welcomed so soon?" He looked toward the porch. She directed a glance there, too, seeing her father still standing like a sentinel on watch.

"Oh, Papa? He won't mind." She doubted that, but she hoped he would soon come around. "And I know Mother will be pleased." Although she might not be happy to hear Christiana had allowed her tongue to get away from her again, in asking Noah to write the story.

"Then I accept."

"Lovely. At noon tomorrow, then?"

"Noon tomorrow. I should be going." He darted another glance toward the house then again looked at Christiana and took her hand in his, lifting it.

Christiana sensed sudden movement from the porch.

"Good night, Christiana." Noah touched his warm lips to her trembling hand then straightened, looked at her once more, and left.

Christiana felt the tingle in her fingers during her entire walk to the porch. She ignored her father's gruff demeanor and kissed his whiskered cheek. "Good night, Papa."

He patted her shoulder as she moved inside, gently muttering something she couldn't make out, but she thought she caught the tail end of his words: "At least that's over and done with."

No, Papa, not even close, she silently answered.

Minutes later, in the kitchen, once Christiana admitted her deed, her mother shook her head.

"You should have asked me first."

"I know, Mama. I was just so excited." She lifted her downcast eyes. "Although Jillian *did* seem comfortable with the idea. . . ," she added hopefully.

"Yes, I imagine she would be," her mother mused. "She was once a thespian and enjoys an audience. Well, never mind. What's done is done." She smiled. "I, for one, like the young man and would enjoy having him sit at our table."

"Do you think Papa will mind?" A foolish question, but she felt compelled to ask.

"Don't worry about Papa, darling." Her mother laid her hand against Christiana's cheek. "It's not that he dislikes Noah. If he did, Noah wouldn't have stepped two feet from this house with you, even accompanied. Your father would have seen to that. He simply must learn to accept that you're now a young woman. You've always been his little girl."

Christiana gave a careful nod. She only hoped Papa's revelation would occur before Noah became weary of the whole ordeal to see her and lost interest in trying.

Chapter 7

Noah could not believe his good fortune. He hurried to catch up to the pretty brunette who walked ahead of him.

"Hello." He tipped his hat with a grin.

"Noah!" Christiana's answering smile assured him of her pleasure to see him, though he had no cause to doubt it after last night's invitation to a meal. Beneath her yellow parasol, her cheeks flushed a delicate pink. "You attend this church, too?"

"Yes, when I'm in town." Relieved to see that papa lion stalked nowhere nearby, he extended his bent arm. "Would you do me the honor of sitting beside me?"

Her eyes were shy as she nodded and took his arm. He didn't want to spoil the moment but had to know. "Are your parents here today?" He wanted no confrontation with her father right before the service but wished to be prepared.

"They went inside. I was talking with another woman I plan for you to interview. She wishes to talk it over with her husband first, but Jillian, the woman you met yesterday, is in absolute favor of the idea." Her words came out in a rush, the interviews clearly exciting to her with the manner in which her blue-gray eyes sparkled.

He doubted his editor would be as enthralled, but he'd told Noah, "It's the controversial issues that sell the most papers." And this idea was all that and more. Nor did Noah feel that doing this for Christiana would be time wasted, on more than one count.

"How are Lanie and the baby?" she asked as they walked through the entryway into the quiet, dimly lit building.

"They're doing well...."

Inside, Noah wished for the peace to extend to his soul. Christiana's father looked shocked, angry, then frustrated as Noah greeted them and Christiana pulled him to sit beside her at the end of the pew. To his credit, her father didn't glare at him during the service, and Noah was able to concentrate on the minister's message of patience and endurance. It appeared he certainly would be learning more of that today.

The glaring came afterward, when they were again outside and Christiana's mother expressed her delight that Noah would be spending the afternoon dining with them. By her father's initial reaction of surprise, he guessed it was the first he'd heard of it.

As his wife gently nudged her husband toward the direction of their vehicle, Noah walked with Christiana a short distance behind.

"Your father didn't know I was coming?"

"Oh, he knew. Mama told him last night."

"He seemed surprised."

"I think he feels Mama should be on his side in all this.

233

I mean—" She looked at him, embarrassed. "He doesn't understand her reasoning at times. But then, not all couples agree on everything, and it doesn't change their feelings for each other. Does it?" Her face flushed rosy, and she looked away. "Oh, look, there's Maribelle. Doesn't she look nice in that blue feathered hat. Hello!" She gave a little wave, and Noah looked toward the departing carriage and the redhead waving back, wondering who Maribelle was and why Christiana thought he should know her.

By the time they all reached the Leonard home, Noah following her parents' buggy on his horse, Christiana had calmed from whatever so unsettled her. Her father, however, had not.

While the two women worked in the kitchen, Noah sat in the chair across from the uncharacteristically silent, but still glaring, bearded lion, all the while wondering if he was to be the appetizer. His few attempts at conversation were truncated with deliberate monosyllabic answers that prevented further discussion.

Once Mrs. Leonard announced that dinner was ready, Noah practically leaped from the chair.

The lion remained quiet during the meal, concentrating on his food. His kind wife was gracious, bringing up the Exposition and the displays that appealed to her. Christiana was talkative as well, darting looks at Noah as she spoke, and Noah tried to converse with both women, eat his meal, and keep a wary eye on the sleeping lion.

"What did you like best, sir?" Noah surprised himself and the others by asking.

Mr. Leonard looked full at him, narrowing his eyes. Noah

swallowed hard.

"Portland's exhibition, of course," he declared as if that should be obvious.

He then went into another recounting of each item on exhibit and those who helped him put it together. Noah could almost hear the collective sigh of relief from the ladies as the master of the den relaxed and spoke of the topic he enjoyed best.

The atmosphere around the table lightened considerably, and the dessert of lemon meringue pie was a pleasure.

"I thought we could sit outside on the porch and discuss the interviews," Christiana said to Noah.

"Interviews?" her father suddenly barked. "What interviews? It's too hot outside."

"That sounds like a splendid idea, dear," her mother said. "I'll bring lemonade."

"What blasted interviews?"

"Noah plans to interview a few of our clients for a piece he's writing in his newspaper," Mrs. Leonard said in the same mild tone.

The look in Mr. Leonard's eyes impaled Noah, like a moth pinned to a board. He could almost hear his mind issuing the angry words: *That is why you have an interest in my daughter—to use her for your paper?*

"Actually, it was my idea. I thought it would be splendid for Noah to get the midwife perspective from our angle." Christiana quickly rose from the table and looked at Noah. "Shall we go outside?"

"There's nothing wrong with the parlor!"

Noah couldn't imagine trying to concentrate on what Christiana said to him with a threatening pair of topaz eyes focused on him the entire time.

"There's nothing wrong with the porch either, dear."

Mr. Leonard brooded. Noah stood to his feet and thanked Christiana's mother for the meal, uncertain if the matter was settled but not wishing to wait around to ask.

He followed Christiana to the porch and took a seat next to her on the glider, leaving a socially acceptable amount of space between them. Movement caught his attention. He looked toward the house.

Christiana's father stood at the window and stared from between parted curtains. The lemon curdled in his stomach, and Noah curbed the insane urge to let out a miserable laugh.

Christiana also turned to look. "Pa-pa. . . ," she enunciated in a softly pleading fashion.

He didn't move away, but a pale, slender hand appeared at his sleeve. He turned his head to answer then moved aside, and the drape fell back in place.

Christiana sighed. "He's really a very nice person. Everyone at the university loves him, both his students and the other professors."

"Ah." Noah smiled politely, unable to say much else.

"Yes, well, Mother and I will be visiting Jillian on Tuesday. Does that work for you?"

"I don't expect you to arrange your appointments around me," he teased lightly. "I'll make it work."

"I'm still waiting to hear back from Mrs. Radcliffe. There's also another lady I'd like to ask—she gave birth a little over two months ago. I think she also would be amenable to the idea."

"What about you? Are you amenable to it?"

"Pardon?" His enigmatic smile made her heart turn over.

"To an interview."

"You want to interview me?" she squeaked nervously.

"Of course, since the article will be based around your work. Any objection?"

"No, I just didn't think you'd want to. . ." Flustered, she let her words trail off as she watched him pull a pad and pencil from his pocket. "What—*now*?"

He chuckled softly. "Can you think of a better time? A reporter's always working, Christiana. The news stops for no man."

"No, of course not. . ." She just didn't realize *she* would be the news.

"Relax." His voice was soothing. "If we were getting to know each other, we would ask questions, right? It's the same sort of idea."

"Is that what we're doing?" She offered an uncertain smile.

"Well. . .yes."

"All right then." Her smile grew more confident. "How do we do this?"

"I'll ask a question and you answer. Like. . .how long have you done this sort of thing?"

"Midwifery?" At his nod, she continued: "I started assisting Mother when I was fifteen, almost three years ago. My first actual delivery, I told you, was Lanie's. Mother said that she long knew I was ready for the next step. I just had to know and exert the courage to try—oh, but don't write that! That's just a minor confession for the getting-to-know-you part of this."

He grinned, crossing out what he'd last written. "And your mother? How long has she been involved?"

"Since before I was born, I imagine. I don't remember her not being a midwife."

His brows arched. "How does your father feel about your mother engaged in a job that could interfere with her duties at home?"

Christiana resolved not to take offense at the question; he was conducting an interview, after all. She wondered if he should ask Papa then immediately thought better of it. "He has no problem with what Mama does. There are no true duties that she's taken away from. We have a maid and cook, though she's on a vacation of sorts, visiting her sister who's ill. While she's gone, Mama is tending to meals and keeping house."

"Hmm." He jotted something down.

Christiana wasn't sure she liked the sound of his *hmm*.

She straightened her spine. "As long as the home is well kept and the husbands and children don't starve, I see no reason that women, no matter their social status, cannot be allowed to work outside the home. Do you?"

He looked up from writing to smile. "I'm not the one being interviewed."

She let out an irritated breath then chided herself. She already knew his answer; it matched what most men thought. She couldn't fault him for a gender-shared attitude.

"What interested you in the occupation?"

"Oh, it's much more than an 'occupation.' It's my godly calling. My grandmother, who took the Oregon Trail, and her mother before her, and even before that, into several generations, all were midwives. My mother gave me their journal filled with advice to those who followed after them, along with their bits of inspiration. Would you like to see it?"

"Yes, but later. Why do you consider it your calling?"

She struggled with how to explain. "It's nested inside my heart. Every mother is special to me and every child born. Helping to bring life into the world is an exhilarating experience—sometimes frightening. But each time I look at a newborn's face, I wonder how anyone can question the existence of God. Midwifery keeps me humble, and yet at the same time confident that God watches out for His own." She made a mental note to jot that down in the journal also, for her own wisdom to share.

He nodded slowly. "I can understand that, having just been through the experience—and never wanting to go through it again."

"It's a good thing you weren't called to be a midwife, then," she teased.

"Or a doctor."

He posed other questions, his responses polite, when asked, but also letting her know he didn't agree, and in her frustration she spoke without thinking: "Since you're clearly not in favor of women working outside the home, I suppose you're also opposed to women gaining the vote?"

"I never said that. As a matter of fact, I think women should be given that right."

She blinked at him like an owl. "You do?"

"Certainly. Most men opposed are worried that if women are given the vote, the first thing they'll do is revoke liquor, because of the existence of the women's temperance groups.

Since I don't drink, it doesn't affect me either way." He grinned.

She was still fighting disbelief. "You support women voting but are against them working?"

"A vote generally takes place once a year. Women who work do so every day. Some women neglect their families to work."

"And what about those women—like my mother—who don't? I agree with you, families should come first. Mother is adamant about that. They are the ones God gave to us, aren't they? But some women have no choice. They must work in factories or secure whatever means available to be able to live and help support their families. It's been that way throughout history."

He gave a short nod. "Poverty has been around since the days of Moses, long before that. There are always extenuating circumstances. But I speak of those who have no need to work and do so out of desire alone."

"Like my mother?" She couldn't help the bitter edge to her tone.

He sighed. "From all I've seen and heard, your mother isn't one to neglect her family."

"She most certainly is not."

"I know. I was agreeing with you. Christiana, I don't want to argue about this. Can we just get back to the interview?"

She nodded, struggling to control her wretched temper. "Yet despite Mother's good example, you are still opposed to the idea in general?"

His silence provided her answer.

"I imagine that once you marry, you won't allow your wife to work?" Her face warmed. Where had that question popped from?

"She won't need to."

"But if she should wish to?"

He stared at her a long time. Christiana held her breath, wishing she could retract the question, though her heart raced to hear his answer.

"I was raised by my father and his father before him to believe that women shouldn't work outside the home. So no, I wouldn't wish my wife to work."

His answer given, Christiana felt worse. She gave a little nod and looked him in the eye. "As I said, I consider midwifery a godly calling, one that's been in my family for generations, and especially necessary to those mothers who prefer a woman tending them. I don't plan to quit anytime soon, if ever."

"And if your husband should disapprove?" he asked softly.

She swallowed hard. "If he is of that opinion, then I would save us both a good deal of grief and never marry him in the first place."

The silence grew so thick she could hear the flies buzzing off the porch. They stared at each other a long time, Christiana's heart beating fast.

Noah flipped his pad closed. "Thank you for the interview. I think I have all I need." He stood up.

She bounced up from the glider, sending it into motion. "Do you wish to see the journal?" She didn't want him to go, as foolish as it was to wish he would stay.

He hesitated as if he might refuse but nodded. "Yes."

"I won't be but a moment."

It would be more polite to invite him back inside, but she didn't want her father's beastly attitude to scare Noah away. She slipped into the house, located the journal, and hurried back outside, handing it to him.

He eyed the plain worn cover and opened the book to the first yellowed page. He read for a moment then looked up. "Would you mind if I borrowed this? I'd like to read it in my own time. I'll take good care of it."

"I know you will." She hated letting it go, even for a few days. It was hers to do with as she pleased, since her mother had given it to her on the eve of her seventeenth birthday—wishing to share the wisdom of it with Christiana now, as she had then told her, rather than after her death. Christiana looked in the book every morning after her devotions. Both always helped her outlook for the day. Still, if reading it would help Noah to understand. . .

"Yes, all right."

He closed the journal. "If you would rather I didn't take it. . ."

"No, that's fine. I trust you, Noah."

Long after they said their farewells, the tender but sad look in Noah's eyes lingered in her memory. Did that look mean he saw no hope for a future for them? Perhaps Christiana *was* rushing things—they had known each other a matter of weeks—but she couldn't help how her heart felt. And it was immersed in Noah.

Christiana approached her father where he sat in the parlor. Immediately he took off his reading glasses, slipped them into his pocket, and laid down his book.

"Ah, Christiana, how are you, my girl?"

"I could be better," she said, taking a seat across from him.

"What seems to be the problem?" His bushy brows slanted downward. "That Rafferty fellow isn't giving you grief, is he?"

"It's Cafferty, Papa. Noah Cafferty. And he's not the one causing me pain. You are," she admitted softly.

He glanced down at his lap, his face going stony.

"What is it about him that you dislike so?"

"He's a reporter, isn't he? And they're not good news."

She didn't smile at his wry pun. "You're judging Noah based on a generalization of men in his career? Is that fair?"

"Blast it, Christie, I don't need this from you, too!"

He reverted to his girlhood name for her, a sign that he was troubled.

"Papa..." She moved off the chair and sat on the floor beside his, as she had done when she was little. She laid her hand over his large one. "You're never going to lose me. I'll always be your little girl at heart, even after I marry and make a life of my own."

Moisture made his eyes shine. He swallowed convulsively. "No man will ever be good enough for my little girl."

"One man has to be. You *would* like me to know the joys of marriage and, one day, childbirth, as I see women experience all the time, wouldn't you? I want to know all of that, all of what Mama had. I don't want to be an old maid."

He sighed. "You're barely seventeen."

"No, Papa, I'm approaching eighteen. This Christmas."

He shook his head softly. "Time is a cursed villain that robs us of life so quickly."

Alarm made her eyes widen. "You're not ill?"

"No, I'm right as rain. Forgive an old man his reminiscences,

Christiana. It seemed only yesterday I bounced you on my knee, and now you speak of bouncing your own children on your knee...."

"Time doesn't have to be the enemy, Papa. Grandmother Polly wrote that time is a gift to be treasured and used wisely. Only then will the treasure hold true value."

He patted her hand. "Your ancestors were wise."

"Just because I'm growing up doesn't mean we won't have other moments to hold dear. Different, but just as special. One day you'll be bouncing your grandchild on your knee, creating a new and beautiful memory."

His gaze sharpened. "You're not *that* interested in this boy, are you? You've only just met!"

"I don't necessarily mean Noah...." She avoided the question. "It's much too early to consider that. Just please, won't you lower the shotgun always aimed his way and give him a chance? For me?"

He looked at her long and hard then let out a weary sigh.

"For your sake, I'll try, Christie. I ask one favor in return. Don't grow up too quickly? Don't throw out your dolls and tea set just yet?"

At his hopeful response both knew to be impossible, for time had a way of rushing things along, she stood and kissed his cheek. "For you, Papa. I'll try. I promise to keep my dolls." She wanted to pass them on to her daughter. "As for the tea party... would you like to have one with me? For old time's sake?"

"You're a sweet girl to humor a pathetic old fool," he said gruffly.

"Pathetic? No. Not a fool, either, and certainly not old. We had such fun with our parties, didn't we? We talked of everything under the sun—well, what was then my sun. All those things important in my little-girl world. And this time I shall make *real tea*, since I'm now old enough to use the kettle."

"Yes, do that. I look forward to it." He picked up his book again and glanced at the table then at his lap then at the floor. "Have you seen my glasses?"

"Right here, Papa." She plucked them out of his pocket and set them behind his ears with a grin then scurried to the kitchen. She hoped this revisit to a dear childhood memory would help ease her father's heart and make her transition into womanhood a little easier for him to bear.

Chapter 8

N oah stared at the words of the journal's final written page.

The women of Christiana's family were strong, courageous, full of hopes and dreams. None of them considered midwifery true work but instead their godly calling, as if they were doing a great mission for the Lord's people.

He looked at the last entry, the ink newer and bolder than the others. This entry bore a different handwriting than the previous ones, the letters graceful and flowing, and there was only one small notation from this last writer to add to the journal. Christiana, no doubt.

I have learned that to fear a problem takes a greater toll on the heart and more effort than it does to trust for the best, even the miraculous. My first delivery was solo and frightening in that respect, as it was thrust upon me. I received help from an outside source, who proved invaluable, but I could not escape the reality that if anything went wrong, the consequences would be upon my shoulders to bear. As the poor woman, a dear friend to me, was in such travail, the revelation suddenly came: I was

not the one in charge. I was merely God's handmaiden, His
chosen vessel, and it was through me that He would make
His glory known. I only had to allow Him to do so, to trust
in His power, and to submit to His greater authority. With
that new understanding, everything fell into place and I
was no longer afraid.

Noah stared at the entry for some time. He'd been unable to get Christiana out of his thoughts all week, since he'd last seen her. It was foolish, he knew. To think of her in any capacity other than friendship would be disastrous; she had made clear her feelings on the subject of women and work. So had he. He was not one to form a dalliance with the ladies as some of his associates did. He wanted to find a woman to make a life with, to share his home and his name. It would be a *mistake* to continue to see her.

But every time they met, he found something else about her he admired, and this journal entry was no exception. A godly woman, humble, but strong of spirit and willing to stand her ground—wasn't that what he always hoped to find in a wife? Yet the very tenacity he admired in her worked in opposition to what he'd been taught by his father. His mother died when he was three, so he'd never gained her insight.

Looking at the time, Noah grabbed his coat and hat and drove his buggy to Christiana's home. His heart gave a little jump as she came through the door. The sunlight hit her face, giving it the luster of a pearl. Her eyes were glowing, her smile for him.

He managed to peel his attention away from her and greet her mother as she came behind, her loveliness a mature version of her daughter's beauty. He helped both women into his buggy.

"Am I that late?" he asked, curious that they had not waited for him to ring the bell.

"I was watching and thought I'd save you the effort and us some time," Christiana said with a little smile.

Clearly she was sparing his feelings. He knew he was at least five minutes late, the writings of the journal having captured his interest.

Jillian Merriweather proved to be a colorful character to interview. After showing Noah an album of old photographs from when she'd taken the stage and telling of some of her more memorable endeavors as a singer, she moved right into the subject of women's right to vote. As if she were the interviewer, she asked Noah's opinion. She was as shocked as Christiana had been to learn he had no opposition to it—did they really view him as so hardnosed?—then his interviewee asked if he would be in favor of speaking at a women's meeting. Remembering the last suffragist gathering and his feeling of being a trapped and despised beast with the women approaching for the kill, he adroitly evaded the topic and moved to the reason for his presence there.

He asked various questions, also urging her to speak freely, jotting notes all the while. "To sum it all up," he said at last, "why do you think the occupation of midwifery is so vital to maintain in this progressive era of our nation?"

She laughed at that. "Oh, I can give you plenty of reasons, Mr. Cafferty, but the chief one for me is that most midwives have been through the ordeal. Men have not. Mrs. Leonard knows the pain involved, being a mother herself. I am more inclined to trust my body to a woman who knows what it *feels* like to experience all one does during pregnancy and childbirth than I am to a man who cannot begin to imagine all of what occurs."

Jillian Merriweather also had a flair for complete candor. Noah busily jotted, his face going a shade warmer at her expressive words.

Once the interview ended, he thanked her and went outside on the porch to wait. Jillian had been so excited to be interviewed, she asked to do that before her checkup, though they had planned it the other way around.

As Noah waited for the Leonard women to join him, he went through his notes, his mind weighing all he had learned against all he'd been taught.

A week and a half after the first interview, Christiana again waited for Noah to arrive. He had been quiet after speaking with Jillian, when he took Christiana and her mother home. Polite. Kind. But quiet. At church the past Sunday, he had been the same.

It frustrated Christiana that he'd not shared his feelings with her, and she hoped today would be different. She would *make* it different!

She would be going alone. Her mother was needed at home to make Papa's lunch, as she'd done every day since the term ended and the university closed. That should make Noah happy—to see firsthand that her mother put her family before work.

Once he arrived, this time she waited until he came to the door. Her father came in from the parlor and gruffly shared a few words with him. But to Christiana's relief he did not interfere with her going alone with Noah, though he did tell her mother he could see to lunch himself and she could go along, too.

"Yes, dear, I've seen how well you cope in the kitchen," she gently replied and looked at Christiana. "Be sure and tell Helen that I'll visit her tomorrow. Her time is nigh, and she might wish to know information you cannot give."

Christiana reassured her mother, and Noah drove her to Mrs. Radcliffe's.

The woman's time was not only nigh, but after her appointment and in the middle of the interview—she doubled over in sudden pain.

Noah was out of the chair and by her side before Christiana could blink.

"Mrs. Radcliffe, are you all right?" he asked.

She looked up, horrified. "I think the baby's coming. I had light pains this morning, but I thought it was indigestion. They weren't like last time and went away after a few hours. . . ."

Christiana immediately took charge, helping Mrs. Radcliffe out of her chair, Noah on the other side of her. They walked with her to the bedroom, and Noah helped ease her to the bed.

He turned to Christiana. "A phone?" he asked hopefully.

Mrs. Radcliffe, still suffering through her pain, gritted out, "We have no phone. Neighbor does. Across the street."

"You're going to call a doctor?" Christiana took him aside and whispered so the woman couldn't hear.

"I'm going to call your mother."

Christiana nodded in gratitude. She felt more assured as a midwife since Lanie's delivery, but assistance was always better, and Noah had often made it clear he didn't wish to repeat the role he once played.

"The twins...," Mrs. Radcliffe muttered.

Noah sharply turned. "You're having *twins?*"

Christiana hoped she wouldn't have to try to catch him since he looked about ready to fall.

"Mrs. Radcliffe *has* twins—Mark and Mary—three years old. They're sleeping."

"I can't leave them alone. They'll be up from their nap soon. And my husband won't be home from the Expo for some time."

"Leave it to me, Mrs. Radcliffe. I'll call Mrs. Leonard, and then I'll watch the twins."

"Don't you have to report to the office?" Christiana wondered if he had any idea what he had just signed to. He had seen how many hours labor could take, and they had arrived toward the end of Lanie's travail. Yet Christiana also could see no other way.

"You don't have to do that," Mrs. Radcliffe said. "Mrs. O'Brien, my neighbor across the street, said she wouldn't mind watching them when needed."

Noah nodded in relief and headed for the neighbor's house. The elderly Mrs. O'Brien, kind as she appeared, barely held on to the door as she opened it. One look at her bleary eyes and reddened nose and Noah realized he might be sitting with the twins after all.

"Feeling a bit under the weather," she admitted when he

asked about her condition in concern. "Not to worry, dear boy. I'll be all right."

Once Mrs. O'Brien heard the news, she led him to her phone. First, Noah called Mrs. Leonard, who assured him she would come immediately. Second, he called his boss. He had to hold the earpiece away from his ear at the man's irate reply, but the crusty geezer had developed a reputation for being a hardnosed editor. Noah often suspected that beneath beat a softer heart, and he found proof of it when the man told him in a quiet voice to do what he had to do to help the women.

Thanking the widow O'Brien, he settled his hat more firmly on his head and approached his newest challenge— entertaining two three-year-old children.

Surely that couldn't be as much of a strain on the mind and emotions as the one time fate had forced him to become a midwife's assistant.

To Christiana's relief, her mother soon arrived. Helen Radcliffe's labor pains came more intense at this stage than Christiana would have expected, but after a first child that sometimes happened. To her absolute shock, her mother quietly told her she would assist and Christiana would deliver. Knowing that her mother sat near helped to ease the sudden lurch of dread, which then faded when she remembered she'd done this once before. She had learned then that God was her supplier to give her all she needed. They prayed for the mother and the child and for guidance and prepared for the long wait.

While Christiana fed Mrs. Radcliffe ice chips, she wondered

how Noah was faring. The twins woke up two hours ago, their excited voices heard on the opposite side of the door. As Mother encouraged their patient, Christiana glanced out the bedroom window, shocked to see her answer: Noah pushing a wheelbarrow with both children inside. Absent of his sack coat, his shirtsleeves pushed up to the elbows, he careened back and forth over the lawn while the towheaded tots squealed in glee, the girl holding to the sides of the wheelbarrow, the boy in front of her, clapping his hands.

Mrs. Radcliffe's latest spasm of pain subsided, and she also turned her head to look. "He seems like a fine young man," she whispered to Christiana.

"He is," Christiana said somewhat dreamily as she watched Noah with the twins.

Mrs. Radcliffe soon had another pain, and Noah was temporarily forgotten.

Six hours and twenty-three minutes later, Tobias Radcliffe entered the world. Squalling and red, he was not one bit happy about it, until he found solace in his mother's waiting arms.

Exhausted but happy that there'd been few complications and both mother and baby were well, Christiana left the bedroom to find more towels to clean up. She came to a sudden halt as she entered the parlor.

Thoroughly mussed, Noah sat sprawled on the sofa, his head back and eyes closed. Mary also slept and clung to his middle, resting her head on his chest. Mark sat on the other side of Noah, wide awake and holding a bowl of what looked like applesauce. He pulled the spoon from his mouth and held it out to Christiana. "Wan' some?" he asked. Applesauce spotted the two children and

Noah, as well as the sofa and floor and anything else within the vicinity of Mark's waving spoon.

Her heart twisted in amusement at the tender sight, and in that instant Christiana knew: she had fallen deeply in love with Noah Cafferty.

Chapter 9

Three weeks had passed since Mrs. Radcliffe delivered her son. In that time, Noah interviewed one other expectant mother, spoke with Christiana twice more at church, and immersed himself in the news stories his editor assigned to him.

He told himself he wasn't avoiding her, but that was a lie. Since she had opened the door to his frantic knocking on that first night, what seemed ages ago, she had disrupted his well-ordered, long-conceived notions with her opposing views. She had shaken the tenets of his male existence with every nuance of her feminine personality. When he closed his eyes at night, it was her bright, intelligent eyes and coy smile that he saw. And when he opened them, she was always the first thought on his mind. He was, in a word, hopelessly and completely besotted.

He prayed over his dilemma and spent hours poring over her journal, which he had yet to return. He spent equal time recalling how perfect Christiana was in her role, how happy she had been with giving herself to others. His interviewees had all offered diverse but sound reasons why they preferred a midwife. He would be a heel to ask Christiana to quit what she felt God had chosen her to do, what Noah had seen with his own eyes—a fearsome task he doubted that many, if any, men had experienced, save for Adam and the physicians, of course. And he had witnessed her confidence each time she spoke of her vocation.

At last, coming to a decision, Noah gathered his notes. He stayed late at the office and spent the next two hours writing out his story. His editor showed surprise the following morning but to Noah's relief agreed to print it in the next edition. He hadn't been sure what the crusty man would say to Noah's unusual approach.

But it was really Christiana's reaction that concerned him.

Christiana opened the door to Noah. Her heart gave a little jump of delight to see him. It had been so long!

"Noah, what a pleasant surprise. Come in." She held the door open.

"Actually, I was hoping you might come outside. I have something to show you."

Her heart beating fast at his peculiar behavior, she nodded and closed the door behind her.

"Since your father doesn't get the *Portland New Age*. . ." He held out a newspaper. "Page two."

She felt she should apologize for her father reading a rival paper and almost admitted that she'd bought every newspaper of his since they met, just to read his articles, but his serious expression stalled further comment.

Her eyes narrowing in puzzlement, she opened to the page, giving a little gasp when she read the title and byline: MIDWIFERY IN THIS PROGRESSIVE ERA BY NOAH CAFFERTY.

Excited, she read the succinct article, creatively written, citing the interviews with quotes and bringing up the controversy, touching on it from both angles. But it was the personal addendum at the end, which she had never seen him use in any of his articles, that had her mouth drop open in shock:

> . . . I have always been led to believe that women should not work outside of hearth and home, and in some cases, I still adhere to that belief. However, after spending time in the Leonard women's company while witnessing the differences they make, the lives they touch, and the skills they possess, I am convinced no physician could have done a worthier job. It is this reporter's belief that midwifery is still as important as it was thousands of years ago. In conclusion, perhaps the true progression of our era is to open our minds to novel ideas, not only in technology but also with regard to our women in society.

Stunned, Christiana looked up and blinked. "I don't know what to say."

"Say you'll go with me to the Exposition again. This weekend."

She gave a soft laugh, slightly shaking her head no then nodding yes in confusion.

"I stayed away because I didn't think it would be fair to

either of us to continue seeing each other after you made your position clear. I've had time to consider, and that"—he glanced down at the paper she still held—"is my answer."

Tears welled in her eyes. "Are you saying. . . ?"

He took the newspaper from her and dropped it to the ground, taking her left hand in both of his and holding it up between them. "I am saying, my dear Christiana, that one day I hope for the honor of calling you my wife. I have found that a life without you is no life worth living. I am hopelessly in love with you, you understand. So now I must ask, is there a chance you might put me out of my misery and agree again to let me court you?"

Her smile grew with each moment of his nervous avowal, and her heart soared at his declaration of love. "Oh yes, Noah, I think there is much more than a chance."

His bright smile soon faded. "And now, to ask your father's permission."

Both of them glanced at the window to see the curtain remained closed.

"One step at a time," she said softly, bringing his hands still clasping hers to her lips and kissing his thumb.

She felt a little shock as he moved his hand away, and his fingertips tilted her chin. A thrill surged through her at the anticipated touch of his warm lips on hers.

Their first kiss. . .

His, a kiss of promise. Hers, a kiss of hope.

And the first of many to come. . .

She would see to that.

Epilogue

Two years later

Noah's father-in-law slapped him on the back, keeping his hand there in comfort. "She'll be fine, son. The good Lord knows she and her mother have plenty of experience at this sort of thing."

"Yes, I know. You're right." But this was different. . . .

This was Christiana.

"I think I'd like more lemonade. Fill your glass, sir?"

"You don't need to be taking care of me. Just relax."

"I feel better when I'm active," Noah admitted, and the older man nodded in understanding.

Noah headed to the kitchen. It had taken six months into his yearlong courtship with Christiana before he became comfortable around the gruff professor, and two months after their marriage before they became friends. While he felt relief that he was no longer considered the enemy, he had bigger problems at the moment.

Instead of lemonade, he found himself chipping ice into a glass. He had thought that *being there* was the greater trial—but not being there, not knowing, was ten times worse.

This was Christiana!

Uncertain of his reception, he approached the second landing and hovered at their bedroom door. She panted heavily then softly moaned and clutched her distended belly.

Propriety was the least of Noah's concerns as he rushed to her side and knelt on the floor near her.

"Noah?" her mother said in surprise from the foot of the bed.

"I thought you might need assistance." His eyes remained on his wife's glistening face. He smoothed the tousled hair from her damp brow as the pain subsided, her strained features slackening in relief.

"This is most unusual," her mother said.

"Yes, I know." He never looked away from Christiana. "But I've done it before."

Christiana smiled tenderly, her eyes glowing. "I want him here, Mama."

"I love you," he whispered, kissing her hair, her cheek, her lips.

"And I love you. . . ." She stroked his cheek with her hand. "Are you sure you're up to this? You did say you would rather be boiled in oil than go through this again."

"I'm the reporter who writes about supporting novel ideas, if you'll recall. I don't think it gets any more novel than having the father at the delivery." He grew serious. "I *want* to be here, Christiana. I want to be here for you. . . ." His hand lowered to spread gently across the mound of her stomach. "For our child."

She nodded, a tear slipping from her lashes. He kissed it away.

"Well, you won't have much longer to wait," Anna Leonard said with a smile. "I think my grandchild will soon make an entrance."

At the announcement, both excitement and dread filled Noah, but he was determined. Five months into their courtship, when he knelt before Christiana in her mother's rose garden and proposed, he never dreamed he would have succumbed to this.

He held his wife's hand through the worst of her travail, fed ice chips to her in between pains, even sat behind her to help support her when the big moment loomed nearer. Somehow he didn't pass out, though he wanted to weep when Christiana's pains came stronger, and he wished he could take all of her suffering away.

He ceased to breathe as she gave one final push. As long as he lived, Noah would never forget the astounding sight of glimpsing his daughter enter the world, caught in her grandmother's hands. Then and there, he silently vowed that his little girl would always know love and safety. He would protect her with his dying breath, and woe to any rapscallion who ever made his baby girl cry. . . .

For the first time, he understood what Christiana's father must have felt upon meeting Noah.

"She's perfect," Anna said.

"A girl?" Christiana asked with a tired smile.

"A girl," Noah confirmed, his eyes falling shut while he held Christiana against him and kissed her hair, thanking God for the gift of his wife and child. After a moment, he moved away, helping her to lie back among the mound of pillows as he stood to his feet.

Once he straightened, Anna held the infant out to him.

He stared at her in shock.

"You wanted to assist," she said quietly, slipping the feather-light bundle of soft femininity into his arms. "Please take your daughter while I finish things here."

Within the blanket, his child's face was cherry red, her head a trifle squashed, but Noah saw nothing but beauty. Huge blue eyes. Dark hair. Ten fingers. Ten toes. Two tiny hands and feet...

"Noah?"

"...And do let your wife see."

Noah had been so immersed in gaping at the miracle of his daughter that he had not moved. At Anna's teasing prod, he smiled in sheepish apology to Christiana. Carefully, he handed the precious bundle over to her mother.

"Oh, Noah," she breathed. "She's wonderful.... I think she has your beautiful mouth."

"And your eloquent eyes," he added, lowering himself beside the bed.

Christiana tilted her head to rest against his shoulder as they gazed with awe at the culmination of their love.

"Hello, my little Pollyanna. Your papa and I have waited so long to see you. Your grandparents, too. Oh, the life you will have, the love you will know! And when you're older, you'll have tea parties with your grandpapa, and lovely strolls with your papa and me, and your papa will tell you such exciting stories. We'll teach you all you could ever wish to know...."

Noah wasn't sure, but he thought he saw his baby girl smile.

PAMELA GRIFFIN lives in Texas with her family. She fully gave her life to Christ in 1988 after a rebellious young adulthood and owes the fact that she's still alive today to an all-loving and forgiving God and to a mother who steadfastly prayed and had faith that God could bring her wayward daughter "home." Pamela's main goal in writing Christian romance is to help and encourage those who do know the Lord and to plant a seed of hope in those who don't.

LABOR OF LOVE

by Trish Perry

To Bronx and Vinny, my baby's babies. Attending your births was an amazing honor, and being your MayMay is a blessing I'll cherish forever.

Chapter 1

L ike melodic molasses, the impossibly mellow voice poured from the Bose radio on the kitchen counter. "Swing Down Chariot." Kendra Silverstone recognized that one. She warmed up her cup of coffee while her very pregnant patient set a plate of hot muffins on the table in the breakfast nook. Kendra closed her eyes and inhaled their amazing, nutty aroma before she sat down.

Now that she had examined Ellie and assured her that the pregnancy was on track, she would enjoy a quick cup of coffee and treat herself to one of Ellie's famous banana muffins before dashing off to her next patient. She spoke loudly to be heard over Randy Travis's rich country baritone.

"Honestly, Ellie, I think your baby is going to enter the world singing gospel rather than crying."

Ellie turned the radio down and joined Kendra at the table. "I do love me some country. Mike thinks he can force the gal out of the country and into the great Northwest, and I guess he's done that. But you can never get far enough north to force the country out of the gal. Not this one, anyway."

"Is that true? Do you feel like you were forced to move to Oregon?"

"No, not really." Ellie pushed the plate of muffins closer to Kendra. "I didn't have deep ties in Georgia once Mama and Daddy moved to Florida. Mike's my everything. I'd follow him anywhere."

She made Kendra smile. "I hope I feel like that about a man someday. I'm thirty-two, and I still haven't felt anything beyond that first infatuation of dating someone new. And I can't say a man has ever shown me unconditional love like everyone talks about, either. You know what I mean?"

"Oh, honey, I do. Enduring love is sadly rare these days."

"Maybe I need to move to a new area." Kendra broke off a small bite of buttery muffin and popped it into her mouth. Just the right amount of cinnamon and nutmeg. "I've lived in Willamette Valley all my life. A new talent pool might be in order."

Ellie sat up, looked beyond Kendra, and raised her eyebrows. "Hmm. Speaking of which. . ."

A quick tap at the door prompted Kendra to follow Ellie's gaze. She glanced over her shoulder and set her coffee mug back down on the table. For the first time since she arrived at Ellie's to check on the baby's progress, Kendra wondered about her own appearance.

"Okay to come in?" The lanky stranger flashed a smile at both women before stepping inside. "Morning. I just need to get the last of my power tools out of the nursery."

Ellie wrestled her bulk out of her chair and spoke to Kendra under her breath. "Don't dismiss Willamette just yet." Then she turned up the wattage of her smile and the belle of her accent. "Of course you can come in, sugar. Don't mind us." She put her hand on her hip, her brows dipping to a furrow of false confusion. "Now, I don't think you two have met, have you?"

Before Kendra could answer, the man stepped forward and gently took her hand. Why that would startle her, she didn't know, but the rush of heat in her cheeks felt horribly visible. Maybe it was the open interest with which he looked into her eyes. And weren't his as clear and blue as a Cascade lake?

"Steven Nichols. No, we haven't met. You're a friend of Mike and Ellie's?"

"No." Kendra shook her head and released his hand to tuck her dark hair behind her ear. "Or, yes, I'm a friend, but—"

"Kendra's my midwife." Ellie gently patted her belly. "She stopped by to make sure the baby's doing okay. We're having this one here at home."

He lifted his eyebrows, and Kendra readied herself to hear the usual surprise at the very idea of home birth.

"Kendra? That means 'water baby' or something like that, right?"

Well, that just shut her right up. But only for a moment. "How in the world did you know that? *I* barely even knew that until a few years ago." She absolutely could not contain her pleasure and gave up trying to hide that she was flattered.

"I had a client whose little chatterbox of a daughter was named Kendra. She—the chatterbox—told me about the 'water baby' thing. Repeatedly."

"Steven is a carpenter," Ellie said. "A *genius* carpenter. He's the one who did the work in the baby's room—the shelving and that beautiful molding around the top of the walls. And he's building the pretty little nook near the window. And he *made* the rocking chair. *Made* it, Kendra. You've seen it, right?"

"No, you've never—"

"Oh, Steven will show you! Take Kendra on up there, sugar, and show her what you did."

Steven looked at Ellie, and a small, humble smile appeared for a moment and flitted away. He gave a playful shrug to Kendra. "Are you game?"

She fought the mild embarrassment that tried to settle in. After all, she wasn't flirting. Ellie was doing the flirting for her. Still, she found comfort in what seemed like easy camaraderie on Steven's part.

"Go on, Steven." Ellie pointed to the stairs. "You lead the way."

The moment he turned his back, Ellie and Kendra met eyes. Ellie extended her arms, presenting Steven for Kendra's consideration. Ellie said nothing but widened her eyes and opened her mouth to express her enthusiasm about him. Her rapid nod at Kendra all but said, "Is he great, or *what?*"

Kendra grabbed at Ellie's arms to lower them, just as Steven turned, clearly about to say something. He stopped before a single word left his mouth. Kendra and Ellie froze, two grown women apparently on the verge of a wrestling match. They swiftly dropped their arms, and Kendra tucked her hair behind her ears again, even though it was already tucked quite firmly there.

Ellie pointed upstairs. "Well, don't dillydally now, Steven.

Kendra has other pregnant ladies to see. Give her the tour so she can be on her way."

He looked from Ellie to Kendra. He raised one eyebrow at them before he proceeded up the stairs. "Mm-hmm, will do."

Kendra made a similar face at Ellie before following him.

Ellie hadn't exaggerated about his being a genius carpenter. The baby's room was unique in its loveliness. And the rocking chair was a work of art, pickled with a thin white stain that enhanced both the wood's grain and the details etched into the arms and headrest.

Kendra's indrawn breath was audible. "Did you do all of the. . .what do you call this? This detail." She ran her fingers across the etched work.

He shrugged. "It's all just woodwork. Carving with V-tools and gouges. And this detail here is called inlay. The placement of another woodcutting within this larger one."

As he reached to touch the inlay, his fingers accidentally brushed against hers. They both drew their hands back as if they had touched hot coals. A second later, they met eyes and laughed at themselves.

Still, they both jumped when Ellie popped her head into the room and said, "Was I right?"

"Wow," Steven said. He rubbed the back of his neck. "You can be pretty quiet when you want to be."

She chuckled. "I'll have to tell Mike you said that. I think he might give you an argument. But isn't this work something, Kendra?"

Kendra nodded and ran her hand along the arm of the rocking chair again. "It really is." She looked at Steven. "You know, I have a couple of pieces of furniture at home that I inherited. A desk and an armoire. They're antiques that have been stored in a bunch of different attics and storage units over the years. I can't honestly tell if they're worth restoring or not."

"I'd be happy to take a look at them."

"I'll leave you two alone to talk about that." Ellie spoke over her shoulder as she left the room. "But Kendra, you said to not let you be here later than ten, and it's ten now."

"Oh! I've got to go. My next appointment is at Willamette."

"The hospital?" Steven asked. "My brother-in-law is a surgeon there. John Parkham."

She shook her head. "I don't know the name." She shrugged. "It's a big place. But, listen, do you have any free time tomorrow? I'm off, unless one of my moms goes into labor."

"I could make time."

"I have my cards in my purse downstairs. I'll leave one with Ellie to give you before you go. If you call me—"

"I'll definitely call you." He gave her a friendly smile, and those penetrating, interested eyes of his crinkled.

She turned quickly away and spoke as casually as she could: "Okay, then! I'm looking forward to it."

She heard him, not too far behind her, as she left the room.

"You bet. Me, too." He said it in a friendly tone, with the utmost respect. But there was no doubt in her mind that he watched as she walked down the stairs. Every step of the way.

Chapter 2

Steven saw her walk out the hospital's revolving glass door with great purpose in her stride and the breeze in her long, dark hair. He jumped out of his Silverado and waited for her to notice him. She didn't.

"Kendra!"

He loved the ready smile that crossed her face when she recognized him and the way she barely hesitated before walking toward him.

Steady, boy. Don't read too much into this.

They hadn't gotten together—hadn't even spoken—the day after they met at Ellie's a few weeks ago. He had called, only to reach her voice mail. She had called back, only to reach his. And she had taken the ball into her own court with the promise to call him again when her schedule eased up.

Since then she had occupied his thoughts at random moments of his days. Her appreciation of his work played over and over in his memory, and he couldn't help but smile with each new replay.

He wasn't sure if she was involved with anyone. He had been too proud to ask Ellie before he left her house that day. He just took the business card Ellie handed him and thanked her as if he had forgotten about Kendra.

"Kendra? Oh, right, right. Yeah, thanks. I'll call her about that furniture of hers."

He wasn't prone to game playing. But Ellie had seemed too curious, and he was sure she'd interfere somehow if he asked questions about Kendra, no matter how casually he did it. Still, if Kendra wasn't involved with someone already and had the slightest bit of interest in him, he was inclined to work on that.

His sister, Marianne, was forever pushing her single friends on him, and he tried to be open-minded about the possibilities. She meant well. And he didn't really want to be alone the rest of his life. But this was the first time in ages that a woman had turned his head just by looking into his eyes.

And here she was, walking toward him and looking into his eyes again.

At once he remembered the matter he promised his sister about, soon after he mentioned his client's midwife. Today's timing couldn't have worked out better.

"The genius carpenter, right?" Kendra reached out to shake his hand.

"Right, from Ellie's nursery."

It sounded as if he *lived* in Ellie's nursery.

"I mean, we met at—"

She nodded. She remembered. "I'm sorry I didn't call you again. About my furniture? It seems as if all the babies in town decided to arrive at once." She cocked her thumb back toward the hospital. "I was just visiting one of my patients, as a matter of fact."

"I figured. I'm waiting on my sister, Marianne. She's visiting her husband."

"Oh yes, you mentioned he was a surgeon here. Their schedules can get pretty crazy, too. I'll bet he's happy to have his wife visit like that."

"He's divorcing her."

He didn't know why he blurted it out so harshly. He heard the anger in his voice as he said it. Not the way he wanted to come across to this attractive woman who now struggled with an expression of uncomfortable shock.

"Oh, I'm so sorry." She glanced down, as if the divorce were her fault.

He shook his head. "No, I—I shouldn't be so blunt." He exhaled exasperation and ran his hand over the back of his neck. "I guess I'm still pretty angry about it. I just heard this week. I don't know what kind of man would walk out on his wife at all, let alone—" He stopped when he looked up and saw Marianne approach them. "Uh, could you excuse me for a second, Kendra?"

She looked into his eyes quickly before she started to walk away. "Sure. I'll call you later. About the desk and armoire."

"No, but could you wait a minute? I want you to meet my sister." He went to Marianne without waiting for Kendra's answer. By the time he reached Marianne, she seemed composed, if not a little moist around the eyes.

"You all right?" He put his arm around her.

She nodded. "I'm fine. I'm glad I came. I think it helps me to let him go when he's so awful to me."

Steven nearly groaned. "Marianne, don't tell me stuff like that when I'm right outside his office. It's all I can do to stay out here and keep my hands off the jerk."

She laughed softly and gave his chest an affectionate pat. "You've always been more like a big brother than a little one, Stevie. Don't worry. It's all going to work out." With eyes sad and tired, she looked at Kendra. "Who's your pretty friend?"

They reached Kendra, and Steven introduced them. "Kendra is the midwife I mentioned to you."

The women shook hands, but Kendra looked at Marianne's stomach, surprised. "Your brother didn't tell me you were pregnant!"

Marianne rested her hands on her swollen abdomen. "Ah. But he told you about my husband, I take it?"

"Well, we just ran across each other before you walked out," Steven said. He looked at Kendra and raised his palms to present his sister's condition. "See, this is why I wanted. . .well, why Marianne wanted to meet you."

Kendra frowned, even while she smiled. "I'm not sure I understand. Surely you haven't gone this far into your pregnancy without getting prenatal care? You must be, what? In your seventh month?"

"Thirty-two weeks." Marianne drew her shoulders back in a stretch. "But things have become a little complicated. I hope I can be candid with you?"

Kendra nodded, but Steven could see she had no other choice. She was going to think his family situation was a regular soap opera. And the whole ugly saga was going to be dumped in her lap before they had really gotten to know each other at all.

Marianne said, "My husband's decision to end our marriage has everything to do with his dalliance with Gina Chastain. The OB/GYN?"

Kendra gasped. "Please tell me she's not your doctor."

"No. Just my husband's girlfriend. And my doctor's partner. When Steven told me about you, I thought maybe God had answered my prayers about that part of my problem. I'm not really all that comfortable with Antoine Zibarro—my doctor—anymore, just because of his partnership with. . .that *woman*. And his friendship with my husband. I'd just as soon get as far away as possible from that little group of people, you know?"

"Dr. Zibarro." Kendra bit her lip. "He's not a big fan of midwifery."

Marianne shrugged. "Well, then, he doesn't have to use a midwife. But I'm sold."

"But you don't even know me."

"Don't worry. I'm no flighty mama. After Steven mentioned you, I asked around, and everyone raves about you." Marianne cocked her head toward Steven. "And you seem to have made a good impression on my baby brother here, too."

Kendra chuckled. "Baby brother."

She looked at Steven, and he loved what he saw in her expression. She saw him as a man, not someone's baby brother. He wanted more than anything for Kendra to agree to work with his sister. He would be the most involved "baby brother" around, especially if it meant a chance to get better acquainted with this particular midwife.

He lifted his eyebrows at her. "What do you think?"

"Hmm." She grimaced. "I don't know. Marianne, I wouldn't

be able to work with you until you formally sever your relationship with Dr. Zibarro. And he's likely to make trouble when he learns you're turning to a midwife."

"He doesn't need to know who I'm turning to. It's none of his business. I'll simply tell him I'm no longer comfortable working with anyone in Gina Chastain's office." She crossed her arms over her ample belly. "I'd like to see them make a stink about that."

Steven watched Kendra struggle with the pressure they were putting on her.

"You know what?" he said. "We really threw this at you out of the blue. Here you thought you were just heading home after checking on a patient, and we've ambushed you."

"No, it's not that. It's just. . ." But she didn't have anything else to say, apparently.

"How about you give it some thought and give me a call later?" he said.

Marianne said, "Or you could just call me." She glanced at Steven, apparently read his mind, and revised her comment: "Yeah, actually, you should call Steven."

Atta girl, Marianne. He smiled at her before giving Kendra a more serious expression. "No hard feelings either way."

"Right." Marianne reached over and gave Kendra a reassuring pat on the arm. "Except I'll be in a horrible bind if you say no."

"Marianne!" Steven kept from laughing until Kendra laughed herself.

"But no hard feelings." Kendra's eyes twinkled. "Good to know."

"Yeah," Marianne said. "I'm sure plenty of women give birth all by themselves these days without the help of doctors or midwives. I'll just ask my neighbors to swing by and lend a hand. They have a couple of kids. They probably know what to do."

"Ignore her." Steven opened the passenger door of his truck, and Marianne waddled toward it. "She'll be fine with another doctor or another midwife if you're uncomfortable with this idea." He looked at his sister. "I'm going to walk Kendra to her car. You okay stepping up to the seat?"

"Piece of cake. Nice meeting you, Kendra."

Steven stayed to help Marianne into the truck anyway, and then he followed Kendra to her little blue Honda CRV. She faced him after she opened her car door.

"I'll probably be able to take on Marianne, Steven, but—"

"Uh, could you say that one more time?"

She tilted her head. "I'll be able to take on Marianne?"

He shook his head. "No. Just my name. That's the first time you've said my name."

She opened her mouth, clearly caught off guard. And then she lowered her eyes. "Well, I've really only just met you."

He said nothing. She had such thick, dark eyelashes. And such perfect skin.

"Steven." She almost whispered it.

She was right. They'd only just met. But he already hoped to hear her address him in that soft voice for many days to come.

Chapter 3

When Kendra walked into her mother's house that afternoon, she wasn't sure if her upbeat mood was more about the fine health of all her current patients or the way Steven Nichols had flirted with her in the hospital parking lot. But apparently her mood was written in her every movement.

"Well, aren't you bouncy today?" Her mother walked down the stairway to give her a hug. "I assume the baby and mother from last night are doing well, then?"

Kendra hugged her mother back and inhaled that wonderful mix of powdery fragrance and recently baked cookies.

"Oh, that baby boy is the cutest thing, Mom."

"Already? I always think they're kind of ugly this early on. Like pruny little old men."

Kendra gave her a little shove and laughed. "You're awful. They're all beautiful, even the pruny ones. I don't know how the family birthing gene managed to skip your generation, but goodness, you're cynical."

Her mother's eyes widened. She grabbed Kendra's arm and led her toward the kitchen. "That reminds me, your sister's coming home for a visit in a couple weeks." She retrieved a greeting card from the counter and handed it to Kendra.

"Shar actually sent you a card? She took the time to write something by hand? Her cell battery must be missing." Kendra saw what her sister wrote:

Coming for the weekend, June 8. Looky looky!

Yep, that was Shar. Never one to wax prolific.

"She wanted to send me this clipping from her local paper. Look. She's really making a name for herself there in Eugene."

Kendra took the clipping. There was her beautiful sister, shaking hands with some guy in a suit, accepting a certificate of some sort. Shar had followed their father's path and become a cardiologist—a very successful cardiologist. She was five years older than Kendra but seemed much further ahead of her when it came to professional confidence. Kendra had strived to go in the same direction—cardiology seemed the surest route to developing a bond with their father—but she realized years ago that she had more of her mother's generational leanings than her father's. The draw to midwifery was so strong she was willing to sacrifice the closeness with her father for it.

And now, five years since his death, it didn't matter that she had become so successful as a midwife. Dad would never know about it.

She felt her mother's gentle touch on her shoulder.

"What's the matter, honey?"

Kendra shook off her self-pity. "Nothing. I'm just being jealous. Daddy would have been so proud of Shar for this."

She got her second hug of the day for that.

"He was already proud of her. And he was proud of you, too. Don't you realize that?"

Kendra nodded. "I know. I realize we made him proud. I just struggle sometimes with that stigma Daddy felt—no, he did, Mom, and you know it. Just like so many other doctors still feel toward midwives. As if we're wild-haired, fringe-type practitioners wearing Birkenstocks and hippie skirts and chanting around a caldron. Is that why you never went into midwifery?"

Her mother took a seat on one of the bar stools at the kitchen counter, and Kendra joined her.

"No, honey. Thanks to your grandma taking me to so many deliveries, I always came across just as many doctors who supported midwifery as those who opposed it. Maybe you've just met an unusual number of wet blankets. I chose not to pursue midwifery because I wanted more for you and Shar than my brothers and I had as kids."

"What do you mean?"

"Well, you know your grandma loved being a midwife, and so did my Grandma Polly. I don't know how far back the family tradition goes—"

Kendra nodded. "Yeah, someday I'd like to look into that."

"Mm-hmm. I'd like that, too."

"So? What was the problem?"

Her mother sighed. "You mentioned being jealous of Shar? Well, I was jealous of hundreds of other children. All those babies seemed to get more of my mother than I ever did. She was a bit of a zealot about her profession. Even my father complained that she took on more patients than she should have." She pushed at her cuticles as she spoke. "It put a strain on the marriage. On the family." She looked up at Kendra with a sad smile. "I missed my mother. I didn't want you and Shar to feel that way."

Kendra nearly choked up to think of her mother sacrificing her future for her own kids. There was much to admire in that.

"Besides," her mother said, "I was always kind of grossed out by the whole thing."

"Mom!"

Her mother laughed. "I love babies and birth—don't get me wrong. But I think your grandma brought me to one too many home deliveries. By the time I married your father, I only wanted to be present at the deliveries of my own children, and even that out of sheer necessity. And maybe at my grandchildren's births."

Kendra smiled. "We'll talk about that when the time comes. *If* it comes."

She didn't think her mother was aware of suddenly drumming her nails on the counter, but Kendra knew grandchildren were welcome anytime now. Neither Kendra nor Shar had made much progress on that front. The least Kendra could do was toss out a very minor bone.

"I *might* have met someone interesting recently."

Her mother gasped. "No!" She leaned forward and grasped Kendra by the forearms. "Tell me about him! Someone from the hospital? Is he a doctor?"

"Nope. A carpenter. A genius carpenter."

Her mother frowned. "What does that mean? He solves

calculus problems while he builds homes?"

"No, Mom. I mean his carpentry is phenomenal. Beautiful."

"And how about him? Is he beautiful?"

Kendra chuckled. "Not that it should matter, but I guess he's pretty striking. Not like a male model, just really masculine. Tallish. And intense blue eyes. Really seems like a nice guy. He's very protective of his sister, who's pregnant. I think I might take her on as a patient."

"Well, that's terrific. How far along is she?"

"She has less than two months to go." Kendra stood and turned away. She wanted to get the ever-present pitcher of iced tea from the fridge, but she also wished she could just walk away from this part of the conversation. She had a pretty good idea how her mother would react to the whole scenario.

"Two months?"

Kendra studied the inside of the refrigerator. "That's right."

A moment of silence forced Kendra to retrieve the pitcher and turn around. Her mother studied her.

"Okay, honey, what's up with this one? Who are you rescuing this one from?"

"It's not like that. She's Steven's sister, that's all. That's why she heard about me."

"Steven's the math-solving carpenter's name?"

Kendra lifted an eyebrow. "It is. Steven Nichols. And Marianne has to—she wants to use someone else to deliver her baby."

"Someone other than. . . ?"

Kendra sighed, resigned. "Antoine Zibarro."

"Oh, honey." Her mother slid off the stool and pulled

down two glasses from the cabinet. "As if that man isn't already looking for fights to pick with the midwife community."

"I know. But there are personal circumstances that make this a very important favor to Marianne."

"Are those circumstances named Steven Nichols?"

"No, that's just how we met. I'd consider taking her on regardless of whether or not I was interested in her brother."

"Ah, good, then you haven't committed to her yet."

"Not yet. But I don't think I can turn her down, Mom. I completely understand why she wants someone else."

Her mother handed her a glass of tea. "Someone else, fine. Why does it have to be you? Why not another doctor?"

Kendra took a long drink. *Lord, could You please give me some help here? I want my motives to be pure.*

She set her glass on the counter. "She asked me, Mom. She's facing a lot of sadness in her life at the moment. I believe in what I do. I believe I can make this childbirth experience as joyful as possible for her, despite her heartbreak. And I think I'm more likely to do that than anyone else. I can't practice my profession well if I try to stay under the radar just so people like Dr. Zibarro will leave me alone."

And that was when she decided. While her mother nodded her understanding and gave her another hug, Kendra knew she'd take on Marianne's care. She'd trust that God would bless her sense of commitment.

Now if God would just keep Dr. Zibarro at bay, everything just might work out.

Chapter 4

Steven closed the door on Kendra's side of the truck and walked around to the driver's side. He loved that she thanked him for opening her door for her. He'd been raised to treat women with common courtesies like that, but it was nice to be thanked.

He tucked her "home visit bag" behind their seats. He had taken it from her as soon as she walked out the hospital's front door.

"Thanks for picking me up here," she said. She cocked her head toward the hospital. "First-time mom. She just needed a little assurance before checking out."

Steven pulled out of the lot and began the short drive to Marianne's house.

"You can't imagine how much comfort you're giving my sister by taking care of her for the rest of her pregnancy. She really dreaded going back into Zibarro's office again and maybe running across Gina."

"I couldn't turn her down after I thought about it. I'm glad she lives close to the hospital. I normally ask about that, because I don't take on clients who live too far away, just in case of emergencies. But it's awful to carry around the kind of stress Marianne's feeling, especially when you're pregnant. She has enough going on already."

They reached Marianne's driveway in a matter of minutes, and Kendra's gasp turned his head.

"Something wrong?"

She gave him a wide-eyed glance and pointed at the house at the end of the long drive. "You didn't tell me she was. . ."

"Rich?" He chuckled. "I'm not sure where I might have worked that into the conversation. They've done all right for themselves, yeah. Does it matter?"

"No, no. Of course not. I have clients who are well-off. I sound like a bumpkin, don't I? It's just that she seems so down to earth."

"She is. My whole family is like that. Not very aggressive professionally, but we go after what we love."

"Like your woodworking."

"Mm-hmm. I take the smaller, detailed work when I can, because I enjoy it more than big carpentry jobs. Marianne was a fund-raiser before she and John married. Then she decided to focus on him, on making his life as smooth and worry free as she could. But she didn't glitz herself up like some trophy wife. I think that's one of the problems. John probably thinks he's trading up, getting involved with that woman from Zibarro's group. Marianne says Gina acts like she's royalty. Marianne has never behaved that way. I think that's why John takes her for granted."

He studied his sister's grounds and home, long familiar, with fresh eyes. "She'd trade in all these trappings of wealth for a husband who still loves her. I'd still like to deck the guy."

He parked the truck before giving Kendra a chance to respond. Marianne met them at the door, grabbed Kendra, and gave her a big hug.

"You're just a lifesaver! And I love not even having to put on makeup before my exam."

Kendra laughed. "I don't require that for the ladies I see at the hospital, either."

"Yeah, but my vanity kicks in when I have to go down there. Especially now. I feel like everyone on staff is making comparisons between me and Gina."

Steven clenched his teeth. "Yeah, well, one of you is a faithful wife, and the other is a home wrecker."

Marianne gave him a kiss on the cheek and a little shove. "You tell 'em, bro. Kendra and I are going to leave you to your own devices for a while. There's leftover mango chicken in the refrigerator if you want to heat it up. John treated me and seven of my closest girlfriends to a little dinner party last night."

"He did?" What was John buttering her up for?

"Yes, he did. He just doesn't know it yet. But he will when the catering bill arrives next month."

He heard Kendra's soft chuckle and knew his sister had a staunch supporter looking after her now. The knowledge relaxed the tension right out of his body.

The women were gone long enough for him to raid Marianne's refrigerator and reheat some leftovers that must have been very elegant last night to still look so tasty today.

The fruity, spicy smell made his mouth water, and he realized he had actually forgotten to eat breakfast. He had been far too excited about seeing Kendra. What was he, a middle-school kid suffering his first crush?

He put three plates on the kitchen table and was sitting down to wait when the front doorbell rang. "I've got that," he called out.

He struggled to hide his surprise when he opened the door to John. Marianne must have had the locks changed, as she said she would. The moment John gave him his broad, friendly smile, Steven got ahold of reality and overcame the strangeness of standing in this man's home, barring access.

"John. Can I help you?"

John's smile flattened. "Oh. I imagine Marianne's home, then?"

"She is. She's up in your—in her bedroom." No, he didn't want to mention the fact that she was being examined by her new midwife. "What can I do for you, John?" He continued to stand in the doorway, his legs akimbo, hoping to suggest that John's entry wasn't a foregone conclusion.

"Is she, is she all right?" At once John looked contrite. "I haven't heard from her, and I've been so worried. You know, about her and the baby."

Ah. So Zibarro's office must have alerted him to Marianne's withdrawal of business.

"I'll ask her to call you. Just as soon as she's up to coming down here. We were about to have some lunch together. Okay?" He pushed the door a little more closed.

"Uh, I wondered. . .well, actually I need to get my golf clubs.

They're in the sports room."

Steven lowered his head and peered at John through heavy, angry eyelids. "Your golf clubs."

John stood more erect and puffed out his chest like a pigeon. His demeanor became nearly prissy in its defensiveness. "Yes. Not that it's any concern of yours, but I have an important tee time tomorrow morning with several other surgeons."

Steven nodded. "I can see how worried you are about Marianne. Hang on a minute. I'll get your clubs for you."

In the middle of John's indignant response, he closed the door, locked it, and rushed to the sports room to get John's clubs. He wanted to spare Marianne from seeing such a graphic display of John's priorities.

When he got back to the foyer, he could hear Marianne and Kendra laughing about something upstairs. He yanked open the front door, pushed the clubs at John, and said, "I'll ask Marianne to call you. Enjoy your game."

He didn't wait for a response. And moments after he heard John's Jaguar pull away, he heard Kendra and Marianne emerge, still laughing about something. He made an effort to hide his aggravation over John's lack of character.

"Hey, I don't know if pregnancy is supposed to be this much fun, ladies."

Marianne sniffed the air with open passion as they descended the stairs. "Goodness, that smells wonderful. I can't believe the appetite I've had lately." She gave Steven a soft pat on the cheek. "You're going to make someone a fine wife someday, sweetie."

"Hey!" Steven frowned but met eyes with Kendra, who grinned at him as if they had known each other for years.

"In case you were wondering," she said, "Marianne and the baby are right on track."

"That's great to hear."

Marianne headed into the kitchen. "I told Kendra I'm going to gush about her to all my rich friends. We'll bring home birthing back into vogue. They love being on the cutting edge."

Steven shook his head and gave Kendra a smile. "You have time for lunch before we leave, right?"

She nodded. "Unless I get a delivery call, I'm free until my two o'clock appointment."

"Who was that at the door?" Marianne put the mango chicken in the microwave for another quick warm-up.

Steven glanced at Kendra and sighed. "It was John."

He saw Marianne's shoulders sag. "What did he want?"

She faced him, and the trace of hopefulness in her eyes broke his heart. "I think he just wanted to make sure you and the baby were all right."

But when her hopefulness seemed to rise at his comment, he panicked. *Lord, I don't know how to handle this stuff. Help!* "Yeah. He asked about you, Marianne. But. . .he got his golf clubs before he left."

He didn't think her shoulders could drop any lower. He was wrong.

"I'm sorry, sis." He looked to Kendra, as if she could offer comfort in the midst of this clearly dysfunctional marriage she had happened upon.

Kendra grimaced, sighed, and looked at Marianne. "Well. He sounds like a real peach."

Marianne shot a glance at her that held for about five seconds before she burst out laughing. She cried, but she laughed, too. Kendra moved up to her, an affectionate smile spreading, and placed a protective arm across her shoulders.

Steven wasn't sure if the two women could tell, but his heart had just melted.

Chapter 5

"Okay, well, cheers to you, Kendra. That was one of the smartest moves you've made yet."

Shar raised her glass of cranberry juice to salute her younger sister. They were dining at the little bistro near Kendra's McMinnville home. A barely audible Edith Piaf ballad lilted from the restaurant's speakers to mingle in the air with the rich aromas of garlic, onion, and seared beef. The soft lighting colored everything and everyone sepia, as if they had been captured in a 1940s Parisian photograph.

Kendra had just mentioned her newest client, Steven's sister. By the time Shar arrived in Willamette Valley for her family visit, Kendra had learned that Marianne was one of the wealthiest women in the area.

"I can't say I was thinking all that smartly taking Marianne as a patient. My heart just went out to her. I like her a lot."

"And I understand her brother isn't bad, either." Shar's lips turned up in a half smile.

Kendra sat back and matched her sister's expression. "Mom.

You've been talking with Mom. And here I thought I was giving you news you hadn't already heard."

"No way. You know how bad Mom wants grandbabies. She's probably already booked flights to Disneyland for herself and your kids. Anyway, you should've known she'd tell me about the rich sister. She's so proud of how well you've done with your business, even though she says you let your heart rule you a little too much. This time your heart seems to have settled you squarely in the land of plenty."

"Ugh. You sound so mercenary, you know that? Marianne isn't a golden goose. She's just one woman. One patient. Her money doesn't make her more important than anyone else."

"One patient, yeah, but she's probably a terrific contact, especially if everything goes well with her baby's delivery. My practice in Eugene grew like crazy thanks to a few well-connected patients like that. Like it or not, the medical community is as political as any other. It's a good idea for you to be out there schmoozing."

"I prefer to stay away from all that." Kendra raised her hand to stop Shar's immediate rise to argument. "But I know you have a good point about Marianne's possible influence. Her husband is the unfaithful one, and he's insisting on this awful divorce, so Marianne's attorney promised her that she and the baby would be financially comfortable from here on out. I think she has every intention of staying in her gorgeous home and remaining an active member of the community."

"Well, sure," Shar said. "She needs the support of her family and friends more than ever, I'll bet."

"And she's eager to recommend me to anyone who's pregnant

or even *thinking* about being so."

"There you go. Tell me about the brother. Has he asked you out yet?"

Kendra shook her head and thanked the server, who placed their salads and a basket of french bread on the table.

"No, I'm not really sure if that's going to happen. He's single, and he *seems* interested. I mean, just the way he looks at me sometimes. And he's flirted with me a little. But he hasn't actually said he thinks of me that way, you know? The interest could just be my imagination. He might be like that with all women. And now I'm caring for his sister. It would be out of line for me to flirt with him. How awkward would that be, if I've misread him?"

"Yeah, like you'd flirt with him anyway." Shar chuckled into her salad just before taking a bite.

Kendra frowned and set down the forkful she had just taken. "What? I flirt."

Shar simply dipped her chin down and looked up at her sister through doubtful eyes. They both laughed.

"Okay," Kendra said, "so I'm no good at flirting. But—"

A frantic version of "Flight of the Bumblebee" rang from her purse. " 'Scuse me." She retrieved her phone, checked the screen, and widened her eyes at Shar before she answered. "Uh, hello? Steven?"

Shar leaned in, an enthusiastic grin spreading, and Kendra had to turn away to remain focused on the call.

Steven sounded winded. "Sorry, I just got back from a run. I hope I'm not calling too late—"

"No, not at all. But I'm out to dinner at the moment."

"Oh, then I'll let you go. I just thought I'd see if you were free tomorrow."

A date? He was actually going to ask her on a date right after she and Shar discussed that very thing? She looked at Shar and flashed her a big smile.

"Yes, actually, I'm free tomorrow. Unless someone goes into an early labor, of course."

Shar gave her a thumbs-up and speared another forkful of salad.

Kendra heard a light laugh from Steven before he spoke. "I guess that's always a caveat with you, huh?"

"Right."

"I thought I could stop over at your place and take a look at those pieces of furniture you mentioned."

Her optimistic mood dropped down a few beats. "Oh. Yes. That would be fine."

"And then maybe we could run out for lunch. If you're interested, that is."

Kendra met Shar's eyes, and her smile returned. "Lunch would be fun. Sure."

"Great. Around eleven, then?"

"Eleven. Yes."

"Oh, wait. I should mention something while I have you on the phone."

"Yes?"

"Marianne talked with John today. Her husband?"

"Okay."

"She, uh, he confronted her about dropping her care with Dr. Zibarro. They're friends, you know, John and Antoine."

"Yes, I remember that." Again, Kendra's mood felt a pinch.

"Apparently John was pretty upset about her turning to a midwife."

Kendra said nothing. She wasn't sure where Steven was going with this.

"But Marianne stood firm and told him he wasn't in a position to dictate who delivered the baby."

"I see. Well, good for her."

"Right, that's what I said. But I still wanted you to know, since now John knows your name. There's nothing he can do, I'm sure, but I don't want you being blindsided. Marianne is still really excited to be working with you. But John? He can be a real...well, I don't think I have a word that's descriptive enough yet polite enough to say to a lady."

She tried to laugh at that, but the whole issue made her stomach ache a little. "Thanks for letting me know. We'll have to say a prayer and hope for the best." Why did that sound more trite than inspiring when she said it? Didn't she believe God would help? "I'll see you tomorrow, Steven."

"Great. Looking forward to it."

She ended the call and looked up at Shar, who stopped chewing.

"Why don't you look happy? It sounded like he asked you out."

"Yeah, he did. I'm happy about that. But it's sort of like someone handing you a gift and saying, 'Oh, but I should alert you to the unstable bucket of cold water hanging over your head.'"

"What's the bucket of water?"

"Marianne's husband, John. He's upset that she's going to use me for the delivery. And now he has my name."

"Well, so what? You're not doing anything illegal."

"No, but I'd rather not make enemies at the hospital. You said yourself the medical community can be very political."

Shar took a long drink from her glass, set it down slowly, and appeared to be speaking to the glass, rather than to Kendra. "Now, let me get this straight." Then she looked at Kendra, her eyes narrow. "Some surgeon with questionable character takes up with another morally challenged doctor, destroying at least one marriage, if not two. One of the victims of their adultery seeks your help for herself and her baby. You take the high road and step in at the eleventh hour for this poor woman. And *you're* the one making enemies? What's going on at that hospital, anyway?"

Kendra felt her chin jut up as she listened to Shar. "You know, you're right. If anyone has a problem with my helping Marianne, there's something seriously wrong with them. Let John Parkham speak badly about me. Maybe people will consider the source and be supportive of Marianne and me. I'm going to do the right thing here." She took up her salad fork as if it were a battle-ready weapon. "I'm going to lean on God and do the right thing."

"You go, honey!" Shar did the same with her fork.

This time Kendra's belief was all over what she said. Of *course* God would want her to deliver on her promise to Marianne. Maybe there'd be negative consequences to her decision, but as in everything else, they would just have to rest in His always-capable hands.

Chapter 6

Steven arrived at Kendra's house the next morning and took his time before knocking on her door. He was plenty eager to see her, but he couldn't help his surprise when he saw her home. He had expected her to have chosen a fairly modern place to live, like one of the new townhomes built in the area during the past five years or so.

But this was a side of Kendra that surprised him. The house was small, old, and decidedly quaint. Three front steps led to a small porch with the Victorian charm of white balusters, brackets, and spandrels. The porch was just large enough for the two-person swing that hung from the wainscoted ceiling.

He stepped back, stroked his chin, and studied the gable decoration and fish-scale siding. "Huh."

The front door swung open. "What are you *doing* out here?"

She wore a beautiful, sardonic smile, a bright blue top, and gauzy white pants. He realized she probably heard his truck's engine when he first pulled up, so she knew he'd been milling about outside for a while.

He matched her smile and opened his arms, indicating the entirety of her house. "I love your home."

She walked outside and stood beside him, regarding her house as if it belonged to someone else.

"Yeah. Me, too. I've always thought it looked like a gingerbread house. Cute, right?"

He turned away from the house and looked at her. Before he could catch himself, he had given her a swift once-over. "Cute. I don't think I was going for that word, but it seems especially suitable at the moment."

Her face quickly colored and she looked away, a shy smile remaining.

She walked toward the house and glanced at him over her shoulder. "You want to come in and give me the verdict on my desk and armoire?"

"Yep."

He followed her inside. Despite the house's age, the interior felt fresh and contemporary. She had interesting taste, mixing modern pieces with several older ones, pairing refined, upholstered chairs with thick, rustic tables. Steven knew not to make judgments about people based on their home and furnishings, but as a carpenter, he did exactly that on some level. And he liked what he determined about Kendra based on her home. Adventurous, open-minded, and classy.

He realized she had stopped walking because he no longer followed her. She stood in the kitchen waiting for him, her arms folded across her chest. He grinned at her. "You intrigue me."

She straightened and tucked her hair behind her ears. "Thank you. I think."

"Yeah, I meant it as a compliment. Who wants to be predictable, right?" He approached her and was caught up by those eyes of hers. The light in the kitchen brought out their intense ocean blue, and an amused twinkle was replaced by an expression more serious, the closer he got.

He wondered if she would let him kiss her today. Certainly not right now. She turned and approached a stairwell in the corner of the kitchen.

"I store both pieces in the basement. I'd like to use them up here, but I'm not sure if they're worth fixing up or not."

He followed her downstairs and was able to give her an answer almost immediately. "The armoire's had some water damage. See, right down here? Like maybe it was in a basement that flooded. I might have been able to fix that for you, but I suspect someone put it out in the direct sun to dry. That's likely what caused this warping—too much harsh heat too soon."

"So no-go with that one?"

"I wouldn't recommend putting too much money into it, no. I don't think it was a very valuable piece to begin with. But the desk is a different story."

She smiled. "Really? It's a lot older than the armoire. Passed down from way back, my mother says. From my great-grandmother, I think."

He squatted to study the desk more carefully. "Yeah, this is deco." He looked up at Kendra. "From the 1920s or so. Mahogany. Metal and Bakelite handles. Some of the Bakelite is dried up and cracked, but we could replace that."

"Bakelite?"

"It's actually plastic." He opened and closed a drawer. "One of the first plastics ever developed. Really popular in deco trims. And this oval area here on the front drawer probably had a medallion or hand-painted piece in it."

"What a shame." Kendra sighed. "I guess it didn't weather as well as the wood. Or am I wrong about the wood? Did it weather well?"

He stood and rubbed the dust from his hands. "Yeah. This is a beautiful piece. I could definitely refurbish it for you."

She clapped her hands for a second before she caught herself and stopped. She looked like a little girl. She chuckled. "I guess it doesn't take much to make me happy."

He tilted his head. "Nothing wrong with that. How about I fix this in exchange for your helping my sister? I mean, she'll pay you, of course, but—"

"Oh no, I couldn't let you do that. Your time is valuable, too. You *are* a genius, after all."

Steven laughed. "Sometimes I forget. Okay, let's go get some lunch, and then I'll load this up and take it to my workshop when I bring you back. We could even swing by my workshop while we're out, if you'd like. I'll show you some of the things I'm working on."

The clear June weather prompted them to enjoy lunch outdoors. They walked out of a deli with drinks, chips, and sandwiches and walked across the street to a lush green park.

"You sure you prefer this over a restaurant?" Steven didn't want her to think he was some oaf who shied away from anything remotely elegant.

Kendra took a sip of her soda and sat across from him on a picnic bench. "Honestly, I spend enough time indoors. This is a treat. And your workshop is nearby?"

"Right down the road." He pointed with a sandwich. And when he looked in the direction of his shop, he caught sight of his sister's car parking nearby. "Oh." He stood back up and took a few steps to see better.

"What's wrong?" Kendra stood, too.

He pointed again. "That's Marianne parking her car down there. The black Mercedes. You mind if I run down and tell her we're here?"

"Not at all. More chips for me."

He chuckled and gave her shoulders a quick squeeze before he started to leave. Then he turned back, shot her a mischievous grin, and grabbed his bag of chips before dashing away. He heard her wonderful laugh as he ran toward the Mercedes.

He met eyes with Marianne well before he reached her, and she opened her window. "Who are you running away from?"

Steven got in on the passenger's side and extended his bag of chips toward her.

"Come on and drive up to the park there. Kendra's waiting for us."

She took a chip. "Oh, good, that's perfect. I need to talk with her." She handed him a handful of magazine photos. "These are the nursery ideas I wanted you to look at." She pulled away and headed to the other end of the street. "Why are you two in the park?"

"We're having lunch."

"I thought you were going to ask her *out* to lunch."

"I did." He pointed to the park as they pulled into a space. "*This* is out."

Marianne turned in her seat. "Please tell me you're kidding."

He laughed, got out of the car, and ran around to her side. "We changed our minds once we left her place. It's nice out today. And I wanted to show her my workshop, so we just came here. We'll go to a restaurant another time."

He helped her move her awkward bulk out of the car. "Wow. How do pregnant women do this on their own?"

She grunted with the effort but gave him a heavy-lidded gaze once she emerged. "Word to the wise, little brother. Try to avoid the word 'wow' when you talk about a woman's size— pregnant or otherwise."

Before he could respond, she waved at Kendra and waddled in her direction.

Kendra met her halfway. "How do you feel today?" She placed her hand on Marianne's shoulder.

"Like six weeks is an eternity. How about you?" She lowered her voice as if she didn't want Steven to hear. "I see Steven is pulling out all the stops in his efforts to charm you."

"Hey!" Steven said. "I heard that."

The women laughed, and at the same time he heard what sounded like distant thunder.

"Listen, Kendra," Marianne said, "I wanted to warn you. John made a big stink about my switching to you for my birthing care."

"Yes, Steven told me. I'm sorry if that's caused you problems. Are you still sure you want to—"

"Oh, absolutely. Even more so than before. But what I

wanted to warn you about is that John gave Dr. Z. your name."

Steven saw the immediate concern in Kendra's expression. But he also saw her work to dispel that concern. She smiled, tilted her head, and gave Marianne a gentle shrug.

"I expected that would happen sooner or later. Maybe Dr. Zibarro has too many patients to concern himself with losing one to me."

"I hope so," Marianne said. She pointed at Kendra. "You know, what you really need is a clinic of your own."

"Now that sounds like a good idea." Steven rested against the picnic bench and felt several drops of rain fall through the trees.

Kendra and Marianne must have felt the same. Marianne looked upward. Kendra put her hand out. "Did I just feel—?"

Within seconds, a downpour opened, and the three of them scrambled.

"Steven, go ahead and help Marianne to her car!" Kendra grabbed at their food and shoved it quickly back into the deli bags.

Steven gave Marianne his arm, but she could move just so quickly these days. They were drenched but laughing by the time they reached her car. He only hoped Kendra was as lighthearted about Oregon's sudden weather.

And she was. She ran toward them with her long dark hair plastered against her head, her wet clothes clinging to her body, and her arms full of soggy, disintegrating bags of food. She laughed as if this were exactly how she had hoped to spend her afternoon.

Marianne opened her window a crack. "Get in, get in!"

Kendra and Steven piled into the backseat. Kendra released her hold on the food, a limp pile in her lap. Steven reached over to help her get her hair pushed back from her face. She was the prettiest mess he'd seen in a long time, especially as their laughter slacked off and she met eyes with him.

"Maybe we should just finish lunch at my workshop," he said. "I'll pick up your furniture later so it doesn't get wet."

She bit her lip. "Um, actually, I think we need to postpone lunch, and Marianne, I need to ask you for a ride home."

"Sure, I can do that." Marianne looked back at the two of them. "You're probably pretty uncomfortable in those wet clothes. And that wet food."

Steven didn't completely understand. "Well, I'd be happy to drive you home to change. You still look beautiful. Just get some dry clothes and—"

"Thanks, but that's not going to work out." She smiled at him, and her cheeks colored. "I'm drenched. And I'm, uh, wearing white."

"Oh," Marianne said. "Got it."

He frowned. "I still don't get it."

Marianne sighed. "Steven, give the girl a break. She's trying to remain modest. White clothes don't do well in the rain."

When awareness finally dawned, he was embarrassed to have pressed to get his own way. He rolled his eyes. "Oh, man, what a dolt. I'm sorry. Yeah, let's reschedule. Maybe dinner?"

At least he saw disappointment in her eyes.

"I'm teaching a childbirth class tonight. But I'll call you when I get home, and we can plan."

He smiled. "Sure."

He didn't know how much good it would do to plan, though. Between their surprising weather and her unpredictable patients, he was starting to see that *he* was the one who needed to remain lighthearted when their plans went awry. The surprise at seeing Kendra's charming old home was just a taste of how unexpected dating Kendra might be.

Chapter 7

A week later Kendra approached Marianne's front door, her home visit bag slung over her shoulder. She stepped back when the door swung open. A pregnant, fortyish blond nearly squealed and took Kendra's hand to pull her inside.

"I am *so* excited to meet you! You're Kendra, right? Of course you are. I'm Alice." She called deeper into the house. "Lonnie! Lonnie, come here and meet Kendra. Turn off that game, babe, and come in here."

Dumbfounded, Kendra glanced around the foyer. This was definitely Marianne's home. She awaited Lonnie's appearance and the possible explanation it might bring. But the blond babbled on.

"When Marianne told me—well, told *us* really—about you, I just quit Dr. Zibarro immediately. I mean, *right. Away.*"

"Uh, Dr. Zibarro?"

Marianne finally toddled down the stairs. "Alice, sweetie, let Kendra breathe. She thought she was just coming to examine me, not field your unbridled enthusiasm."

"Hey." A burly young man in a Seattle Mariners T-shirt walked in. He had to be a decade younger than Alice. "You're Kendra? The midwife?" He put his hand out.

"Kendra the midwife. That's me." She shook his hand.

Marianne steered Kendra toward the guest bedroom area. "See, I told you I was going to rave about you. And Alice and Lonnie here are six months along and haven't been at all happy with Dr. Zibarro."

"He's mean," Alice said behind them.

"Mean?" Kendra knew Zibarro could be brusque, but she had never heard of his being mean.

Marianne waved the comment away. "Alice's feelings are easily hurt. Well, they are, Alice. See? Lonnie's nodding. Anyway, Kendra, you'll take her as a patient, won't you?"

Kendra looked from Marianne to Alice. Lonnie had already quietly headed back to the television. "I don't know, Alice. We'll have to talk about it."

"That's fine. I'm not due for another exam for a few more weeks."

Kendra tried not to let Alice see her frown. It wasn't that she wanted to turn anyone away. But she also wasn't a one-woman campaign against Antoine Zibarro's practice. The man was a perfectly good OB/GYN.

"You don't mind Alice sitting in on this exam, do you?" Marianne opened the door to the bedroom, and Alice waited for Kendra to follow before she joined them.

"I don't mind if you don't." She set her bag on the dresser and unpacked her stethoscope and blood pressure cuff. "But Marianne, maybe you could refrain from talking me up to people who are already associated with other doctors for their deliveries. There are plenty of women out there getting pregnant. I don't want to become known for stealing away doctors' patients, okay?" She reached back into her bag.

Alice sat in a chair near the window. "But I thought you'd be happy to meet people like me. You know, who are still eager to use a midwife, even after that article came out."

Kendra stopped digging in her bag and looked up at Alice. "What article?" Acid suddenly burned her stomach.

Marianne lay back and again waved away the comment. "It's nothing. Just some squeaky wheels looking for attention."

"And Zibarro is right there, squeaking with the best of them. I left it on the kitchen counter." Alice headed for the door.

"No, Alice," Marianne said, "don't bother Kendra with that."

Kendra approached Marianne but looked over her shoulder at Alice. "Actually, I would like to see it, but let me take care of Marianne's exam first."

The article was not what Kendra would have called "nothing," as Marianne had. A few local obstetricians, Antoine Zibarro included, had provided quotes for a piece about the possible dangers of relying on midwives and especially of delivering babies at home. It didn't look as if Zibarro had prompted the article, but he was front and center in a group position that sounded rather crusadelike.

"This is awful." She set the paper down on the kitchen counter while Marianne poured three cups of tea.

"But they showed both sides, don't you think? They

included two couples who used midwives and were happy with the results."

Alice tapped on the paper. "They certainly didn't talk me out of the idea. I'm thrilled Lonnie and I will be able to deliver at home."

"Alice, you and I still have to interview, okay? I can't commit to your care until we do that." Kendra looked at the paper again and sighed. "I guess it wasn't a complete hatchet job. But it doesn't encourage me to rush into opening my own clinic, that's for sure."

Marianne gasped. "So you've been thinking about my idea?"

With a mild chuckle, Kendra said, "I've wanted my own clinic for as long as I can remember. I know a couple of midwives who would love to partner with me. But there are so many things involved, not the least of which is money. And now this." She pointed to the paper. "I'm going to have to see if there are repercussions in the community because of this."

"Listen, you believe you're doing what God wants you to do, don't you?" Marianne asked.

"Yes." Kendra sipped her tea. "At least I *try* to listen for His guidance." After reading that article, she had to admit some shakiness to her conviction. But not out loud.

Alice smiled. "Then all you need are enough patients who believe in *you*." She waved her finger between Marianne and herself. "We'll help you there, and I'll bet lots of your past patients would, too. Referrals, you know?"

"Maybe we can even help with the money situation," Marianne said. "I've done quite a lot of fund-raising in my day, you know. I also have connections with people in finance.

I didn't spend my married years watching TV and eating Cheese Doodles. And Alice here can be mighty pushy when she wants to be."

Kendra set her cup down and gathered her bags to leave. "I need to get back to work. But you two are really wonderful. Every time I get depressed tonight about that article, I'm going to think about this conversation. I can't believe how supportive you both are."

Alice gave her a wink. "Anything for my new midwife."

Marianne laughed, and Kendra gave Alice a look of mock admonishment. "Marianne's right. You *can* be mighty pushy. I'll give you a call, and we'll get together in the next couple of days to talk about your pregnancy."

Alice shrugged, holding her palms up. "That's all I'm asking."

That wasn't exactly true, but Kendra would leave it at that for now. She needed to get away and pray about Alice and about the women and babies currently in her care. There was a chance some of her patients would have questions after seeing that article. She wanted to make sure she gave them the answers God wanted her to give.

Chapter 8

The next evening Steven sat across from Kendra at JORY, one of his favorite restaurants, at the Allison Inn in the heart of Oregon's Willamette Valley.

"I love this place," Kendra had said when they pulled up to the valet. They took the time to look out beyond the inn, to appreciate its lush vineyards and elegant gardens. "My sister, Shar, and I did a weekend at the spa here last year."

He had watched her relax visibly during the past hour or so since he picked her up. Once they entered the restaurant and were shown to their table, she sat back against the upholstered booth. Steven smiled back at her. "I'm glad you agreed to come out tonight."

She sighed. "I needed this like you wouldn't believe." She unfolded her napkin and arranged it in her lap. When she smiled, he saw weariness giving way to contentment. "And thank you for the tour of your workshop. With no thunderstorms!"

"But I noticed you chose not to wear white."

"I'm no fool."

"That was already clear. You agreed to go out with me, didn't you?"

Her chuckle had a lazy, laid-back sound to it. She leaned forward and rested her chin on her hand, as if she were in class and he were the subject she studied. "You know what I think I like about you?"

He mirrored her gesture, a twinkle in his eye. "There are so many possibilities, I can't even begin to guess."

She sat up straight and laughed out loud. "I'll narrow it down for you, then. I like that you're always so calm. You bring out the calm in me."

"You do mean calm? Not boring? I mean, cadavers are calm."

"I didn't say you were *lifeless*. Far from it. But so often I'm surrounded by people in a panic, you know? It just goes with the territory for a midwife. And you're. . ." She put her hands just over the table and slowly moved them away from each other, as if she were playing the piano. "You're mellow." This last she said in a spacey, hippie voice.

He let his expression go goofy. "Dude."

For dinner they enjoyed Manila clams and watercress soup, Atherton lamb and sea scallops, fresh, hot coffee, and each other's company.

"You still want me to restore your great-grandmother's desk, right?"

"Definitely. Especially after seeing the things you had in your workshop."

"I don't have anything in there with the kind of finish your desk needs. A lot of the furniture from the deco era has a real polished finish to it, more than anything you saw in my shop.

I think we should do that deco finish with your desk. It'll highlight the wood's grain better. And the inlay."

She lifted her palm to him. "I defer to your wisdom and brilliance."

"Cool. I'm happy you like what I do. My folks worry sometimes because I often turn down the more commercial, construction-type jobs. That's where the quicker growth in business comes from. The better money. But these individual jobs are the kind of work I look forward to when I wake up each morning."

"They're more artistic, aren't they?"

He nodded. "Yeah. So it's a trade-off. I enjoy it more, but the income isn't usually as good." He shrugged. "I take on commercial work when I have to, though."

Why was he yammering on about money to her? They barely knew each other, and he was starting to sound like he was interviewing for something. Maybe he was. He knew her profession would make it difficult for her to juggle several guys at once, but he couldn't believe she didn't have her pick of men. She was smart, kind, funny, and beautiful.

As they walked out of the restaurant, a woman passed them and broke into a big grin when she saw Kendra.

"Kendra!" She gave her a hug as if they were the closest of friends, and Kendra said hello, but Steven didn't see a lot of recognition in her eyes. Apparently, the woman noticed that as well.

"Jill Maxwell? Five years ago? Twin boys? Fraternal?"

Jackpot. Recognition dawned on Kendra's face, and she hugged the woman back again. "How *are* you? How are the boys?"

"Fantastic. Starting kindergarten in September, can you believe it?"

"No, it feels like yesterday." She glanced at Steven. "This is my friend Steven Nichols. Jill was one of my surprise home deliveries." She and Jill grinned at each other.

"Surprise?"

Jill said, "I was supposed to deliver at the hospital, but the boys had other plans. They came way early—"

"And way fast," Kendra said.

Jill placed her hand on Kendra's shoulder. "After reading that article this week, I feel like I really dodged a bullet. Or two bullets, I guess!"

"What do you mean?" Kendra's smile faltered. Steven didn't like the sudden change of direction in the conversation any more than she seemed to.

Jill shrugged. "Well, I never realized how risky home births were."

Kendra looked as if the woman had just slapped her. "They're not—"

"They haven't seated you yet?" A man the size of a linebacker walked in and interrupted the conversation.

"I haven't given them our name yet, Brad. Look who I ran into, honey. You remember Kendra. She delivered the twins. And her boyfriend, Steven." Jill chuckled. "She didn't deliver Steven, just the twins. Ignore me."

"Oh, hey, yeah. Nice to see you again." Brad gave both Kendra and Steven a powerful handshake.

Steven placed his hand against Kendra's back and thought he felt her shaking. He looked at her face and could tell her mind was elsewhere, or at least unsettled.

"Sorry, Jill. Brad," he said. "We need to be someplace right away, so. . ."

"Oh, sure," Jill said. She gave Kendra's arm a little squeeze. "You'll have to come see the twins sometime."

Kendra nodded. "Yes. I'd like that."

As soon as she and Steven walked out of the restaurant, she teared up. Steven handed his ticket to the valet and gently put an arm around her. She turned into his chest, so he completed the embrace. He spoke softly into her hair. "You should do just as she said. Ignore her."

"What am I going to do?" She pulled back and looked into his eyes. "She even experienced an emergency home birth that went well, and *she's* turned off by midwives, thanks to that article."

"I'm sure she's not the norm, Kendra." He wiped her tears away with his thumb. "Anyway, she didn't mention midwives. Just home births."

She puffed out an exasperated sigh and shook her head. "Most people just lump the two together in their minds. This could ruin my business."

The valet pulled up, and Kendra turned away to get into the Silverado. Steven followed her and silently closed her door for her.

She looked at him when he got in the car. She had stopped crying, but that wonderful contented expression from the restaurant was long gone.

"Steven, do you mind if we just play that nice classical CD you played before? I mean, no talking for a while? I need to gather my thoughts. Is that all right?"

"Sure."

But as they drove back to her house, he tried to think of suggestions for how she might combat the article's possible effect on her business. He wished he could just make it all better for her. When they reached her house, he walked her to her door, a protective arm over her shoulder.

"You know, when you decided to help Marianne, and then John got upset about it, you said you were just going to say a prayer and hope for the best. Maybe that's the best thing to do now. Until you feel more certain about doing anything else, that is."

She sighed. "Of course I need to pray about it. But this timing couldn't be worse. I was talking with a couple of other midwives about opening a clinic."

"Don't give up too soon. That could still happen."

They ended their evening on a solemn note. The last thing he wanted was for their first kiss to be connected to worry or sadness. The moment was far from romantic. So he just gave her a quick kiss on the head.

"I still need to come pick up your desk. I'll call you to schedule that. And to see how you're feeling, too."

She nodded. "Good night. Thanks. It was fun."

They exchanged a rueful laugh.

And as Steven drove away, he tried very hard to focus on the actual fun of the evening, rather than creeping feelings about his brother-in-law and the trouble he had likely stirred up for Kendra. He tried not to dwell on the possibility that, by introducing Kendra to Marianne, he had indirectly drawn her into a battle she shouldn't have had to join.

Chapter 9

Kendra's mother and sister were in no hurry to leave her house.

"Nothing doing," Shar said. "If Steven is on his way over, we need to stick around long enough to meet him."

Their mother remained on the couch and crossed her legs. "I second that motion."

"That's fine." Kendra sat back down as soon as she checked herself in the foyer mirror. "I want you to meet him anyway. Especially with you heading home tomorrow, Shar. Just don't embarrass me. No stories about past boyfriends or stupid things I've done. I'm already feeling at odds because of the whole stink of that article."

"What stink?" Shar took another sip of lemonade. "I think you've taken all of that too personally. Don't get Mom all worried. You haven't lost any patients over it, have you?"

"No. I guess I just feel kind of defensive. Yeah, don't worry, Mom."

Shar stood and looked out the window. "Besides, from the

way you describe him, Steven doesn't sound like the type to give you a hard time about *anything*."

"Get away from there, nosy. And you're right. He's actually called a few times this week and encouraged me to ignore the article and move forward with the clinic idea. My midwife friends feel the same way. We're going to look at some properties tomorrow."

"Yes, I like this man, Kendra." Her mother stood and joined Shar at the window.

"Will you two please get away from—"

"Ooo, there he is!" Shar jumped back, which made their mother jump as well, and the two women practically knocked each other down running back to the couch.

"Oh, for goodness' sake." Kendra laughed at them, and they joined her. "I said don't embarrass me, okay?"

She was still smiling when she answered the door. Steven had a young man with him and rolled a hand truck behind himself. He returned her smile.

"That's what I like to see. You look a lot happier than the last time I saw you." He and the young man walked in. "Marty here is going to help me load your desk—oh, sorry, I didn't realize you had guests."

"We're not guests; we're family." Shar strode up to him and shook his hand.

Kendra took care of introductions and took Steven and Marty downstairs. The men took their time with the desk and loaded it onto the truck, Kendra right behind them.

"Will you and Marty stay for some iced tea or lemonade? Just long enough for my mom and sister to chat with you a little."

"Sure, for a few minutes. I don't want to leave the desk out here too long. But yeah, that would be nice. Am I auditioning for anything I should know about?"

Marty snorted and then looked down, his smile shy.

The three of them walked back to the house.

"I think they're already sold on you," Kendra said. "They like that you've been encouraging me about the clinic."

"You're going to work on that, then?" He broke into a big grin and gave her an affectionate rub on the back. "That's terrific. Marianne told me she wanted to help you find investors or financiers or something like that. She's your second biggest fan."

"Who's her second biggest fan?" Shar walked out from the kitchen, a pitcher of lemonade in her hand.

"Steven's sister—you know, Marianne? I've mentioned her. She's a real dynamo, too. She's offering to help me get the clinic going, and she's already brought me another patient—"

"Is that Alice?" Steven asked. "Thanks." He took a glass of lemonade from Shar and handed it to Marty. "You just might empty out Dr. Z.'s office at this rate."

Kendra looked at her mother, whose expression immediately showed worry. "Dr. Z.? As in Zibarro? As in that article?"

"Yes, but Steven's kidding, Mom. Alice is the only other Zibarro client I'm taking on."

Steven took the second glass from Shar. "I'm sorry, did I say something wrong?"

"Mom's afraid Zibarro will come after me."

Her mother rubbed her arms as if she were cold. "The man's notoriously anti-midwife. You don't want to go making a powerful enemy."

Steven nodded. "I understand that, Mrs. Silverstone. But I can tell you my sister would have left him even if it meant going to another doctor. She couldn't go to that office anymore—I'm not sure if Kendra told you about that."

"Mom, I didn't feel like I could turn Alice down, either. I didn't agree to her request without a lot of thought and prayer. She's really uncomfortable with Zibarro's bedside manner—or lack thereof, I should say. And she wants to try a home delivery. She fired him as her doctor before I even met her. And I examined her earlier this week and checked on her case history. I couldn't find any reason to turn her down. Cowering about Dr. Zibarro just doesn't seem like a good enough reason."

"She'll be fine, Mom," Shar said. "Especially if she and her midwife friends get this clinic together." She looked at Kendra. "I think that will give you more clout in the medical community. There are probably plenty of people at the hospital who think of you as a nurse and nothing more."

"She'll still need her hospital privileges," their mother said. "She needs to be able to handle the emergency births and the births for women who want to deliver in the hospital."

Kendra noticed Steven's helper, Marty, looking uncomfortable. Or possibly just bored.

"We should let Steven and Marty get going. That desk isn't going to refinish itself."

"Right." Steven took Marty's glass and started to walk in the direction of the kitchen. "Back here, right?"

Shar stepped forward. "Here, I'll take those." She made a cutesy face at Kendra. "You kids go on out there and say your good-byes. And pipe down there, Marty. It's hard to get a word in edgewise with you around."

Steven chuckled and shook hands with Shar and her mother. "Nice meeting you both. I'll see you later."

He and Kendra walked out the door with Marty. Kendra heard Shar talking to their mother as the door closed: "Don't worry, Mom. It's all going to work out great. And how cute is *he*, huh?"

Kendra shot a glance at Steven. He seemed busy with the keys to his truck. "Did you hear that?" she asked.

A concentrated focus on the keys. "Hear what?"

She kept her eye on him. "Nothing."

"You mean how cute I am?"

Kendra laughed and lowered her voice. "Actually, I think she was talking about Marty."

Steven looked over at Marty, who had already climbed into the truck's passenger seat and shut the door. "He's a good kid. Studying design at the University of Oregon. He wants to learn woodworking, so I'm letting him apprentice with me for the rest of the summer. He's a hard worker."

Kendra simply nodded. They looked at each other for a moment. She was never quite sure how to say good-bye to him. Their circumstances didn't seem to allow for even the hint of a good-bye kiss, even if they were ready for that. There was always some interruption, it seemed.

"Speaking of which," he said.

For a moment she was afraid she had just thought out loud. "Uh, speaking of what?"

"Hard workers. Like you. When do I get to take you out again? Surely you can't be delivering babies *every* day. Can we schedule an evening soon? Like tonight?"

She laughed, and he rubbed the back of his neck, pretending chagrin. "Not that I'm desperate or anything." He gave her a genuine smile. "I have a very full life, you know. Hugely popular. Lots of stuff going on."

"I can see that." Yes, she would certainly appreciate his giving her a kiss right now. She hadn't noticed before that he got dimples in his cheeks when he smiled just so. "Um, yeah. How about this weekend? I'm free Saturday."

"Perfect. And I wanted to find out if you had Fourth of July plans. Marianne is having a big cookout before the fireworks."

"Yes, she mentioned that to me."

He stepped away as he spoke. "Let's go together. Shock the townsfolk."

"Oh, I'm sure tongues will wag." She started back toward the house, but she turned to speak again. "We're pretty fascinating people, after all."

He stood at his door and opened his arms to gesture toward her and back toward himself, drawing a line of connection between them. "What's not to love, right?" He flashed a smile and got in the truck.

She tilted her head and spoke softly: "I haven't come across anything yet."

Chapter 10

"Here, Kendra. You've got to taste this. Marianne made it from scratch, she says."

Steven extended a spoonful of peach ice cream to her, and she swallowed it with pleasure. Marianne never ceased to amaze her.

"Oh, that's terrific. I should have gotten that. But the cheesecake brownies looked too good."

"Hey, it's July Fourth." He stretched out his long legs. "Have both. I'll share this with you. I kind of enjoy feeding you."

She gave him a half smile. "I kind of enjoy it, too."

Noisy, happy people surrounded them as they lounged near Marianne's pool, but they acted as if they were completely alone. They had no other choice.

Since the day Steven met her mother and sister, they had managed two dates. The first one had ended with his rushing her to Ellie's delivery. Ellie had introduced Steven and Kendra in the first place, and she invited Steven to wait downstairs— an offer he promptly chose to decline. The second date started at his workshop, where they decided to meet before going elsewhere, but Marianne showed up unannounced, all hormonal and needing Steven's company. So they brought her along with them for the evening, despite her embarrassed protests.

Now he leaned toward her as if he were going to tell her a secret, so she leaned forward, too. He had brought her to that calmness she told him about before. It was one of the qualities she liked the most about him.

"You know, we always start out just fine when we get together," he said.

"That's true."

"But there's something about the second half of our dates—"

"You noticed that, too, huh?"

He nodded. "I did. So I was thinking. I know we have, what, maybe three hours left tonight? Who knows what might happen? So I was wondering if I might ask for my good-night kiss right now—you know, just to play it safe."

A rush of heat ran up her neck. Silly, really. She felt they were far overdue. But by their putting it off as they had, it had become more special. "Well, I don't know. If we have to discuss it—"

He bridged the short distance between them, hesitated for a moment as if assuring permission, and gave her a soft, warm kiss that tasted like peach ice cream and felt like heaven.

Marianne's voice broke through the moment: "I'm so sorry, you two."

They looked at each other for a second before chuckling. Steven gave a subtle shake of his head. "Told you."

Kendra sat up straight. "No problem, Marianne." She saw genuine concern in Marianne's face then and felt bad for their cavalier response to her interruption. "Is something wrong?"

"It's Alice. I think her water broke."

Kendra stood at once. "Where is she?"

Marianne turned, and both Kendra and Steven followed her. They rushed through the crowd. It was obvious no one knew anything was amiss.

Steven spoke over Kendra's shoulder. "Is this serious?"

They reached one of the bathrooms, and Marianne tapped quickly on the door.

Kendra turned to him. "It is if her water broke. She's not even seven months along yet. This is way too soon. We might need you to get us to the hospital. Can you run out to your truck and get my bag?"

She went into the bathroom and found Alice in the empty tub. She was obviously in pain. Not good.

"Are you having contractions, Alice?" Kendra dropped to her knees beside the tub.

Alice spoke through clenched teeth: "I don't know if that's what this is or not. It hurts."

"Let me check you—" And the moment she did, she knew. *Dear Lord, help us. Please help us now.* "Okay, Marianne, get me a robe or something we can drape around Alice. And tell Steven we're definitely going to need him to drive us to the hospital."

"Should I call 911?"

"No, we can get her there faster. But get me a phone, okay? Alice, was the water clear?"

"Huh?"

"When your water broke. Did you notice if it was clear or not?"

"Oh." She grimaced with pain. "No. Not clear. It was nasty."

Alice's husband, Lonnie, opened the door, panic in his eyes. He held Kendra's bag. "Alice? You okay, baby?"

Marianne stopped him. "Got your phone on you, Lonnie? Give it to Kendra, quick. Steven—"

Marianne shut the door as she left, and Lonnie dropped to his knees next to Kendra, fumbling to get his phone out of his pocket. The normally husky man looked suddenly small, as if he were folding in on himself.

Kendra took his phone and her bag. "Lonnie, put your hand here on the baby's head. Just apply gentle pressure."

He gasped when he did what she asked. "That's the baby's head?"

"Yes, I'm afraid so. Alice, I know you're hurting, but try not to push, okay?"

She called the hospital and yanked her stethoscope from her bag. She tried to hold the small cell phone between her shoulder and ear while she searched for the baby's heartbeat. She spoke the moment the emergency room receptionist answered with the standard greeting. "Is this Tanya?"

"This is Tanya, yes."

Good, one of the more quick-witted ones.

"This is Kendra Silverstone. I'm five miles from the hospital with a severely distressed twenty-six weeks with a possible prolapsed cord."

Alice started crying, and Kendra raised her voice to talk over her.

"The mom's nearly complete, and her water broke. Meconium present. Have the obstetrician-on-call waiting for us."

"Got it. Heartbeat?"

Kendra had been searching with her stethoscope. "I haven't found one yet." She grabbed at the phone and tossed it on the floor.

Marianne barged in, a large white terry-cloth robe in her arms. "Here you go, Alice, honey, it's my maternity robe. It'll cover everything. Steven will drive you in my car." She looked at Kendra as they wrapped the robe around Alice. "The Mercedes will be easier for her to get in and out of."

Kendra nodded and mouthed the word *pray*. "Lonnie, switch places with me. Can you lift her out of there and go with me to the car?"

He lifted Alice as if she were a feather.

"Good," Kendra said. "I'm going to stay right next to you and keep pressure against the baby's head. Marianne, can you grab my bag there?"

They followed Marianne through the house, which had become still, despite the crowd of people there. Everyone had moved toward the back of the house to get out of the way.

Kendra spotted Steven in the foyer. Their eyes met, and for a flash of a second she remembered the first time they saw each other. His eyes now held the same intensity she noticed then. But the playfulness was gone. He held the front door open and then got to the car ahead of them, opening doors and helping to get Alice and Kendra in the back.

"Steven, drive as safely as you can, but get us there yesterday."

Twenty minutes later Kendra and the doctor confirmed what

Kendra had feared the moment she examined Alice. The baby had been dead for hours. Alice was inconsolable, but Lonnie, sobbing, stayed with her to try.

Kendra held herself together until she left Alice's room, but when she entered the waiting room and saw Steven, she broke down. Marianne had followed them in his truck, and the three of them embraced.

"What happened?" Marianne asked between tears. "I thought she was doing well with the pregnancy."

"She was. I examined her last week, and she was fine. She said she felt good until this afternoon, when she—"

"Yeah, that's right. When they got to my place, she said she felt a little sick to her stomach. A little feverish. Should she have told you?"

"Yes, but I think it was already too late. I think this happened yesterday. That's the last time she remembers the baby moving. She just didn't realize that until the labor started."

"So what happens now?" Steven asked.

"They're keeping her overnight at least. Lonnie wants to stay in her room, and they're going to let him. The doctor wants to observe Alice, and the coroner..." She choked on her emotion and had to stop talking.

Steven had his arm around her and squeezed her to himself. "Let me drive you home."

She nodded. "Thanks. Oh, Marianne. I should tell you." She put her hand on Marianne's shoulder. "The OB on call is Gina Chastain."

Marianne stiffened. The woman responsible for ruining her marriage was just on the other side of the door. Kendra didn't know why she told Marianne, but she simply felt she should know. "She did everything she should have done for Alice."

Marianne's lips were thin when she looked to the ground. She said nothing.

Neither Steven nor Kendra spoke much on the way to her house. Kendra felt she carried so many sad issues on her shoulders when they walked to her door. Finally she spoke, and she felt the weight in her voice. "On top of Alice and Lonnie's horrible heartbreak, this incident will obviously be reported to Dr. Zibarro by morning, if Dr. Chastain hasn't already called him."

Steven hugged her and kissed the top of her head. "Don't think about that tonight. That kind of pressure will diminish for you once you have your own clinic."

She pushed away from him. "Don't you get it? There's no way I can hope for a clinic after this."

"But this wasn't your fault. Right?"

"That won't matter."

He tried to hug her again. She could tell he was trying to make her feel better, but she wasn't ready for that. The hug felt suffocating.

He said, "You're just upset right now, like we all are. But don't give up so easily. Tomorrow—"

She pushed away again. "Don't tell me not to give up. It's not like you're out there blazing a trail in the construction business."

He frowned. "What?"

"Just don't tell me what to do." She heard herself and knew she was being mean and childish, but she couldn't seem to stop. "Look, I need to be alone right now. Thanks for the ride. Thanks for helping."

She turned away from him and half expected him to try to stop her. But he didn't. When she looked over her shoulder, she noticed his angry stomp back to the truck.

The first thing she saw when she trudged across her threshold was the light on her answering machine. The *last* thing she wanted to do was check messages, but there was always a chance the call was about Alice, so she hit PLAY.

"Hello, Kendra Silverstone? This is Vance Chaney with the *Willamette Gazette*. I wondered if I might talk with you about the incident at the hospital tonight. I'd appreciate it if you could give me a call."

Chapter 11

S he didn't return the reporter's call. She called Shar the
next morning, after a sleepless night.

"I guarantee Alice was perfectly healthy, Shar. The
baby was perfectly healthy."

"Come on, Kendra, go easy on yourself. Of course they
were healthy, right up until they weren't. You've had years of
experience. You know sometimes pregnancies go wrong. This
can't be the first time one of your patients miscarried."

She shook her head. "Preterm delivery. Alice was twenty-six
weeks. But no, you're right. It's rare and horrible, but it happens.
It's just the other circumstances around this loss. I don't even
feel like I can give Alice proper attention, because I'm hesitant
to run into that reporter or Zibarro or who knows who else."

"Well, you're just going to have to tough it up, sister. You
need to go see Alice."

Kendra nodded. "I know. I have every intention of going to
her this morning. But pray I say the words she needs to hear,
okay?"

"You got it. It's going to be all right. Remember, you didn't do anything wrong. Praying is a good idea."

Kendra heard from her mother shortly thereafter. She realized it might have been a good idea to ask Shar to keep the awful news quiet for a while.

"Honey, I'm so worried about you. This is exactly the kind of thing Antoine Zibarro was waiting for—"

"Mom, don't you think I know that? Could we please talk later? I need to try to wake up and get into the hospital to check on Alice. Her situation is more important than mine right now."

"Well, I think they're pretty well intertwined, don't you? You shouldn't have taken on—"

"I'm sorry, Mom. I don't want to interrupt you. But I honestly have to talk with you later. Okay?"

A sigh. "I'm sorry, too, honey. You don't need to hear this right now. Tell me what I can do for you."

"Pray. Alice needs comfort and hope. And I need guidance and protection."

She didn't hear from Steven. Or Marianne. That was certainly no surprise. She figured he had probably told Marianne how horrible she was to him.

Every time she thought about how vicious she sounded, she wanted to crawl under a rock. How could she have struck at the one remotely vulnerable thing he had told her? She knew his parents pushed him to be more aggressive, or at least more commercial, with his carpentry. She understood her own relationship with her parents well enough to know Steven probably hurt a little at his parents' pressing him like that. If they thought he should be doing something other than what he was doing, he probably sensed some disappointment on their part. Grown man or not, that was likely a tender spot. So, of course, that's exactly where she hit him. How dark was *her* heart, to come up with such a harsh comment?

Before she left to visit Alice, she spent some time on her knees: *Lord, soften my heart. You know what Alice needs to hear from me today. Please put the words in my mouth that will help her now. You and I both know how poorly I can choose my words, especially when I'm tired and emotional, which I am right now. And guide me, Lord. Please. Are You trying to guide me away from what I've always thought was my calling? Is that what's happening here?*

Alice and Lonnie were amazing. Their hearts were broken. But Dr. Chastain had assured them that the baby was lost because something wasn't developing as it should.

"God showed mercy on our little sweetheart. Our Theresa," Alice said through her tears. "She would have had a hard life if she had made it—" And she stopped to cry again.

Kendra cried, too, especially hearing the baby's name. She reached out to brush Alice's hair away from her face. "Alice, I'm so sorry. I'm so—" She stopped to swallow down the thickness in her throat. And to pray quickly again. She searched for the right words.

"Kendra." Lonnie put his hand on her shoulder. "We don't blame you. Is that what you think?" He wiped his hand across his eyes. "We don't."

Alice shook her head. She was crying too much to speak.

And Kendra joined her in that struggle. This couple—the

lively, fast-talking blond and the laid-back sports-watching couch potato—had undergone what was probably the worst thing a couple can endure. And they were actually making an effort to comfort *her*.

It took only two more days for the article to hit the paper. This time Kendra was watching for it. As she expected, Dr. Zibarro was quoted, and he was virulent and far more vocal this time around. Now he attached an incident—an unnamed forty-one-year-old mother's sudden loss of her child on July 4—and a name—Kendra's—to the dangers of relying on midwifery. He was careful but damaging in his wording. Without pointing the finger specifically at Kendra, he said that "losses like this one are often connected to inexperience and the lack of proper care and facilities."

Marianne finally called.

"Don't let him get to you, Kendra. People who know you still believe in you. You know that, right? And they'll talk you up. I'm going to see to that."

Zibarro's suggestions were wrong, but Kendra knew people tended to believe what they read in print. "You mean you still want me as your midwife?" After what happened to Alice and with Steven, she was honestly shocked.

"Why wouldn't I? Everyone knows Alice's situation had nothing to do with you. You had barely even taken her on as a patient. Antoine knows that, too, believe me. He's covering his own skin just as much as he's trying to tar and feather you. He was her caregiver a *lot* longer than you were."

She hadn't thought of that. Should she make an issue of that? Call the reporter and defend herself?

The very thought of engaging in a public argument like that felt wrong somehow. Maybe that was some of the guidance she'd prayed for.

Marianne's comment cut through her thoughts. "We start weekly exams this week, right? How's this weekend? I could make dinner for you and Steven after."

Clearly Steven had said nothing to Marianne about how mean Kendra had been to him. She felt a sudden urge to see him. To apologize and make sure he would forgive her. "Uh, that works for me, Marianne, if it works for Steven."

She wasn't one for impromptu visits, but she was on full-guidance mode, and this felt right. She knew Steven had a lot of projects going, including her desk, so she rushed to his shop. She saw him through the window, placing a call. Just as she tapped on the window, her cell phone rang.

She ignored it. Just this once, she was going to ignore it. She watched him turn, and delight actually lit his eyes when he saw her. He set his phone on a workbench and came to the door.

Kendra spoke the moment he opened it. "Please forgive me. Please." She almost started crying again, especially when she realized he meant to embrace her. She spoke into his chest. "That was one of the worst things I've ever said to anyone. And you've been so wonderful. Your *work* is wonderful. I'm just self-centered and—"

He chuckled and pulled back to look into her eyes. "I was

calling you just now. You didn't answer."

She hesitated. "Oh. No. I didn't. I was too worried you wouldn't come to the door. Do you forgive me?"

He nodded. "You were having a rough day. You think that's the worst I've ever heard?"

"Well, it's the worst you've heard from me. I'm so sorry."

He gave her a kiss on the forehead. "I need to show you something."

He guided her into the shop, toward her desk. She couldn't believe how nonchalantly he had treated what she struggled with for days. He had sanded her desk, and the drawers lay about on a workbench. "I have a feeling you didn't know about this," he said.

He had removed the upper left side of the desk, as if he were dismantling it. But from that spot he pulled out a drawer.

Kendra frowned. "I didn't think those top drawers were actual drawers. Let alone drawers that pull out the *side*. Why would they make it like that?"

"It's a secret drawer. One of the coolest I've ever come across." He picked up the side panel that normally covered the drawer. "This covers it, and you have to pull up on it and remove it from the desk to find the drawer."

She broke into a grin. "That's completely awesome!"

He laughed. "There's the smile I've been missing. But that's only half of what I wanted to show you." He picked up a package and handed it to her. "This was in the drawer."

It felt like a book, but a layer of soft, pale leather was wrapped around it, and the open edge was sealed with wax. The wax had broken and flaked enough that Kendra could peek inside. "It's a book."

He nodded. "Didn't you say this desk belonged to—"

"My great-grandmother. Or great-great, I don't remember."

Steven leaned against a worktable. "So. You going to open it or keep it sealed for future generations?"

She tsked. "Are you kidding? Didn't I just tell you I was self-centered?"

She broke away the remaining wax and gently unfolded the leather. The book inside was in surprisingly good condition. The cover was also leather, but it had no title. She set the book down, gently opened it, and touched the top page. "This paper almost feels like fabric."

"High rag content," Steven said. "That's why old books usually last longer."

"How do you know things like that?"

He shrugged. "You know. It's a wood thing. I've studied papermaking, too."

She gasped when she turned a few more pages. "Steven, I think this is a journal." She rubbed down the goose bumps erupting along her arms. "And look!" She read aloud. "March 2, 1843. A midwife means 'with woman'—Steven! She was a midwife!"

"I am *so* floored." Steven stared at the journal as if it had just dropped down from heaven. "I've been praying about how I don't want to tell you what to do, but I want you to get some..."

"Comfort?"

"Yeah."

"And guidance?"

He smiled. "Uh-huh."

She tenderly wrapped the leather back around the journal and held it against her chest. "Me, too."

Chapter 12

Over the following week, Kendra felt as if her ancestors had come calling—not just one, but a group of women who understood her in a different way than any other family member had. Grandma, yes, she was Kendra's early inspiration and her mentor of sorts. But Kendra's mother had been right. Even when Grandma no longer saw her own patients, she always seemed involved with other people more than her own family. As a child Kendra felt special to have been chosen as Grandma's favorite, the one to whom many of the delivery stories had been told.

Still, this journal made her feel as if she were there as the stories unfolded. As odd as that sounded, Kendra knew it was true. Grandma's stories were a wizened old woman's memories. Sadly, she hadn't been aware of the journal's existence. These entries were written at the moment they impacted Kendra's ancestors, and they pulled her in. There were entries filled with joy, but Kendra was most ministered to by the words written during the tougher times.

There was Adele, a Wisconsin widow in the mid-1800s who remarried but continued to help birthing mothers, her daughter, Polly, by her side. She wrote no account of losing a baby in the birthing process, but she did lose one of the mothers under her care. She described the sorrow in that loss, writing, *At times I feel helpless in being "with woman" during times of uncertainty and fear. . .a faithful midwife learns to love, to cry, to pray, and to say good-bye.*

And Adele's daughter, Polly, embraced the journal as a family tradition as she traveled the Oregon Trail. She wrote about a patient whose loss was similar to Alice's:

> *Katie Jo lost the baby two nights ago, just five months into her time. We don't know why it happened, but the Lord does. I couldn't write about it until now, when the Lord moved me to record the sadness, so that next time I'll know that He moves us beyond it. I'll read this later and remember. He does move us so.*

Polly's daughter contributed her wisdom as well, but it was Christiana, Polly's granddaughter—Kendra's great-grandmother—who wrote the simple line Kendra most needed to hear at this point in her calling: *I was not the one in charge. I was merely God's handmaiden.*

Kendra was seeking comfort. And guidance. And protection from people like Dr. Zibarro. But this was exactly how she needed to see herself if she hoped to experience any of those things. She wasn't in control. God was.

Lord, I'm going to do my best, always, to help these women—

these mommies—deliver healthy babies. But I surrender my efforts to Your will and control. Please help me to accept and communicate the love behind Your will, regardless of the circumstances. I love that You entrust these women and children to me, Your handmaiden. And I trust You, Lord, in all things. Amen.

As if on cue, her cell phone rang upon her "Amen." Marianne, sounding chipper as always. "Hey, Kendra, are you feeling any better? I tried to give you a good solid week before calling—"

"No, that's fine. We're still on for your exam tomorrow, right?"

"Well, see, that's why I'm calling. I think we need to reschedule."

Kendra grabbed pen and paper. "Okay, just as long as we don't go too far down the road, with you due in less than a week."

"Yeah, that's the thing. I think we might have to push that date up a bit."

Kendra sat up straight. "Are you saying—?"

"Five minutes apart. That's okay at this stage of the game, right?"

Kendra stood to gather her things. She laughed. "Yes. Marianne, I swear you're the calmest pregnant lady I've ever met. Oh, but wasn't Alice going to be your birth partner?"

"Yeah, that's my problem. I went ahead and called her, just in case for some crazy reason she wanted to be a part of this, but I guessed correctly the first time that she wasn't up for it. My mother is on her way, but she hadn't planned to be here already. She'll take three hours."

Kendra nodded. "Sure. Okay, don't worry about it. I'm sure I can bring one of the midwives I'm going to open the clinic with."

"Perfect. Hey, that reminds me. Did you see the—hang on—"

Kendra heard Marianne breathing through a contraction.

"Huh," Marianne said when she was able to talk again. "That was only four minutes."

Kendra dashed out the door, lugging her boxes of equipment while she juggled the phone. "Okay, let me hang up so I can get help. You can tell me whatever you were going to say once I get there. If the pains get bad enough that you might not be able to open the front door, be sure to unlock it."

"Key's under the mat."

❧

In the short drive between her home and Marianne's, Kendra called one of her midwife colleagues and Steven, both of whom headed to Marianne's—one to assist and one to pace.

Between ever-closer contractions, Marianne told Kendra what she tried to tell her earlier: "The paper." She pointed toward the bedroom doorway. "On the kitchen counter. The *Gazette*. Letters to the Editor."

"Ugh. What now?" At least Kendra felt better equipped to read bad press after the strength she had gained from her journal. And from God.

"No, it's good," Marianne said. "And you're not going to believe who—oh, here comes another one."

The paper had to wait. But not for long. Marianne's birthing experience was one of the good ones. Intense but smooth and quick, with no complications. Kendra had little doubt Marianne felt the pain of carrying and delivering her child without the support of a spouse. But her eyes were full of joy when her daughter loudly announced her arrival into the world.

As soon as Marianne was presentable, they let Steven come in. Marianne cooed to her baby, "Callie Marie, this is your big, strong uncle Steven. I know you're just going to love him to death."

Steven wouldn't take hold of the baby until Marianne bullied him into it.

"You do delicate, detailed work with your hands all day long. I think you can be trusted with Callie. And you'd better hold her while you can. Once Mom arrives to help out, *I'll* be lucky to hold her again."

He laughed. "All right, give her here."

Kendra watched him. She had a hunch about how he might react to holding that tiny bundle, and she was right. She saw him clench his jaw, swallow, and try to blink away the moisture in his eyes.

She walked her colleague to the front door and took the time to flip to the back of the newspaper Marianne wanted her to see. She found the Letters to the Editor page and had to sit down. Normally a one-page item, this week's edition covered three pages because of all the letters Kendra's patients had written, supporting her and defusing the damage done by the past two articles. Unlike Steven, Kendra didn't fight her tears.

But her tears didn't keep her from homing in on one of the writers' names. Dr. Gina Chastain. Dr. Zibarro's partner, the woman who destroyed Marianne's marriage, and the doctor in charge when Kendra and Alice arrived in the emergency room on the Fourth of July. Kendra braced herself for this one, most assuredly one that would differ from all the others.

But it didn't.

As the obstetrician on call when midwife Kendra Silverstone's patient suffered the tragic loss of her baby, I must respectfully disagree with my colleague, Dr. Antoine Zibarro. The loss of the baby was tragic but was in no regard connected to the care the mother received from Ms. Silverstone or from the OB/GYN practice of Zibarro and Chastain, the mother's previous medical team, of which I am a partner. In fact, Ms. Silverstone's swift actions prevented the mother from suffering any further medical complications as a result of her tragic loss. She is to be commended.

Kendra walked back into Marianne's room, holding the rolled-up paper aloft. She caught Marianne's eye, and Marianne widened hers to match Kendra's expression.

"Ah! You read that hussy's letter! Isn't that a kick in the pants?"

Kendra huffed. "I'm so conflicted about her now. I mean, she—"

Marianne waved her comment away. "I know. Don't worry about it. Even a messed-up clock is right twice a day, right? Some people have very selective consciences. Steven, I want my sweet baby girl back. And go away now so Kendra can teach me what to do. Poor little Callie has a first-time mommy."

"She has the perfect mommy," Kendra said.

Steven appeared reluctant to surrender the baby. He looked at Kendra and chuckled. "I want one."

They laughed together, but when their laughter stopped, their eyes remained focused on each other. Warmth spread over Kendra like a warm summer shower.

Kendra sighed and looked from Steven to the child in his arms. *Yes, please, Lord. One of each would be just fine.*

Chapter 13

Eight months later

The clinic was in utter chaos. But it was a good chaos. Glorious weather allowed for milling about, both inside and outside. Bright balloons and streamers, buttery popcorn, steamy hot dogs, and even the local high school cheerleading squad kept the visiting families entertained, while Kendra and her business partners played hosts and gave impromptu tours of the new facility.

Kendra stopped interacting at one point and simply surveyed the scene before her.

A warm, deep voice interrupted her thoughts. "I suppose a lot of these kids are your babies, huh?" Steven's arms wrapped around her from behind, and he nestled his head next to hers. She rested her arms on his and leaned comfortably into him.

"Mm-hmm. Not the cheerleaders, of course. But a few of their younger siblings. A lot of the tweeners and most of these little ragamuffins running around are mine or Shelly's or Rita's." She sighed. "We're going to work so well together."

"I like that you'll have more steady backup for your patients.

You think that might make your schedule less hectic? Less. . . unpredictable?"

She gently pulled out of his embrace so she could face him. She looked intently into his eyes. "Is it starting to get to you? My crazy, baby-impulsive lifestyle?" Not a month went by when they didn't have something interrupted by a delivery.

He held her gaze. "Not at all. I've never known you otherwise, so I'm used to it. It's just. . ."

She struggled not to worry. He had always been completely up front with her when anything bothered him. It was one of the qualities she most loved about him. "Just what? You can tell me."

"I like to think that now you'll have time to plan things."

She smiled. "I'm always planning things. Sometimes they get interrupted, that's all."

"Yeah, but now that you're partnering with Rita and Shelly, maybe you'll be able to take that trip to Fiji we've always talked about."

They had never talked about a trip to Fiji. She laughed. "Oh. Right. That."

His mouth twitched. She just loved when he tried not to smile. He forced a serious expression. "And if you plan to go to Fiji with me, there would be a couple other things you'd have to plan for, too."

What in the world?

In one swift movement, he reached into his pocket and lowered to one knee.

A yelp from someone was so loud, Kendra thought maybe *she* had done it. Both she and Steven shot a glance in that direction, as did many other people.

Marianne stood facing them, Callie perched on her hip, and her hand over her mouth. She dropped her hand and grimaced. "Sorry. So sorry. Go ahead."

Now all eyes turned to Kendra and Steven, and Kendra heard gasps all around. She looked back at Steven and realized she was crying. "Steven. . ."

He held a brilliant solitaire ring between his fingers. His voice was soft, intimate, and just for her to hear. "Kendra, I cherish you. And I love you. I need to know you're safely back home in the middle of the night after those babies decide to show up. I need to know we'll have time together when the babies leave you alone. I. . .I just need you."

She couldn't speak. She reached forward and grazed her palm over his cheek, loving the manly stubble on it. Loving him.

"So, I thought you might marry me," he said. "Will you marry me?"

Kendra still felt she would be unable to answer, so she nodded several times before she finally swallowed her emotions and found her voice. "Yes!"

The moment Steven stood and they embraced, the crowd enveloped them. The already celebratory atmosphere took on an even stronger feel of family. Kendra couldn't have loved the moment more.

She kissed Steven, shocked and thrilled to imagine him her husband. She pulled away and whispered to him. "Perfect. How did you know this was the perfect time and place to do this?"

He kissed her again. "Have you forgotten already? Ellie told you the day we met." His smile drew her to him. "I'm a genius."

She laughed and hugged him again, a prayer pouring from

her heart: *Thank You, Lord. You have truly blessed me. You protected me from lasting harm and led me to new love. And the clinic! How I wish Adele, Polly, and Christiana were here today. In many ways I feel they are. Thank You, Lord, for giving me their words, for reminding me that ours is a labor of love.*

TRISH PERRY turned to writing after a time in the stock exchange and DC law firms, as well as raising two children. Using a degree in psychology, she writes award-winning contemporary fiction that delves into her characters' minds and emotions. She serves on the board of directors of CCW and is a member of both American Christian Fiction Writers and Romance Writers of America. Visit her at www.trishperry.com.